D1282505

Plowshare in Heaven

PLOWSHARE
IN HEAVEN

Stories by
Jesse Stuart

With an Introduction by
Ruel E. Foster

Jesse Stuart Foundation
PLOWSHARE IN HEAVEN

ISBN 0-945084-21-8

Library of Congress Catalog Card Number: 90-62718

Published by:
The Jesse Stuart Foundation
P.O. Box 391
Ashland, KY 41114
1991

*To the
Honorable Order
of
Kentucky Colonels*

CONTENTS

INTRODUCTION

The stories in *Plowshare in Heaven,* all written before 1956, are drawn from the deep well of Jesse Stuart's youth. They are fresh, spontaneous, and full of youthful energy. Stuart manifested throughout the first half of his writing career a genuine ambivalence toward the mountain life of his short stories. There was a kind of "mountain glory" in the rock-bright waters of a mountain stream and in the pristine beauty of a clearing-in-the-sky cornfield. Stuart gloried in such scenes. But there was also a deep "mountain gloom" in the dark hills surrounding and shutting him in and in the casual brutality of a mountain crowd, his people, enjoying with callous hilarity the spectacle of a poor devil being hanged at a "Sunday afternoon hanging." There is a real conflict within him as he is torn between mountain gloom and glory, a conflict which can be found from time to time in the stories of *Plowshare in Heaven.*

Even a casual reading of this book shows how deeply Stuart was concerned in his writing with things-that-pass-away. In spite of the turbulence of his early writing, there is an ever present undertone of sadness for the days that will not come again. His story, "Walk in the Moon Shadows," begins "Where are we goin' Mom? I said, ... Where can we go when the moon is up and the lightning bugs are above the meadows?" After this wonderfully evocative opening, Stuart goes on to record a long ago walk through the lovely moon shadows of a mountain night. The young boy narrator and his sister imbibe this magic. They thrill with the knowledge that the abandoned cabin they come to deep in the forest had been the home of a long dead couple who were friends of their mother in her youth. The mother expects their phantoms to emerge from the house to greet them. The mother, drawn by some obscure psychic urge, makes this spectral visit before each child is born.

It is interesting to note certain parallels between Stuart's work and that of William Faulkner. Take the story, "Zeke Hammertight," which opens *Plowshare in Heaven*. This is a serio-comic story of a half-crazed old mountaineer, Zeke Hammertight. He is the patriarch of a wild mountain clan, a clan that devours all the nuts, berries, and animals in the neighboring hills. They are like a plague of locusts scorching the earth. Sheriff Watkins leads a big posse out to Hammertight country and runs old Zeke down in a farcical battle against an acre of the half-human Hammertights. At the close of the story, the fat sheriff rides at the head of his rabble army followed by a wagon with old Zeke on it imprisoned in a hog crate.

As happens so often in a Stuart story, behind the broad frontier humor lies faintly heard what Wordsworth called "the still, sad music of humanity." And this does remind us of Faulkner. Note the following parallels. The Hammertights are all over the hills; the hills are overrun with sassafras sprouts and the Hammertights. Wars can't kill them; droughts can't starve them. They keep on coming. This, of course, is a perfect description of Faulkner's rapacious Flem Snopes and all of his spawning breed. What the Snopeses are to Yoknapatawpha county of Northern Mississippi, the Hammertights are to the hill country of Eastern Kentucky. They take over everything—they are like kudzu.

Introduction

Jesse, like Faulkner, had both a fascination and a love for his common folk. Both authors present their characters without sentimentality and often comically. In both authors, there is frequently a deep undercurrent of sadness for their characters' comic sin and sorrow. They both write sad-comic pastorales of poor families caught in the turbulence of acute social change and not realizing the why of all the turbulence.

There is indeed, for Stuart's several million readers, a magnetic quality to his work which draws them into his stories. This quality is present in *Plowshare in Heaven*. Jesse tells a fast-moving story, a technique he had learned from Harry Kroll, his writing teacher at Lincoln Memorial University. Professor Kroll told Jesse many times, "Write as you talk. Turn it on and pour it out." This advice gave Jesse one of the elements of his "talk style," as we see in "Zeke Hammertight" and "A Land Beyond the River." A later writing teacher, Donald Davidson of Vanderbilt University, a charter member of the famous "Fugitive" and "Agrarian" movements there, taught him another lesson when he turned back to Jesse some of the pseudo-sophisticated and highly imitative poetry the young mountain poet had written in 1930. "Don't be a pretty boy, Jesse. Go back to the hills, Jesse, and write about the people you know and the sheriffs and constables you hate. Write of your country as Yeats wrote of Ireland. Your country is your material." This advice got through to Jesse at a crucial time in his writing career, and the present stories in this book are the result of his heeding that advice. These stories are his country as it was before the 20th Century technological bomb had exploded in his world. They preserve a vanished way of life. In *Plowshare in Heaven*, Stuart is truly the elegist of a lost world.

Plowshare in Heaven is like a rich montage of vanished scenes of mountain life passed through and colored by Stuart's imagination and personality. Millions of readers have fallen in love with the curious and unique nature of Jesse's created world. Stuart is definitely one of the folk, a man of the people. His grandmother on his maternal side was a full-blooded Cherokee Indian and some of the Indian affinity with nature comes through in Stuart's loving embrace of nature and the earth.

Like the 16th Century poet John Skelton, Jesse loved the great vocal, lusty, low-brow masses. Like Skelton, he loved scenes of peasant revelry. He loved to bring together common people and set them to cathartic release, as in the roistering, boozer-mourners of "Sylvania Is Dead." Jesse could have written Skelton's memorable poem, "The Tunning of Elinour Rumming" with its realistic picture of a low-life tavern in an English village of 1600, thronged by all the thirsty trots, boozeheads, and village gossips of that era. The rich peasant life steams up from the babble of voices floating through the tavern, uttering their survival cries, their great unconscious affirmation of life. And Jesse presents his own equally earthy and primeval affirmation of life in the drunken burial crew of "Sylvania Is Dead," as well as in the defiant shouts of the Sixeymore brothers to the mob gloating over their hanging in the story, "Sunday Afternoon Hanging." The death motif is very strong in Stuart's own life history, and it looms large in *Plowshare in Heaven*.

The death motif continues through story after story— "Sylvania Is Dead," "Sunday Afternoon Hanging," "The Reaper and the Flowers," "Bird-Neck," and several others. This death motif represents the "Mountain Gloom" aspect of Jesse's writing. Jesse's satire is frequently an implicit criticism of mountain traits he finds reprehensible but does not want to denounce openly. This is clearly evident in "Sunday Afternoon Hanging," his satirical portrayal of the public's joy and delight in "a good old-fashioned hanging" in the Kentucky mountains after the Civil War. Grandpa tells the story in the first person to his young grandson with a wealth of savory detail that conveys the thinly veiled sadism of the thrilled mob of men, women, children, and babies. "It was as much fun to see a hanging in them days as it is to see a baseball game nowadays here in Kentucky," says reminiscent Grandpa. Grandpa's brilliant monologue illustrates with marvelous detail one of the dominant strains in Jesse's work – a strain of violence, brutality, and lack of compassion mingled with a kind of bizarre humor. Grandpa tells with great relish the story of the biggest hanging they ever had in Blakesburg.

It is a tale of the democracy of death. Three co-conspirators with the depraved Sixeymore brothers, Jake and Tim, bludgeon to death aged Uncle Jim Murphy and his wife. The murderers are caught and all five are hanged in sequence on Sunday afternoon. The climactic moment is the hanging of Tim Sixeymore. The crowd taunts each murderer and watches the hangman, Bert Blivins, adjust his noose – "Bert was a whiz at this hanging business." The old women taunt the killers as they go up to the gallows, and the fierce ladies shout as the neckbone cracks and the hanged turn blue-black and the tongue extrudes from the mouth. The classic drama rises to its fore-ordained pitch as the ringleader of the crime, giant Tim Sixeymore, rides astride the biggest coffin ever seen in Blakesburg. The Sheriff gives him his final drink of liquor and chew of tobacco and calls for his ritual confession. Tim rises like a black demon, looks scornfully at the crowd and tongue-lashes them. "I hope to hand everyone of you a cup of water in hell." So saying, he lets the wagon be driven out from under him and the weight of his massive body breaks the rope. Tim laughs loud enough to be heard a mile away. They get a bigger rope, which holds, and Tim Sixeymore is hanged. A fight then starts in the crowd. Grandpa says, "God, it had been an awful day. Women pulling hair and shouting and praying, singing, screaming till you couldn't hear your ears."

Jesse had no first-hand knowledge of these hangings, but he had good sources. Both his mother and his landlady at South Shore, Mrs. Forrest King, told him stories of the old hangings seen when they were young. "We'd get all dressed up to go to a hanging. Schools turned out to go to a hanging. . .like going to an all-state game." In this democracy of death everybody got to see and laugh or faint or curse or cry—to do just as he pleased. The emotions so carefully bottled up on most public occasions found their purgation at funerals or hangings.

One other example of the death motif in Stuart is his story, "Sylvania Is Dead." It is also a sterling example of his affinity for the tall-tale strain in American frontier humor running back to Davy Crockett's autobiography and the Sut Lovingood stories of George Washington Harris. Sylvania is a 650-pound moonshiner who lives atop a precipitous mountain in East Tennessee. When she dies, the neighboring mountaineers and their wives assemble to bury her, but Sylvania is much too big to get through the door. Sylvania hasn't been out of the house since she was a girl. This has also protected her from arrest by the revenue agents because they would have to tear out one wall to get her out. Even if they did this, they would still have to get her off the precipitous mountain somehow, and if they accomplished this, they still couldn't get her through the jail door. So for years she has plied her trade, heedless of the law. Now, after her death, her former customers are there to bury her and it takes about all of them. They knock the chimney down and remove one end of the shack to get the coffin in and out. Twenty men hold on to the plowlines under the coffin to lower the huge weight into the grave. The mourners drink dipper after dipper from Sylvania's last barrel of moonshine and weep liquidly for their lost bootlegger. The extravagance and hyperbole of this story is characteristic of America's tall-tale humor and of much of

Stuart's humor. The tragic aspects of death are drowned in the comic.

Some fine day a historian of American culture will write a monograph on the parallels between Stuart's fiction and Al Capp's comic strip, Li'l Abner. Li'l Abner ran from 1934 till the 1960's and was immensely popular here and abroad. It appealed to a mass audience primarily but was also read by various intellectuals. It was set in the mountains of Kentucky, at the mythical town of Dogpatch, whereas most of Stuart's fiction is set in the Kentucky hills in or near W-Hollow, the actual locale where Stuart grew up and lived most of his life. The heyday of the careers of these two men was roughly the same—from the 1930's to about 1960. Each had a strong public appeal. Li'l Abner was for ten years the most popular comic strip in the U.S.A. and was also widely read abroad, having an estimated total readership of 60 to 80 million people. Stuart, operating in a much more limited medium, had a smaller audience. But within his own medium of fiction he had a considerable popularity. His most successful novel, Taps for Private Tussie, sold over 2 million copies in the 1940s.

Both Stuart and Al Capp liked to do hilarious parody. Stuart's parody often has overtones of pathos, as in "Zeke Hammertight" and in "Sylvania Is Dead", the parody of a bootlegger's funeral. Each writer also deals with the quality of innocence. Capp's Li'l Abner goes through the world with an innocence that is indestructible. His world is full of con men who cheat, defraud, and deride him, yet he remains kind, loyal, generous, and patriotic. Li'l Abner's world is like the South in its emphasis on kinship and family, the acceptance of the individual, the emphasis on the grotesque, and a reliance on violence. There is a depleted agrarian economy that annually brings near-starvation when the turnip crop is destroyed. Al Capp relies heavily for his humor on dialect, exaggeration, and a lively narrative action. Yet, as a number of commentators have pointed out, all the ridiculous and scabrous con men who traipse through the comic strip are right out of the real world and can be documented by a casual search of the morning paper.

There were differences, of course, between them, one being that Stuart's folk culture was indigenous and genuine, while Capp's was a synthetic folk culture. There is no indication that the two artists knew each other's work, so their similarities cannot be explained on the grounds of mutual influence. The striking parallels between the two remain, however, of paramount interest to the cultural historian. For that matter, they help the reader who comes to *Plowshare in Heaven* for the first time to gain an additional insight into the world Stuart has spun out in his stories.

Plowshare in Heaven gives clear evidence of that great vitalism, that elemental love of life and of the mystery of the life force, which burned brightly in Stuart before his heart attack in 1954. One feels this in Stuart's comment, "I wouldn't give an extra day of life for the best short story I've ever written." After that heart attack in 1954, life put a halter on Jesse, but it didn't put a halter on his humor, which continued to bubble up vibrantly, as in the story, "Before the Grand Jury": "The other day I saw him [old Fred Sizemore] all dressed up and started to town and I said to him, "Where are you going, Fred?" 'Going to town to get drunk, and Lord God, how I do dread it!' "

When Stuart died in 1984, the death certificate stated that he died, "of intractable heart failure." Like his character, Phoeby, the dead mountain wife in this volume's title story, Jesse in death hoped to spend his eternity on Kentucky earth. For him, Heaven was, in the words of the oldtime preacher, a "Kentucky of a place." *Plowshare in Heaven* grants us copious visions of this Heaven for our present and future pleasure.

Ruel E. Foster

PLOWSHARE IN HEAVEN

Stories by
Jesse Stuart

ZEKE HAMMERTIGHT

Do you believe there are sassafras sprouts on the Kentucky hills? Do you believe there are eternal rocks and tough-butted shaggy-branched white-oaks growing among Kentucky's eternal rocks? Do you believe there is the whisper of winds in the wild-rose bushes and the wild-gooseberry sprouts in these Kentucky hills where skies immeasurable float above like a flock of buzzards in the sky? Do you believe there is a hill-Kentucky with her bony acres where the lizards crawl on the burnt-black logs and the snails leave silvery traces on old moss-infested stumps? If you believe these things are here and that there are buzzards, lizards, blacksnakes, copperheads, and crows, then you can believe we have the Hammertights here — plentiful as the crows and the buzzards, all the time slipping through the woods with shotguns across their shoulders, sly as the wind in the brush and curious as a hounddog on a cold trail.

"I'll tell you what is the matter with this hill country," says Cousin Milt. "It's overrun with sassafras sprouts and the Hammertights. Every way you turn here you run into a Hammertight. They are thicker than sassafras sprouts. They are thicker than pawpaw sprouts and they are harder to get rid of than persimmon sprouts in a pasture where the cattle won't eat them. W'y, they have been here, I guess, long as the rocks have

1

been here. You know a Hammertight is tough as a hickory withe you burn and twist to tie up bundles of fodder."

When a body walks down a path here he is liable to meet a Hammertight. He might be carrying a gun across his shoulder just by chance he sees a squirrel.

"I'll tell you," says Cousin Milt, "if some kind of plague don't come and sweep out the Hammertights this country is not going to have any squirrels, groundhogs, possums, foxes, rabbits left to tell the tale. W'y, I was out on the hill this morning and saw old Zeke Hammertight dig a old she-groundhog out of a hole and took off four suckling young groundhogs about the size of kittens, knocked the old she-groundhog in the head with a mattock handle. Put her in his sack. Guess he's cooked her in the pot by now with green beans and taters—guess he's et her by now. Shame the way the Hammertights and the sassafras sprouts have took to Kentucky. Can't get rid of 'em any more than you can get rid of the rocks on the Kentucky hills—or the tough-butted white-oaks that grow like blackberry briers on the Kentucky claybanks."

Old Zeke Hammertight—you ought to see him. Six-feet-four with a cupped-in face—a face bent in like a half-moon with a long chin and a handful of dead-looking white beard, wind-scattered and falling over his shirt-unbuttoned hairy chest. White beard with the stain of bright amber—the color of red-oak leaf-stain—mixed with the white bridle-tassel of corn silk. You ought to see his long dangling arms with the big blue veins running like little mountain streams of water on the winter flank of a mountain. You ought to see his steady blue eyes that the years cannot dim any more than they can the eternal Kentucky rocks—wear a little, tear a little—just a little by the wind, the sun, the rain, the sleet, and the snow. Freeze a little, thaw a little, and fade a little as the years roll by. No wonder the Hammertights keep coming like the young sassafras sprouts on the Kentucky hills—the sassafras sprouts are rooted in the Kentucky earth and the cattle can't kill them; and the fire that burns over the earth and kills their bodies can't kill them. They come again in the spring: ten young sassafras sprouts for the old one that dies. That's the way of the Hammertights. The wars can't kill them; the drouths can't starve them out; the earth can be cruel to them or kind to them—the high hill earth—and people can fight them—but they keep on coming. They grow like the timber here; and there is something in their blood that makes them tough as a hickory withe or a tough-butted white-oak.

Cousin Milt says:

Old Zeke Hammertight,
The daddy o' 'em all,
Fed 'em on groundhog
Before they could crawl.

"Well," says Cousin Milt to me, "guess you've heard the latest. Old Zeke Hammertight's not nigh all there. He's losing his mind. Body's as good as it ever was, but he's got something wrong on the inside of his head."

"It can't be," I says to Cousin Milt.

"W'y, it can be, too. Guess I know what I saw with my own eyes this morning."

"Saw what?" I says to Cousin Milt.

"You know where my garden is," Cousin Milt answers. "I was working there early this morning. Zeke comes up the road with that old shotgun across his shoulder that he always carries around wherever he goes. He comes up to the palings where I was cutting crab grass out'n the pole beans. He says to me, 'Say, you know that young nephew of mine, young Zeke Hammertight.' And I says: 'Which one of the Zeke Hammertights? I know a whole slew o' 'em.' And he says, 'Brother Zeke's Zeke.'

3

And I says: 'W'y, sure I know him.' Then he comes right up to the palings and he says, 'Come over here. I got something to tell you.' He laid his gun down there among the milkweeds—that old scarred-barrel Columbia single-barrel he carries everyplace he goes. I was glad he laid it down. Didn't know what he might be up to. He says: 'W'y, that young Zeke—my brother Zeke's Zeke—has been trying to pizen my cattle.' And I says: 'You don't mean it.' He says, 'W'y, it's the gospel truth.' He cupped his hands up beside his mouth and whispered it to me through his cupped hands and there wasn't anybody in a mile to hear. And he says, 'I met him awhile ago and told him he was trying to pizen my cattle. He got mad and said he'd pour the hot lead to me. W'y, I know he's trying to pizen my cattle. I saw him across the meadow last night—walk right through that little patch of white-oaks by the barn. Walked right up among my cattle and he had rat pizen spread on fried Irish taters and tried to give it to my milk cows. That's the kind of pizen you give to foxhounds. So I takes out after him. He gets away. I know he was there—I know the way he come and the way he left, down among the milkweeds and the sassafras sprouts by that little patch of sprouts. Yes, my own brother's boy trying to pizen my cattle.' W'y, the man is crazy. He's dangerous, too. Too much inbreeding there—heads no bigger than drinking-gourds. Cousins a-marrying first cousins, and uncles marrying nieces, and nephews a-marrying aunts. W'y, it's the awfulest mix-up in that family of Hammertights you ever saw. You know that, Quinn."

And I says, "Yes, it's a terrible mix-up. It's just sassafras sprouts mixing with sassafras sprouts, though."

"That's it," says Cousin Milt. "Ought to mix the sassafras sprouts with the pawpaw sprouts and that mixture with the persimmon sprouts. Then we would have one of the dad-durndest mix-ups you ever heard tell of. W'y, old Zeke went on up the road from the garden this morning. Went up past my

4

barn. I heard a shot blast out'n my barn like a bolt of thunder. I turned and saw old Zeke in the road kicking and cussing, hollering he was shot in the heart. I saw young Zeke running right around the pint over there back of my barn with his gun on his shoulder—just a-flying off the earth. Old Zeke down in the road a-kicking and hollering he was shot in the heart. I left my work in the garden. I ran to him fast as I could get there. I didn't see any blood. He says, 'Look at my heart, Milt.' I tore his shirt open and looked and I couldn't see a mark. And I says, 'W'y, Zeke, you ain't shot in no heart.' And he says, 'ook at both panels o' my ribs.' So I took his shirt off and unbuttoned his undershirt. Wasn't a mark there. And I says, 'You ain't shot there, Zeke.' And he started cussing and hollering and crying and says, 'Look at my legs then. I'm shot someplace.' So I pulled his overalls down and looked at his legs. 'Not a mark there,' I says to Zeke. Well, he jumped up and never took time to put his overall galluses over his shoulders. He run right out'n his overalls—just in that old heavy long underwear he wears of a summertime. Took time to put that old shotgun across his shoulder—just in his underwear, hat, and shoes—and he took around that hill the way young Zeke went, just a-hollering and a-cussing and crying. He made better time than any mule could a made that I got on this place. Big and tall as he is and in that white underwear, w'y, he skeered every horse to death on the road. Had 'em a-raring up and breaking out wagon tongues and express shafts. I never saw a old man run like he run around that hill. It's just been a hour or two since he run around there."

"We'd better go over the hill and cut 'em off next to the post office and see what has happened," I says to Cousin Milt. "Might go over there and kill one another or kill somebody."

"No such good luck," says Cousin Milt, "as for a Hammertight to kill a Hammertight. One sassafras sprout won't kill another. It might draw some stuff from the ground that the

5

other sprout wanted where they are so thick on a bank—but even at that, one sprout can't starve out another sassafras sprout. That's the way of the Hammertights. Look how he missed old Zeke back there. Missed him with that old cock-eyed rifle he carries around here across his shoulder."

Cousin Milt Zorns is big at the middle and little on each end. He is like a calf that was weaned too soon and gluttoned on grass. Just wobbles as he walks and when he talks he wiggles his ears like a rabbit wiggles its ears. Cousin Milt never cared much about me. Only he gets good when the Hammertights give him trouble. Uses me then for a cousin. He needs my help.

We walk up the path by the barn. Cousin Milt is in front and he says, "Whee! God, it's hot as a roasted tater out here under these trees—no air a-stirring and this uphill pull."

Cousin Milt walks in front, swinging his arms. He has his thirty-two in his hip pocket.

"May not be able," says Cousin Milt, fingering it, "to kill a man with this the first crack, but I know I can stop him."

We walk right on up the hill—right up the cowpath under the trees whose leaves hang down like wilted pepper-pods.

"Young Zeke and old Zeke went around the horseshoe road," I says to Cousin Milt, "and when we walk across this backbone ridge here and drop down the other side we'll just about be at the other cork of the horseshoe where the post office is. The other side of the horseshoe runs right along up beside Sandy River. They're right over there now."

We walk up the hill. The buzzards sail in circles over the ridge, over the wilted leaves and the lean cattle. They sail in circles over us. They swoop and swerve in the high hot air, over the lean cattle and over us. They can't get Cousin Milt and me. We'll feed 'em the hot lead until they'll be buzzard meat for the ants. It is easy walking downhill—easy for me.

Cousin Milt says, "My knees rattle like the wheels of our

6

old buggy. And it ain't had no axle grease on it for years."

We walk down the hill under the trees and the buzzards and the hot wind and the mare-tailed sky.

"I see them," says Cousin Milt. "W'y, look yander. They're not fighting. Coming up the road. Look yander. Each one o' 'em's got a sack o' meal on his shoulder."

And I look around the edge of the brush by the path. There they come—coming up the path toward us—talking. Old Zeke is talking with the point of his shotgun that he is carrying in his left hand. He is holding a sack of meal, of a sack of flour, on his shoulder with his right hand. Young Zeke is carrying a sack of meal or flour on his right shoulder, holding it with his right hand and trying to talk with his left hand where he holds the long-barreled rifle.

"Are we going to meet them?" I says to Cousin Milt.

And he says, "Hell, yes. Why not? The crazy damned Hammertights and the sassafras sprouts are taking this country. They are taking Kentucky."

The wind lap-laps the poplar leaves about our heads. It is a lazy wind. The sun is hot and the lizards are sleepy on the rocks. They lift their heads when a green fly passes over and swallow the green flies like a toad frog catching yellow jackets. The ground sparrows twitter in the seeding crab grass. The voices of the men are lazy as the wind. We can understand their words now just about the same as we can understand words of the wind. They are coming up the path from the post office.

"I didn't say it was you, young Zeke," says old Zeke, "trying to pizen my milk cows. I didn't say it at all. You just thought I said it. I know you wouldn't pizen my stock."

"W'y, you did say it," says young Zeke. "You told Milt Zorns I was trying to pizen your milk cows. You've told it everyplace and got people afraid of me. No wonder we can't marry women in other families. We have to marry one of our kind—we have to

7

marry a Hammertight. No wonder our heads are getting to be simpling heads. Our hands our getting small. We are losing our minds. No wonder. We are all going to seed like these straw hats go to seed. Get big at the bottom and little at the top. W'y, we have to marry one of our kind. We are Hammertights. You go around and put out all this talk about me—your brother's boy— about me pizening your stock."

"W'y," says old Zeke, "I'll tell you who is pizening my stock. I'll tell you who is right after my milk cows. Oh, I know he is the one. He's not a Hammertight. I'll tell you, young Zeke, who he is. Hold over here and I will tell you."

And they stop over the hill, down below us in the middle of the path. Old Zeke drops his shotgun—lets it drop on the ground by the wild ferns and the crab grass. Above them on the rugged slope is the croaking rain crow. Above them are the eternal Kentucky rocks, the tough-butted oaks, the saw briers, the greenbriers and the blackberry briers. Above them in the air the buzzards are watching, and the crows are watching; the lizard is watching too, and Cousin Milt and I are watching. We are all out on the hill together. The lazy wind is listening as old Zeke cups his left hand and puts it up beside his mouth so as to keep his words from getting away when he whispers his secret loud enough for all the hills to hear.

He says: "W'y, young Zeke, I never said you was trying to pizen my stock. I never said it at all. I can tell you who it was, though. I know, for I seen them going right across that little bottom—right up through the milkweeds to my milk cows. Oh, I know who it was. I know who it was. And I am going to get him. I am going to get him at the pint of this gun."

Cousin Milt nudges me in the ribs. He whispers, "Wonder who it was this time trying to kill the old fool's cattle? Going around here and putting that out every day. Somebody that don't know he's crazy as a bedbug might believe him. Listen.

Let's see if we can hear what he says."

And we listen as he cups his hand a little closer, draws in his big fingers and makes them tight as a rail pen so the words can't get out. They stand there in the path and the hills listen; the rocks listen, and the lizards. And the wind slips through the green wilted leaves and listens.

"Oh, it's the Zornses that's pizening everybody's cattle. Just going over the country and killing them in heaps. Shooting them between the eyes when the pizen won't take. Shooting them! Going right over the country and giving them rat pizen on fried taters. It's the God Almighty's truth, young Zeke. It is that Milt Zorns the leader of it all. Didn't I see him cross that little bottom of mine, come right up through the milkweeds? He had on a white apron and he had it filled with fried taters. Had them soaked in rat pizen. He went right up where my cows was. And he says:, 'Swooke Gypsy. Swooke Star.' And they come up to him—licked out their tongues—and he pulluted their tongues with rat pizen on them old taters and they spit it out. I hollered at him and of all tearing out of there—you never seen the like in your life. God, he took off that pasture like a racer snake and I told him that I'd see him in the courthouse for trying to pizen my milk cows."

Cousin Milt pulls out his thirty-two. He steadies his quivering hands by putting the pistol across a stump. He takes aim. He wants to be sure and get old Zeke.

"The old lying crazy sonofabitch," says Cousin Milt, "I'll make him think I pizened his cattle. I'll give him a surer dose of rat pizen. I'll give him a dose he can't carry—a dose of hot lead."

And Cousin Milt holds the pistol steady. Pow. The smoke puffs up before our eyes. The lazy wind will not take the smoke out so we can see.

"Did I get him?" says Cousin Milt.

9

"You sure didn't," I says, "by all the cussing I hear. Just listen to that, won't you?"

And of all the cussing any man ever heard, we heard it. The smoke thins and we see them running, old Zeke with his sack of meal or flour and a white stream pouring from it.

"Put a hole through the sack," says Cousin Milt. "Never got him."

And young Zeke is running with a sack on his shoulder and a rifle in his hand. They are running and cussing. Cousin Milt holds the pistol up and aims: pow. They just run faster. Cousin Milt takes aim again: pow. And a stream of meal or flour pours out of the sack on young Zeke's shoulder.

"We can track them," says Cousin Milt. "We can track them by the flour and meal. I'm sorry I didn't kill that old crazy devil. When a man goes crazy he ain't any more for the hills. Ain't no use to send him to the asylum. Just work him to death down there to get his mind off worry. Just as well kill him here and give him to the ants, crows, and buzzards. W'y, a crazy man is dangerous. Sheriff Watkins has been told and told about this man Zeke Hammertight and he's afraid to arrest him. He's afraid of him. We don't want a sheriff like Watkins any more. He's going to get us all killed by Zeke Hammertight. The man going around here crazy as a bedbug. Come on and I'll get him. He'll not charge another Zorns of pizening his cattle."

We take over the hill, down the path, across the rocks, the stumps, the fallen trees, Cousin Milt in front with the pistol in is hand. The sweat is pouring off him like clear warm water; Cousin Milt's middle is too big for him to do much running, and he is too small on both ends. Maybe the lizard is watching us, maybe the rocks that have seen men kill before and men go crazy. Rocks that have seen stories they've no tongues to tell.

"Here's the meal," says Cousin Milt. "Might a knowed awhile ago a Hammertight never buys flour. He don't know what good biscuits taste like. Have corn bread for dinner, breakfast, and supper. Come on, now. We got a hot track and I'll bet you it'll take us to Greenbriar. There's where they went. Went to get the sheriff."

So we run the meal track, a white streak over the dusty road. Rocks looking down on us from the high hill whence we came – down in the pleasant valley now where the post office is – down where the waters of the Little Sandy moan.

"A warm track we got," I say.

"Yes, a damn hot track," says Cousin Milt. We run down the road.

"Better watch one of them old Indian tricks old Zeke might pull," I says to Cousin Milt.

"He's not going to hide in the brush and bushwhack nobody," says Cousin Milt. "He's too afraid now. He's going after the sheriff...."

Cousin Milt has his pistol in his hand. People pass us on horseback, in buggy, express, jolt wagon, and old T-models. They don't pay much attention, though – only at the stream of meal poured along the road. It is bread from the high hills spilt along the valley, bread from the high hill earth, for the Hammertights live among the hills and they raise their own corn and have it ground at the mill by the post office.

"Here's the end of the meal," I says to Cousin Milt. And it does end by the falls of Little Sandy, the place where the wagons ford the river only when we have had a big rain.

"No meal up the other side," says Cousin Milt. "Guess the meal all run out on 'em. And they've just throwed their meal sacks in the river. Either this or they caught a ride into Greenbriar."

We wade the river, the muddy water not up to our knees. Now we walk on the main road that leads us to Greenbriar. They will beat us to Sheriff Watkins. But anybody knows a Hammertight here. Anybody can tell you old Zeke is crazy as a bedbug and our word will go further with the Law.

"Who ever heard of a crazy Zorns?" says Cousin Milt. "W'y, if I go crazy I hope somebody gets me. I don't want to be crazy. Somebody get me out here and work me for ten cents a day like a lot of crazy people that are hired out. W'y, old Zeke would be better off dead."

And we take down the dusty road beneath the sun. Our clothes are wet with sweat. Walking over the hills in the July hot sun is work where you have a lot to carry like Cousin Milt.

"They've just been here," says Sheriff Watkins, "just been here. Yes, two of the Hammertight boys. Old Zeke and young Zeke. Young Zeke said you scalped his shoulder with a ball— showed me the mark. You just cut a trench in the skin and his meal sack with the same ball. Getting mighty close. And you broke one of old Zeke's slats—bullet just grazed his side and broke a slat for him. He said you shot through his sack of meal, too, and tried to kill him. Said he left his gun out on the Runyan Hill."

"W'y," says Cousin Milt, "he's crazy as a bedbug and putting out all over the country that I'm pizening his cattle. I can just tell you the whole story, Sheriff."

And Cousin Milt tell Sheriff Watkins the whole story.

Sheriff Watkins just sits here and he says, "Huh and u-huh. That's right." His jaws are fat and rosy as a pink morning-glory in the sun. He is bigger in the middle than Cousin Milt. He has little stubby hands and fingers like a groundmole's fingers. He bites off his fingernails. He has a blue eye that has a twinkle in it, and he has a row of gold teeth. "And that's the way it was?" says Sheriff Watkins.

And Cousin Milt says, "That's exactly the way it was. I thought, Sheriff, if I got to come in here and explain it to you, w'y, you'd understand."

12

"But he'll kill me if I undertake to arrest him by myself,"
says Sheriff Watkins. "Too many of them Hammertights. You
can't tell what they'll do. Might bunch on me and kill me. Just
because I'm sheriff they'll think that is a big thing to do. Don't
like to take any chances on that Hammertight bunch."

"W'y, we'll help you, Sheriff. We'll help you clean out the
whole Hammertight bunch," says Cousin Milt. "I'll tell you it is
dangerous to live among the Hammertights. I wouldn't have
one of my blood to marry among them for nothing in this wide
world. All losing their minds and going crazy. Just because they
marry their kinfolks. Don't the Bible say that you shall not marry
the second cousin? W'y, they marry their first cousins, their
uncles and aunts. W'y, it's a sight the way they carry on. They
are just taking Kentucky, too. Just the Hammertights and the
sassafras sprouts. You know, Sheriff, before you come to this
office you used to be a farm boy. You know you couldn't whop
the sassafras sprouts out."

"Good God Almighty no," says Sheriff Watkins. "Them
sassafras sprouts. I go up in smoke when I think about the way
I used to fight them. Pap fit them before he died. W'y, they took
our farm. Got a start on us and we couldn't whop 'em out."

"That's what I am trying to tell you, Sheriff," says Cousin
Milt. "The sassafras sprouts and the Hammertights are taking
Kentucky. Old Zeke, the daddy of 'em all, is crazy. We got to get
him in jail. Get him to the asylum. Or get rid of him one."

You would a laughed to have seen Sheriff Watkins when he
came out to Cousin Milt's house. Here he was, sitting up there
on a sorrel horse with a blazed face and a nice tied-up tail, sitting
there big and fat in the middle as he was, his starn-end just
filling one of these cowboy saddles and his short legs resting in
the stirrups, a big Winchester in his right hand resting across
the saddle horn, two bloodhounds that booed-booed all the
time, raring to go, chained to the pommel of the saddle with a

13

bright strong chain.

"Well," says Sheriff Watkins, "I've come, Milt, to take back the bacon. If he runs I've got the dogs that'll put him up a sapling quick as a hound-dog will tree a squirrel. I've just thought it over – damn fool crazy as he is – w'y, he's dangerous to the people here in the hills."

"I've told you that," says Cousin Milt, "all the time. I've told you that the man was dangerous."

"Well," says Sheriff Watkins, his blue eyes twinkling under his brassy eyebrows and above his pink morning-glory cheeks, "I'll tell you the truth, Milt. Come a little closer so I won't have to speak too loud."

"What about them bloodhounds?" says Cousin Milt. "I believe they are after man meat."

And the bloodhounds snap and growl and rare against the chain.

"Be still, Queen. Be quiet, Lope." And Sheriff Watkins jerks on the chain. The hounds keep quiet now. "They won't bite you," says Sheriff Watkins. "They are just like old quiet rabbit hounds. They want to take a track and jump their meat. They'll never bother you. These are smart dogs. They just about know who is innocent and who is guilty. Just come over here, I want to tell you something."

And Sheriff Watkins whispers to Cousin Milt so the trees will hear and the rocks will hear and the lizards. He cups his hand by the side of his mouth and he whispers to the world, "W'y, Milt, I bought that Hammertight vote. I bought it from old Zeke. You know what old Zeke does they all do. It was what elected me. I give forty dollars for all their votes. I have just hated to come out here and chase old Zeke like he was a rabbit. But I have to. He's a dangerous man. A sheriff can't take any chances on a man dangerous as he is and a man crazy as a bedbug. W'y, he won't have sense enough any more to sell the

14

family vote. So it doesn't matter much. I've got to run him down like a rabbit or get him."

"Just exactly what you'll have to do, Sheriff," says Cousin Milt. "We've just got to go Hammertight-hunting. Got my gun all greased up here and I brought a couple of the Raymond boys here. He's been going around and saying that old man Raymond has been pizening his cattle, too. So we just intend to clean up these hills and make them a decent place to live. Got to get rid of the Hammertights and the sassafras sprouts."

"We got to watch in this hunt," says Sheriff Watkins, sitting high on the sorrel horse, "and keep ourselves in the clear. Let the dogs strike up a cold trail. Do you know where old Zeke has been in the past three days or the past three hours till we can give these dogs the scent? They'll fetch him around like a rabbit. Can't help it if he is crazy."

"Yes," says Cousin Milt, "let's go down to his own milk gap. There's where he hangs out of a morning. Just about ten after nine now. They've just milked their cows a little while ago. I believe the dogs can get a fresh track."

"W'y, they tell me," says Sheriff Watkins, "that old Zeke lost his mind on cattle and horses. You know when a man loses his mind it is always on some one thing. A woman come in to my office only last night and said she saw old Zeke out there by a patch of bushes trying to ride a horse and there wasn't any horse there. Said he'd get up like he was getting on a stump so he could jump on the horse's back. Then he would act like he was a-hold of the bridle reins. He would heave on the reins and holler:, 'Get up there, hossy. Get up, Cob. Whoa back, Cob, pet! Whoa back, boy! Good old Cob.' Just-a-cutting all kinds of crazy didos right there and there wasn't a sign of a horse. She said it was right laughable to see him riding the wind."

We follow Sheriff Watkins toward Zeke's milk gap. It is right up by the edge of the river and a hill. Sheriff Watkins leads

15

the way, Cousin Milt walks behind him with his rifle, and I walk behind Cousin Milt. The Raymond boys are behind me with a couple of little twenty-twos that wouldn't stop a blue jay, let alone a big man like Zeke Hammertight. Old Queen and Lope boo-boo and charge against the chain.

"They're a-raring to go," says Sheriff Watkins. "Turn 'em loose right here, boys. I believe they'll get the old pup's track. He ain't gone from this milk gap more than thirty minutes. I can still smell him. Don't be afraid, Milt. They won't hurt you. Just unsnap the chain. They are after fresh Hammertight meat."

Boo-boo—boo-boo—ough-ough-ough—boo-boo. Around the milk gap they circle, sniffing the Hammertight scent. I just wonder how they can trail that scent when there are piles of smelly droppings from the cattle, little black heaps among the ragweeds and the sand briers at the milk gap. I wonder how they know what we want—why they chase man and don't go out in the weed fields and jump a rabbit. They have hit a track—boo-boo—boo-boo—ough-ough-ough—and around the hill.

"They have him. They've got his scent," says Sheriff Watkins. "Got him a-going sure as God made little apples. Now, boys, you fellows have all rabbit-hunted. You know just what it is. You know how to watch for the rabbit. Just place yourself so you won't shoot one another. You know a rabbit always comes back where you jump it from. Or it goes to its den. Now, old Zeke might go to his den. Or he might circle back here. And you know what to do when you see a rabbit coming, don't you?"

"Boy, listen to them hounds, won't you," says Cousin Milt, "just plaim-blank like rabbit hounds. Ain't they bringing that old boy through the bushes. Going right to the house. Come on, Sheriff, up there at the top of the hill if we want to get a shot. They're making for the Hammertight house. Hurry up, Sheriff."

And we take up the hill, Sheriff Watkins up there on a

horse's back, his starn-end covering one of them little cowboy saddles, his belly going up and down as the horse lopes through the wind, over the grassy hill, the wind blowing fresh over the saw briers on the pasture hill. And, lord, the chase is on: the boo-boo and the ough-ough of the bloodhounds, the bellering of the pasture bull and the moo of the cows, the cracking of our feet against the earth as we follow the chase.

"Take care," says Sheriff Watkins. "Yander he goes. Yander he goes. There goes the rabbit we want."

Sheriff Watkins brings his horse to a quick stop. His fore-feet skive up the earth. Sheriff Watkins takes a quivering aim. Pow. And the blue smoke spits from the long tongue of his Winchester. The man keeps running. It is old Zeke, all right — gun in his hand — running for the barn. Pow. The smoke is in little clouds in the bright air. Zeke dives in at a hole in the side of the barn. Pow. Pow. Pow. And our bullets splinter the planks on the barn.

"Got in a hole on us," says Sheriff Watkins. "The old rabbit is in his hole. Got him in his hole."

Sheriff rides and we run toward the barn. The blood-hounds go up the hill; it looks like the tips of their four feet are tied together under them, the way they are running up the hill.

"Youp — youp — you —" and the bloodhound falls back from the hole where it is trying to get in after Zeke.

"Hit my dog with his gun barrel," says Sheriff Watkins.

"Boo-boo — boooooo." And the other bloodhound tumbles in a half-dozen fits over the hill.

"God, he's hurt my dogs. Come here, Lope. Come here, Queeny girl. I guess we'd better fire that barn and bring him out of there. W'y, he's dangerous. He's a dangerous criminal."

"What did you say, Sheriff?" says Cousin Milt.

"I says," says Sheriff Watkins, "that he is a dangerous criminal. That the best way to get a rabbit from a brush pile is to set fire to it. Let's fire the barn."

"What about the livestock?" says Cousin Milt. "You don't want to burn a lot of innocent cows and mules and maybe little pigs with a crazy man!"

"Right," says Sheriff Watkins, "right you are."

Whinnnnnnnnnn.

"Bullet through my horse's ear from that barn," says Sheriff Watkins. "Look how it tore it open. Put the shots to the side of the barn. Maybe one will go through a poplar plank and get that old polecat between the eyes."

Pow. Pow. Pow. Pow. Pow. And the blue smoke swirls on the fresh morning wind.

"Got him in a hole," says Sheriff Watkins.

"He's down in behind the manger," says Cousin Milt, "two-plank deep. That's why the bullets can't reach him."

Whinnnnnnnnnn. Right above our heads. Whinnnnnnnnnn. Just a little closer. The bloodhounds come to us. One with a broken nose. One with a broken jaw. When they started through the hole in the barn into the manger after old Zeke, he raps their noses with his gun barrel. The bloodhounds are breathing through their mouths. They wallow on the grass and whine.

"Tie them to the chain," says Sheriff Watkins to one of the Raymond boys – shooting around with a little twenty-two, worth about as much as a good sand rock to throw in this hunting game. Raymond snaps the chain. Sheriff Watkins rides back across the field.

"Say," says Sheriff Watkins, "come away from that barn. We are all going to get killed. If we could just fire that barn. If we could just smoke him out of the hole like you do a rabbit or possum."

Sheriff Watkins rides out across the field. His belly goes up and down like a leaf in the wind. The Raymond boys are behind the horse. Cousin Milt and I are behind the horse. We are breathing hard.

Cousin Milt looks back. He says, "Look yander, won't ye, around that barn."

And we stop and look back. If you could only see the Hammertights around that barn. More than a acre of sassafras sprouts on a Kentucky yellow-clay bank. A whole army of Hammertights armed with gooseneck hoes, brier scythes, double-bitted axes, broadaxes, apple-butter stirs, clubs, four-year-old clubs, and two-year-old clubs, rocks – sand rocks and flint rocks – just a whole army of them swarming around the barn. I tell you the Hammertights and the sassafras sprouts are going to get Kentucky in the end.

"Say," says Sheriff Watkins, "this fighting is getting right for me. Just the kind of fighting I like to fool with. I'll conduct this battle like the Father of Our Country, George Washington, when he crossed the Delaware. I'll do it like Teddy did when he charged up the hill of San Juan. We'll call this the battle of the bresh. We'll go right up there among them Hammertights and send 'em back to the bresh. We'll send them back to the sassafras sprouts. I'll stay right here and shoot once in a while and, Milt Zorns, you go to Greenbriar and by this order of Sheriff Watkins you deputize ever man between the years of sixteen and sixty-five able to take bead on a rifle and bring him out here. Also, see Jim Caudill and have him to gear up his mules and bring that big crate out here they hauled that big boar hog with them long tushes to Allcorn in. We're going to need that crate. It held a wild boar and it will hold a crazy man."

"All right, Sheriff," says Cousin Milt. And he runs down the path, past the willows toward the ford.

Sheriff Watkins holds up his Winchester and shoots. He rides out across the field in front of the Hammertights. He rides fast through the purple ironweeds. He shows them he is still here and acts like he is just a little afraid to make the attack. He

is like the Father of Our Country. He has the Hammertights
fooled. When he gets reinforcements he will charge the hill like
Teddy Roosevelt. Sheriff Watkins is a fighter. He might have
pink morning-glory cheeks and a belly that goes up and down
like the wind, but our sheriff is a fighter.

"We can hold out a few minutes longer," says Sheriff. "I am
just praying that Milt hurries with new men. We need them
right now to charge that hill." And Sheriff Watkins rides
around and the horse prances in front of the army of Hammertights gathered around the barn where old Zeke is. "I tell you,"
says Sheriff Watkins, "when the Hammertights want to gather
in their men and women to take up arms, they tell me they ring
a big dinner-bell down there at old Zeke's place. Something
strange it don't take 'em all day to get ready."

"Whooppee! Whooppee!" they holler. It is our men—if you
could only see. The road is filled with them—shotguns across
their shoulders, twenty-two rifles, a few with clubs; all the guns
in Greenbriar have been mustered out to fight the Hammertights.

"I tell you," says one of the Raymond boys, "we ought not
only to run 'em to the bresh but we ought to leave 'em there. W'y,
long as we leave a Hammertight in these hills for seed we won't
be able to find a wild walnut, a butternut, a hazelnut, nor a
chestnut. They even take all the wild blackberries, the raspberries, the dewberries. They find all the wild honey in the woods
and keep the groundhogs killed out till you can't get a mess. I'm
telling you, this country will be better off without a Hammertight left. Sheriff, of course, you can do as you please about it."

"Do you think," says Sheriff Watkins, "that Teddy Roosevelt would have killed the innocent women and children? Do you
think the Father of Our Country would have killed the innocent
women and children? Well, do you think Sheriff Watkins is
going to do it? If you do, you are badly mistaken. Listen to me,

fellow citizens and soldiers for the state. Don't you harm a woman or a child. Get ready for the charge. Make it a charge now!"

"Sheriff, what if a woman comes at you with a club? Must I let her brain me? You know the Hammertight women are tough as the men. Hunt with them. Shoot with them. Ride with them. They are fighters."

"Make them disperse the clubs," says Sheriff Watkins. "Make them disperse the clubs!"

We have an army big as the Hammertights. We are better armed. We are getting ready for the charge. The Hammertights can see us. They shake their hoes, pitchforks, and rakes, and axes at us. They shake their fists. But that does not matter. We are going after them. We are in lines that crook like red worms crawling on the ground in April just before a good time to fish. All of our men are armed better than the Hammertights. You know a double-barrel shotgun shooting number-three shots with black powder is better than fifteen clubs, five pitchforks, ten garden hoes, five brier scythes, and a half-dozen double-bitted axes.

"Boys, when I blow between my fingers that is the signal to charge the hill," says Sheriff Watkins. "Jim Caudill, you be right behind with the mules and the wagon!"

We are all waiting for the charge. The poor crying bloodhounds are with us. Maybe they are waiting for the charge. They sniff with their broken noses. They are waiting for the charge.

"Lord," says Isaac Sneed, "I didn't know Sheriff Watkins was getting me in a battle big as the Battle o' Bunker Hill."

"Wheeeee – tooooo – looooo-dooooo."

We charge up the hill, Sheriff Watkins in the lead, the bloodhounds at his heels. It looks like all their feet are tied together and their ears are spread to the wind. The hill is black with men. We start up the hill hollering, one right after the other, screaming; no wonder the crow flying over changes its course. No wonder the bloodhounds bark and Sheriff Watkins' horse snickers. We are charging up the hill and the screams— the screams of the men: "Whooppee! Whooppee! Whooooooooooooopppppeeeeeeeeeeeee." We are right after the Hammertights.

"Don't shoot yet, boys," says Sheriff Watkins, way up in the lead, his belly going up and down with the wind, his fat little hand holding the bridle rein and his fat little hand holding a Winchester. The boo-boo of the hounds and the ough-ough-ough. Right up the hill toward the barn. Wagon coming right behind us with a crate on it and the mules loping in the harness and the mules cutting up in the harness scared to death. Boy, what a time going up the hill!

Hammertights start to run, right out through the sprouts. Just went east, west, and crooked. Never saw as many Hammertights in one congregation in my life. Just jumped out'n the sassafras sprouts like cottontails. Girls flew out'n the ragweeds like grasshoppers on a hot day. Took to the woods like wild quails. Rakes flew ever such way. Threw them right and left. Garden hoes a-flying through the sassafras sprouts. Broad-axes and double-bitted axes, brier scythes and clubs a-going ever such a way. Never saw anything like it in my life. And the Hammertights on the run, right back to the bushes like rabbits. It suits them there. They are used to the brush and they like the brush.

"Come on to the barn, boys," says Sheriff Watkins. "Come right on to the barn. Got him here in the hole—rabbit in the hole. Bring that wagon right on, Jim Caudill." And the wagon rolls over the rough pasture earth; the mules have their tongues out snorting, and the foam is flying from their thick gummy mule lips. "Get in there, Milt Zorns—you and the Raymond boys—and drag that rabbit from the hole. Get you a pole and twist in the seat of his pants and twist him out like you'd twist out a rabbit. If you can't twist him out, get a bee smoke and some rags and smoke him out. That'll fetch him. It'll fetch out any varmint, even a polecat."

Cousin Milt jumps in the hole right after Zeke, and the bloodhounds right after Cousin Milt. You ought to have seen them working around the hole, just like dogs hot after a polecat. Men rushed on up the hill and waited around to see old Zeke. Some of our men watch the sassafras sprouts to keep the Hammertights scared out.

"Not a man killed so far," says Sheriff Watkins. "Be careful, Milt, and bring old Zeke out alive. We got to take him to Greenbriar in that hog crate. Make people think we all been hunting and got a bear."

Of all the fussing back under that manger and the hollering and cussing—just like a young hound-dog going back in a hole and getting a groundhog. Just a-spitting and biting and fighting. Hounds backed out of the hole first and here come Cousin Milt with old Zeke's leg. Old Zeke with dirt in his whiskers and his long white hair, cussing and spitting and saying to Milt, "You did pizen my milk cows. You know you did. I saw you coming right up across that little bottom out'n that milkweed patch. Oh, you did pizen my milk cows."

And four of our men grab old Zeke and put him in the crate. We twist the old gun from his hand—the old Zeke, the daddy of 'em all, in a crate—and we start to town.

The wagon goes in front with Sheriff Watkins riding beside the wagon and all the men in Greenbriar between the ages of sixteen and sixty-five right behind the wagon with guns on their back. Old Zeke just clawed at the planks on the crate and hollered and cussed.

He'd say, "Let me go back to the woods. You did pizen my

cows. You know you did. Let me go back to the hills. I'll show you where a den of groundhogs is. I'll show you where you can find the good wild raspberries. I'll show you where you can find the walnuts and the butternuts if you'll let me out'n this chicken coop. Where you taking me? Going to kill me and hang me up on a gambling pen like a butchered hog? You going to butcher me for meat?"

"He's not safe among civilized people," says Sheriff Watkins. "He'll know where he is when he wakes up in the asylum. He's lucky to get there. All this expense on the county taking him over there. W'y, he's not any more good. He ought to be left out there among the sassafras sprouts. Out there for the crows and the buzzards. Making us fight the Battle o' Bunker Hill over again to get him."

You ought to see us going to Greenbriar. Like a big bunch of men been to the hills and caught a bear. Just that away: a long line of men behind the wagon and Sheriff Watkins up front, just riding as big with the bloodhounds with broken noses strapped to the saddle.

Maybe the hills know we got old Zeke Hammertight. Maybe the eternal rocks of Kentucky know it and the lizard knows about it. The sassafras sprouts know that we got him. Like the buzzard, the crow, the lizard, and the snake, old Zeke would love to get out of that hog crate and run wild over his Kentucky hills again—run wild forever over the hills that have produced him and his generations thick as the hair on a dog's back, thick as the sassafras sprouts on a Kentucky poor-clay bank and under the Kentucky wind, and sun, and moon and stars.

WALK IN THE MOON SHADOWS

"**W**here are we goin', Mom?" I said, looking up at my tall mother. "Where can we go when the moon is up and the lightning bugs are above the meadows?"

Mom didn't answer me. She was braiding Sophia's hair. Sophia was my oldest sister, twelve years old, with blue eyes, blond hair, and tight lips. Sophia didn't ask Mom any questions. She stood still, never moving her head while Mom finished braiding her hair. Mom had dressed Sophia in a white dress, and she wore a sash of red ribbon instead of a belt to her dress. The sash was tied in a big bowknot. Sophia was dressed like Mom dressed her when we went to Plum Grove's Children's Day once a year.

Mom had scrubbed me from head to foot. She had used more soap and water than she had ever used before. There couldn't have been a speck of dirt on me anyplace. Mom gave me the same kind of scrubbing she gave Sophia. That was the reason I asked her where we were going. Mom had combed my hair, parting it in a straight line, using the long comb for a straightedge to get the part straight.

Mom had dressed me the way she always had before Children's Day. She put on me a little pair of pants that came to my knees and buttoned to my shirt. Mom made all of the clothes that we wore.

"There's no use to go, Sal," my father said. He was sitting in a rocking chair in the room where Mom was getting us ready. Now and then he would turn his head slowly and watch Mom for a minute. Then he would turn his head back and face the empty fireplace. "You're dressin' the children for nothin'. They won't be there when you go. They never have been at home."

"Just because we've gone before, Mick, and they weren't at home, is not any sign they won't be there on an evening as pretty as this one," Mom said. "I'll keep on tryin' until I catch them at home!"

"Where are we goin', Mom?" I asked again.

"I'll tell you later, Shan," she said.

"Sal, we've been there several times since we've been married and we've never found them at home," my father said.

"Where are we goin', Mom?" I asked. Sophia remained silent, pressing her lips tighter than a turtle's. "Who are these people we are goin' to see?"

"Never mind, Shan," Mom said. "I must go in the other room and dress."

"Who are they, Pa?" I asked, turning to him when Mom left the room.

"Just people you don't know," he replied. "But your mother and I know them. And when we go to visit them, they're never there."

"Where do they live?" I asked as Sophia made a face at me.

"Up on a high hill," he told me.

Then I thought we might be going to see Sinnetts. They had two boys, Morris and Everett. If we went there, I'd have somebody to play with. Then I thought we might be going to Welches. They had three boys, Jimmie, Walter, and Ernest. If we went there, I'd have somebody to play with. But Sinnetts lived upon a little bank above Academy Branch and Welches lived in a saddle between the Buzzard Roost Hills and the John Collins Knolls. I thought we might be going to see Alf and Annie Dysard. They lived on a low Plum Grove hill and had a son, Jack, and I could play with him. I didn't have a brother to play with.

When Mom came from the back room, she was dressed as fine as I had ever seen her dress. Mom's black hair was combed and laid in a big knot on the back of her head. Her hair was held there with combs that sparkled in the half-darkness when she walked to the far corner of the big room away from the kerosene lamp. She was wearing a blue dress trimmed in white frilly laces. She had worn this dress before to our Fourth of July celebration in Blakesburg. My mother was beautiful. Pa looked at her and he didn't turn away and look at the empty fireplace this time. He kept on looking at Mom.

"I'll take the children with me, Mick," she said. "You'd better go with us, Mick!"

"I've gone there too many times already," he said. "I've been disappointed too many times. Sal, they're never at home. Not when we go. So I say, what is the use to go? If they can't be at home, if we can never see them, why go and try to look them up? I don't see any use of pestering friends who try to dodge us."

"I want our children to see them," Mom said. "Come, Sophia! Come, Shan!"

"We're going to Sinnetts, Welches, or Dysards," I said happily. "I'll have somebody to play with."

Sophia made another face at me. She was trying to get me to keep still.

"Do you know where we're goin', Sophia?" I asked.

She didn't answer me.

"You'd better go too, Mick," Mom said as she walked toward the front door of the big room with Sophia and me following her. "Mick, I think you want to go but you're afraid."

27

"I'm not afraid to go either," Pa said. "We've never had better neighbors. As friendly a people as we ever lived by. What would they have against me now? That's where you're wrong, Sal. I'm not afraid. I just don't see any use of trying to catch them at home. I'll stay here this time and let you go."

We walked down the field-stone rock walk in front of our big log house. Mom in front and Sophia and I behind. When we came to the winding jolt-wagon road that went up the hollow, I watched to see which way Mom would go. If she went up the hollow, we would be going to Sinnetts. If she went down the hollow we would be going in the direction of Dysards and Welches. Mom turned down the hollow on the jolt-wagon road.

"Not to Sinnetts but to Welches or Dysards," I said. "I'll get to play with Jimmie, Walter, and Ernest. Maybe I'll get to play with Jack."

Mom didn't say a word and Sophia didn't make a face to keep me from talking. Mom took big steps down the road and Sophia hurried to keep up with her and I had to run. Sophia was three years older than I was and she was taller. She could take longer steps. And I looked up at the moon in the high blue sky. It was a big moon the color of a ripe pumpkin I had helped my father gather from the new-ground cornfield and lay on a sled and haul home with our mule. There were a few dim stars in the sky but over the meadows, down where there were long moon shadows from the tall trees, thousands of lightning bugs lighted their ways, going here, there, and nowhere. Upon Press Moore's high hill where Pa had found a wild bee tree, and cut his initial on the bark, a whippoorwill began singing a lonesome song. Somewhere behind us, I heard another whippoorwill start singing too.

Less than a quarter-mile down the hollow, an old road turned right. This road was not used except by hunters. And when we came to this road, Mom turned right.

"Mom, where are we goin'?" I said. "We don't go to Welches or Dysards that way. We can't go anywhere on that road. Not anybody lives on it."

"That's what a lot of people think," Mom said. "But I know people do live on it."

"Do they have any boys?" I asked as I followed Mom over the old road, marked by gullies where the jolt wagons once loaded with coal had rolled along, pulled by oxen and mules in years gone by. I'd never seen the oxen and mules pulling the big coal wagons but Pa had told me about it when he had gone this way in the autumn to shoot rabbits and he had taken me along to carry them.

"No, they don't have any boys," Mom said.

"Then why did you want me to go, Mom?" I asked.

"Shan, I want you to meet them and to remember," Mom replied. "You might see something you will never see again."

"What's that, Mom?" I asked as Sophia walked very close to Mom, and she was as silent as one of the tall trees with the moon shadows.

"Some old friends," Mom said.

Mom wouldn't tell us where we were going. If Sophia knew where we were going she wouldn't tell me. Sophia pretended that she knew. But I never believed that she did because she was afraid of the dark woods on each side of the dim moonlighted wagon road. I watched Sophia step from lighted spot to lighted spot along the road, dodging the deep ruts and the dark long shadows. But the shadows and the ruts didn't bother Mom. She walked proudly and she was as straight as an upright tree. She wasn't afraid of dark shadows and deep ruts. Mom could step over the deep ruts easily.

My mother wasn't afraid of anything at night. She loved the night because I had heard her say she did so many times. I'd heard her talk about old roads beneath the moon and stars, roads

29

where people had walked, ridden horseback, and driven horses hitched to express wagons, surreys, hug-me-tights, and rubber-tired buggies. I'd heard her say she loved the lonesome songs of the whippoorwills and she loved the summer season when the lightning bugs made millions of lights on our meadows up and down the hollow. Mom often sat alone in our front yard and watched them at night. But Pa wouldn't do it. He'd sit whittling, making ax handles of hickory, butter paddles of buckeye, hoe handles of sassafras, and window boxes of yellow locust for her wild flowers. Pa always wanted to make his time count. I knew he would make a window box for Mom while she had taken us on this visit.

"Mom, where in the world are we goin'?" I asked.

I had to run to keep up with her as we climbed gradually up the hill on this deserted road that wound among the tall trees.

"Keep quiet, Shan," Mom said. "We'll soon be there."

Then Sophia turned around and put her fingers over her lips. She told me to keep quiet without using words.

In many places we ran into pockets of darkness under the trees. The moonlight couldn't filter through the dense green leaves rustled by the late April winds. I wondered where Mom was taking us. Soon, after we had staggered and stumbled along, I looked ahead and saw a vast opening beyond the trees. It was like leaving the night and walking into the day to leave the woods and walk into a vast space where only waist-high bushes grew.

"We'll soon be there," Mom said, breathing a little harder.

We followed Mom along the ridge road until she came to a stop. In front of us was an old house and around it were a few blooming apple trees. The apple blossoms were very white in the moonlight and more lightning bugs than we had seen above our meadows played over these old fields.

"This is the place," Mom said.

"People don't live there, do they, Mom?" I said. "Half the windowpanes are out, planks are gone from the gable end, and the doors are wide open!"

I could see the windowpanes still in the windows because they shone brightly in the moonlight. And there were deep dark holes where the panes were out.

"Yes, people live there," Mom whispered. "Be quiet, Shan."

"Mom," I whispered, "are we goin' in?"

"No, we'll just wait out here," she said softly.

"Are there any boys here for me to play with?" I said.

"No," she replied very softly as she took a few steps forward. She reached one of the big apple trees that looked like a low white cloud. Mom sat down on a gnarled root beneath the tree. Sophia sat down beside her. And I sat down on the grass.

"I don't guess anyone's at home," Mom said. "We'll wait for them."

"Who are they, Mom?" I asked in a whisper, for I was beginning to get afraid.

"Our neighbors and friends," she said. "Looks like they'd hang some curtains to their windows, plow the garden, and cut the grass in the yard," I said. "Looks like they'd nail the planks back on the house and put panes back in the windows. Pa wouldn't let us live in a house like that."

Mom didn't say anything. She looked toward the front door as if she expected to see somebody walk in or come out.

"Who are they, Mom?" I asked again. I wanted to know.

"Dot and Ted Byrnes," she said. "That is the old Garthee house. Dot used to be Dot Garthee...the prettiest girl among these hills. She and Ted and Mick and I used to be young together. None of us were married then. Many a time we rode down the road we have just walked up in a two-horse surrey together. Many people have seen them at night on this ridge in a two-horse surrey. Old Alec told me he did. Jim Pennix saw them one Sunday morning in the hug-me-tight driving early toward Blakesburg. That's the way they used to go to church every Sunday morning."

"But why don't they ever visit us, Mom?" I asked.

"Because they're not here any longer," she said.

"You mean they're dead?"

"Yes, in 1917, the flu epidemic," Mom said. "They left this world only hours apart."

"I'm afraid of this place, Mom," I said.

"Shhh, be quiet!" she said. "They won't hurt you. If they come in or go out of that house, I'll call to them. I want you children to see them. And I want them to see my children."

"Is that the reason we are all dressed up like we were goin' to Children's Day?" I asked.

Mom didn't answer me. She never took her eyes off the front door. Sophia sat closer to Mom and I got up closer to Sophia. We sat there silently and no one spoke. The April wind shook down a few apple blossoms from the branches above us. And when I saw a white blossom zigzag down toward us, I shivered.

"Mom, I don't believe we're goin' to see them," I said. "I don't believe they're comin' home."

"But they might be in the house," she said. "Dot's great-grandfather, Jim Garthee, built that house. Her grandfather, John, and her father, Jake, lived in that house and raised their families. The well in that yard is ninety feet deep and cut through solid rock. I remember this house when there was a lot of life here. I've had many good times here visiting Dot. Dot was the last Garthee ever to live here. Now she's gone."

"Mom, they're not comin' out," I said. "They don't want to see us. Let's go back home."

Mom wouldn't answer. She sat silently and waited for Ted and Dot Byrnes. I stopped looking at the old house there under the blooming trees. I looked away over the fields where the night wind rustled the leafy tops of the bushes and there were little dots of light everywhere. These fields were covered with lightning bugs. I didn't want to think about Dot and Ted Byrnes. I didn't want to see them and I didn't want to think about them. I wanted to go home and get away from this place. The whippoorwills were singing lonesome songs on the ridges and their singing and the falling apple blossoms made me have strange feelings. I knew Sophia was scared too. I sat close enough to her to feel her shaking. Sophia would do what Mom told her and she would never ask Mom a question.

"When I come back here another life comes back." Mom's words were softer than the April winds. "I can see the buggies filled with young people and the surreys with families going for visits or Sunday drives. I can see young men and women on horseback riding along this ridge. People used to stop here and drink cold water from that well and sit under the shade of the apple trees."

"Did you use to ride horseback here, Mom?" I asked.

"Yes, Dot and I used to ride her father's horses from one end of this ridge to the other," Mom said, looking away from me toward the house. "I'd love to see Dot and Ted. I know they'll never leave here no matter what happened to 'em. If Dot knew I was here with my family waiting, I think she'd come up and speak to us."

"Look, the moon is going over the ridge and it will soon be dark in the woods," I said. "How'll we get home?"

"Don't worry about that," Mom said. "We'll get back all right. Let's wait a while longer. Ted and Dot might be out somewhere on the ridge. And we'll get to see them when they come back."

"Do you want to see them, Sophia?" I said.

Sophia didn't answer me. She shook more than the leaves and blossoms in the wind above us.

"I wonder if Dot will be wearing one of the pretty dresses she used to wear," Mom said. "I think I can remember every dress she wore. Dot was always so pretty in her nice clothes. She knew the colors to wear and she was beautiful."

"Mom, I'm getting cold sitting here in this April wind," I said. "I want to go home."

"Just a few more minutes," Mom said, in a louder voice. "Maybe they'll hear us and come out."

"Could we go in the house and find them?" I asked.

"No, we'd better not try that," Mom said. "Your father and I did that once just before you were born. We didn't find them. I think it's better to let them come to us. But let's watch and see if anyone goes in or out."

While Mom watched the house the moon went down behind the ridge. I knew it must be midnight, for roosters crowed at faraway farmhouses.

"I wish we could have seen 'em," Mom sighed as she got up to leave.

Sophia jumped up and hugged close to Mom.

Mom walked slowly along the ridge and we followed her. We couldn't see the moon now and it was very dark. But we could see better than we thought after we followed the winding road into the deep woods again. We saw Pa coming toward us.

"Sophia, why did we ever come out here to the old Garthee house?" I said.

Then Sophia walked close to me. She whispered in my ear as Mom walked on with Pa. "Shan, Mom is going to have a baby. She did this before you were born. Pa said she did before I was born."

I couldn't answer Sophia as we ran in the darkness to catch

34

up. A baby brother, I thought as I ran. I will have somebody to play with me now.

A LAND BEYOND THE RIVER

My Pop was the best water dog that ever rode a raft of logs from the Levisa Fork down the Big Sandy. He was the captain of a crew of water dogs. He got the job because he could holler the loudest, and shoot the straightest. Pop was a big man with iron jaws and mullein-leaf-gray eyes. His hair was the color of a yellow-clay clod. His arms were big and where the sleeves were torn out of his shirt his big muscles rippled up like where wind bends down the grass in the yard and when the wind passes over it the grass comes up again. Pop was the strongest man on the Big Sandy. People called him Big-Sandy Bill. Nobody along the Big Sandy wouldn't call him a water dog and get by with it either. He shot at them till they got out of sight. If they shot back at him from the woods he'd just stretch out on the raft of logs and answer them long as he had a shell. And Pop always kept plenty of them.

I can see Pop now going down the Big Sandy on a raft of logs—a long train of rafts. I can see Pop standing there waving his hand from the front raft showing the boys the way to dodge the shoals and follow the current—great trains of logs—pine, poplars, oaks, beech, ash, maple, chestnut—great mountains of timber in them days on the Big Sandy and God knows it was the roughest place in Kentucky. Everybody carried a gun. Pop

36

made all his men on the river carry a gun. They couldn't get a
job unless they had a gun and a pole with a spike in the end of
it. They had to be men who could jump from log to log like
squirrels – good swimmers, too, or they'd better stay off the Big
Sandy. It's filled with swirl holes and shoals and mean currents
that twist log trains into the banks and then you have to wait
forever to get a flood to clean the log jams up – a flood in March
or April – sometime in the spring. No man that worked on the
Big Sandy that had any raising would ride a raft of logs and let
a fellow call him a water dog. Pop give his men orders to shoot
the first man down in cold blood that called them water dogs.

God, but them was awful days on the Big Sandy. A lot of
people didn't like Pop. One day when Pop and his crowd was
passing through Evans – a little town on the Big Sandy – some
fellow called Pop a water dog and he swum to the bank, went
up in the town, and run the fellow around the square pouring
the hot lead at him. Pop would a killed him but the Law come
down and told Pop to get back on the Big Sandy where he
belonged.

I remember how we used to hear about Uncle John
Hampton and them old men that lived on the river till their hair
got white. I remember how we used to hear how they'd shoot a
man every now and then and they wouldn't try them for the
killings. These fellers would come out and mess with the river
men. They didn't like the water dogs. Pop was a water dog and
Pop wasn't afraid of the devil. He'd come home and take his
guns off his belt and have Mom to fix him a bite to eat and then
he'd go right back to the river. Pop loved the Big Sandy as every
man that lives on that river loves it. Pop was known from the
Levisa Fork to the Gate City down on the Ohio River where the
Big Sandy gives up her logs to a bigger river. Everybody called
Pop "Big-Sandy Bill who's never died and never will."

Every spring Pop would stay away from Mom. It would be

37

in the rainy season when the logs would have to be floated down the Big Sandy. Pop would never get to come home and stay with us. We'd watch the river day and night for Pop. He had a fox horn he'd blow when he's coming down the Big Sandy and Mom would have a basket of fine grub waiting for Pop about the time he'd come down the Big Sandy. We'd run down to the river and Hilton would take it out to Pop in a john-boat. And Mom would write Pop a letter and have it in the basket. That's all she'd get to say to Pop was what she could say in that letter. Pop would take the basket and grab the letter before he would the cake and fried chicken. His big hand would grab the little letter. He would read it and tears would come to his eyes. Then he would turn and start cussing at the men and tell them to watch the train of rafts—for a mile up the river or more. Pop would read the letter. Then he and his men would eat the chicken and cake. They would walk the raft of logs up to Pop, one at a time while the others watched the rafts. They were afraid to leave the rafts. It was easy to ground a raft of logs on the Big Sandy— river so crooked flowing around the mountains like a blacksnake in a brier patch.

I remember when my sisters, Clara and Grace, and I—we used to stand out on the bank of the Big Sandy and watch the big rafts go down. We'd watch to see if the raft belonged to Pop—if it was Pop or any of Pop's men. We could see the blue water from the house for we lived right upon the bank on the Kentucky side. We lived under a patch of big oaks and my brother Hilton kept his fishing poles hooked under the oak roots right in the yard. He kept his nets further down on the river. He fished from a split-bottom chair in the front yard. We'd lived in this house all of our lives and Pop said his Pop had lived here all his life and raised him and his sisters and brothers here and his Pop's Pop on before his own Pop had come from old Virginia and raised his family here. Our house sagged a little in the middle, but it wasn't the house so much we loved as it was the Big Sandy! We fished in its waters. Pop rafted logs on its back. We went riding on it in our john-boats. To us the Big Sandy was a brother and he was a bad brother at times especially in the spring after the mountain rains. I used to read in my old primary geography about the Don River in a far-off land called Russia and I always thought the Big Sandy in my country was something like the Don River in Russia. The Don River had its Cossacks that rode horses and fought; the Big Sandy had its mountaineers that rafted the logs and fought one another. Big men and tall men with sun-tanned hard iron faces and heads of shaggy hair that never was covered with a hat. And I saw mountains in a far-off land in Italy that come down to the blue waters – high rugged hills covered with trees – that looked something like the mountains that come down to the Big Sandy on the West Virginia side; on the Kentucky side there were fields of corn back on the mountain slopes and in the narrow valley. It was a pretty country. We loved the mountains and the Big Sandy.

Jim Hailey ran the next biggest raft train on the Big Sandy – the next biggest to Pop's. He worked as many men as Pop. He had nine men. Pop and Pop's men didn't like Big-Sandy Jim and his water dogs. They would pass Pop and his men when they was coming down Big Sandy with a raft of logs and Pop and his water dogs would be going back. They wouldn't call Pop anything but they didn't speak. Big-Sandy Jim would just grin at Pop. All Big-Sandy Jim's men would just grin at Pop and Pop's men and keep their hands on their pistols. Big-Sandy Jim's horses always beat Pop's horses at the Evans races every spring, too. Pop bet last spring and lost all he'd made on the river. Pop's not afraid to bet even on a horse he's not sure of. He would say: "I'll take his damn bet. It's a good one even if I lose from that low-down river rat. The Big Sandy River is disgraced to have a thing riding its back like Big Jim Hailey. If ever I get the chance— something he's got agin me—" Then Pop would cool down and smoke his pipe and twist his hands on his knees.

One night in April I saw a light hanging out in our yard. Mom slept in the room next to the river downstairs. She slept there alone. Hilton and I slept in the north room across the hall from the girls upstairs and they slept in the south room just across the upper dogtrot. I got out of the bed and run down and told Mom there was a light on our back porch. I run down the stairs and I broke into Mom's room. She was up in bed. She was wide awake.

I said, "Mom, there is a light on the porch. What's it doing there?"

Mom said: "Go on back upstairs and tend to your own business. I had to draw a bucket of water from the well. I lit the lantern and I forgot to blow it out."

Mom got out of the bed and walked out on the porch. Mom hooked the bale from off the nail, lifted the half-smoked globe, and blew out the quivering blaze. She walked back in the house, and it was light enough until I could see her. She went back to bed, pulled up the cover. I could not understand. There was light enough in a quarter-moon for Mom to go to the well and get bucket of water. The girls and Brother Hilton never did wake up.

I told them about it the next morning and Hilton said, "W'y, you've been dreaming, Don. Never was a light on that porch. I was awake a long time last night. I looked out at the West Virginia mountains; I saw them in moonlight. I looked at the river and thought of all the times I'd swum it and of all the pike I'd caught from it and the jack salmon. I just laid there last night and listened to that old river flowing—the moan of the water and the wind in its willow banks. I thought of Pop, wondered where he was on this old river with a raft train of big logs.... That's what I want to do some day: I want to follow the

40

river like Pop only I want to run a boat on the Big Sandy and let the whistle do my hollering.... Don, I was awake far into the night last night, dreaming, dreaming but with my eyes open. That's a fact, Don. I never saw a light."

And then I thought: "I could not be dreaming. I went downstairs. I remember stepping on the steps. I remember the broken step with the knothole in it. I remember it sagged with my weight. I remember hearing the wind out there in the oak tops. I remember how the light scared me. And I remember going in Mom's room. I remember the words she said to me. That she had used the lantern going to the well and forgot to blow it out. And how she told me to get back to bed. I remember Mom getting up in her nightgown. I remember how pretty Mom looked to me when I went back up the stairs. When she went out and got the lantern she looked so tall and straight. Her hair — pretty and golden as corn silks in an August wind — was loose down her back. Her eyes, big and blue, flashed in the lantern light. I remember. I surely was not dreaming."

And the next night I thought I saw the light again and I was too sleepy to go downstairs and see. I just don't remember. I thought I was going; maybe I went to sleep dreaming I was going down to see about the light. And maybe I just dreamed about the lantern the night before. No one can remember a dream not knowing it was a dream. But I remember the night and the stars, night around the house and the stars over the Big Sandy. I thought about Pop and wondered where he was on the river. Pop traveled nearly two hundred miles on the Big Sandy with the log rafts.

Grace and I were out in the swing on the oak tree in the front yard that day when we saw Pop and his men pulling up Big Sandy in a john-boat. They had gone down the river to Gate City with a raft train of logs. I would swing Grace awhile and she would swing me from a split-pole swing that was fastened with a horseshoe to a limb in the oak tree. We could swing out over the river and look down on the Big Sandy. Our house faces the Big Sandy River. All the houses face the river instead of the road. All the houses on the West Virginia side of the Big Sandy face the river instead of the road. We face one another. And when I swung out over the river and saw Pop coming up the river I told Grace to catch the swing and hold it. She held the swing and I run into the house and told Mom, "Mom, Pop is coming. Pop and his men are coming up the river."

Mom run out in the yard. Pop was the first to get out of the big john-boat and tie it to a willow. He said, "Get out, you fellers, and we'll shade awhile and eat before we mosey on up the river."

Pop led the way up the bank. His beard was out long on his cheeks and chin. His hair fell down on his shoulder, hair the color of a dry yellow-clay clod in August. I wouldn't tell Mom but I thought Big-Sandy Jim Hailey looked better than Pop. He did go shaved. He had a clean face. He wasn't a big man like Pop and he wasn't near as hairy as Pop and didn't look as mean as Pop. Pop's men all looked mean. All had hairy faces like Pop: just a hole in the hair on their face for their mouths that worked when they talked and their eyes flashed blue, black, and gray under heavy ledges of hair. They had big pistols belted around them and they walked up our bank to the house like they owned the Big Sandy.

Pop grabbed Mom and kissed her.

Mom said, "Ah, them old beards, Bill. They don't become you one bit. You look awful in them."

And Pop said, "Honey, they ain't no razors out there on the Big Sandy when a feller has to live for three and four days on a log train. Has to sleep on a raft – catch a wink when he can and when the Big Boy's mad can't catch a wink of sleep. That's what's happened now. Had rain on the head o' Big Sandy and the river is just a-foaming like a mad bull."

And Mom said, "I didn't get the basket to you as you went down. Didn't hear the horn and I'm so sorry, Bill—I had chicken aplenty for you and the men."

And Pop said, "And we missed the chicken too. I thought I saw a light on the porch. That was Thursday night. And I wondered what it was doing there. I thought maybe it might be Hilton that had come from his nets and then I knowed he's got eyes good as a crow's eyes, and I just wondered about that light."

And Mom said, "I don't know anything about a light on that night."

And then I thought: "Well, maybe I was not dreaming. Maybe I did see the light. I dreamed it or saw it, one of the two."

And Pop said, "We saw a light here, didn't we, boys?"

And the men—all nine of them squatted around over the green grassy yard—said: "Yep, we saw a light."

Mom never said another word and Pop said, "Honey, fix us a bite to eat and we'll be getting on up the river. Another big train of logs waiting to be rolled in. Got to get them to the Ohio by Sunday."

I can see Mom, Clara, and Grace yet. They went into the kitchen, put a fire in the stove. They put on every pot. It took grub for ten river men where they'd been eating cold grub on the river. The table looked like it would feed twenty-five men. I remember the steam from the chicken and dumplings. I remember the white chicken dumplings going in at their hairy mouths. I remember how they'd never ask for anything but just reach over the table and if they couldn't reach a thing one would say, "Damn it, Zack, can't you give a body a lift to the dumplings? Can you hand over the beans there? What the hell do you think this is, your birthday?" And they just went on like this and Pop would say, "By God, boys, not so goddam-much cussing around over my grub."

And Mom and Grace would just get out of the dining room

43

and let them have it. They'd clean every plate and sop them out. They'd come out with eggs in their whiskers and gravy all over their vests, picking their teeth with goose quills they carried for that purpose, and they'd light up a long green cigar apiece and pat their stomachs and stretch and make it back for the boat. And we'd see them far up the river. We'd see Pop wave good-by to Mom.

It seemed like Pop just come and went and Mom went about the place hunting for Pop. And the days just come and went – spring on the Big Sandy when the trees leafed along its rippling blue waters – and then the rains and the muddy waters and then blue waters again with mountains that come down, mountains of quivering green clouds of leaves. Then would come a dry season when white clouds would float in the West Virginia and Kentucky skies and the water would get low and a raft of logs would run on a shoal. Water would get low and the river bottoms would look white in the sun. Mare-tails would float in the sky. Pop would wipe his sweating brow and say: "Mare-tails in the sky. Sign of rain in three days." Butterflies would flit along the Big Sandy and water moccasins would sleep along the banks on a log and just plump in the water when they saw the raft coming. Turtles wouldn't move – there were so many of them. And they had been in the Big Sandy so long and knew as much about the river as the men and the snakes.

Another night and I dreamed I saw, or went to sleep dreaming I saw, a light downstairs and a man get out and come up the bank. I dreamed that it was Pop. I just don't remember. But I thought this or I dreamed this: "Now the other time I didn't go down. I don't know whether it was a light or whether I just dreamed it. Tonight I'm going down and see."

But I didn't go down and see. I must have just dreamed it was Pop back to see Mom but he hadn't been gone up the river but three days. He didn't have time to be back.

I told Hilton about it and Hilton told Mom the next day.

And Hilton said, "Don, you must be having nightmares. I never saw a thing and I just sleep right across the room from you."

But it seemed to me like there was something. I just felt it. Something bothered me. It was something very strange. I thought of Pop on the water. I wondered where Pop was and if he'd shot at anybody for calling him a water dog. I just know Pop would kill a man and do it quick. We don't know but we heard once Pop and a feller quarreled over a bottle of licker and they agreed to shoot it out. So they turned their backs, each one holding a pistol of the same kind with the same number of cartridges in it, and they walked so many steps apiece – ten, I believe – and turned and started shooting. Pop got the feller. That was when Pop was a young man, though. Pop's got a big scar on his wrist. We heard there was where he got it. He never told us. We don't know.

When Pop come down the river with the next train of logs and blew his horn it was on a pretty day – sun high in the sky – and Mom just piled in all the grub she had cooked in a basket that she always kept waiting for Pop and the men about the time for them to get back. And Hilton took the basket out in the john-boat. He brought a letter back to Mom. And Pop said in the letter: "Elizabeth, when I was going up the river old Jim Hailey was coming down with a train of logs. He was on the front raft with a white shirt on. He was all dressed up and on the river. And when he passed me he just looked at me and laughed and laughed and the men all laughed and looked at me. I'm not for taking such foolishness. I thought once I'd tell my men to fire on them after I'd bumped Jim off for the signal to start. I thought I'd redden this river to the mouth with their blood. I don't know why he's got the laugh on me. You know the only laugh us river men have on one another is when we get the other

45

man's money playing poker, outshoot or outholler the other feller, or take the other man's wife. This is something Big Jim ain't done to me, can't do to me, and never will do to me long as my pistol will bark." I found the letter in Mom's room. I read it.

Pop and Big Jim both were down the river now. Big Jim had been down the river five days. He'd had time to get to Gate City with his log train. Pop had just passed. He would be down the river at least a week. The next day we saw Big Jim at the head of his big john-boat with a white shirt on and he looked toward the house. Mom was not in the yard. We didn't wave at him. We had been taught to hate Jim Hailey from the day Pop could tell us a word about him. He's getting mighty friendly to us. Pop ought to have been here when he waved. Pop would have killed him like he would shoot a rabbit.

It was five days before Pop got back up the river and we told him Jim Hailey passed and waved at us.

Pop said, "He's getting too smart of his pants. That low-down vile water rat!"

Pop said to Mom, "Fix us a basket of grub and we'll take it to the boat. We'll mosey on up the river. We don't have time to stop long. A train of logs is waiting us up on the Levisa Fork."

Mom and Grace fixed a big basket of grub. Two of Pop's big hairy men took it down to the boat. The rest of the crowd followed. I remember seeing them grabbing into the basket as they pulled away up the Big Sandy; I remember seeing the boat dip and swerve as they hogged into the basket.

Eleven more days and I remember. It was night and a full moon was up. Was I dreaming when I heard a shot fired? I heard a scream! It was not the wind among the oaks this time, the wind that blows from the Big Sandy. It was gunpowder. I smelled it. Hilton and I jumped out of our beds. The girls rolled out on the other side the dogtrot. I heard them.

46

"Who was that that shot?" hollered Hilton, and we run downstairs.

"You low-down vile skunk of a water rat, may God send your soul to hell—trying to break up my home," said Pop and he kicked a man lying on the floor bleeding and he held Mom's hand. "Goddam you and your kind—roast in hell, damn you— and you, Elizabeth, what do you mean! That's what the lantern's been hanging out for and what this sonofabitch has been doing wearing a white shirt on the river! Stopping to see my wife.... You children, get back up them stairs, every last one of you!... No man that is a true river man on the Big Sandy can wear a white shirt and go clean-shaved on a log train—that's why you done it, you lousy river rat. I'd throw you in the river but you are not worthy to pollute the water with blood of your kind!"

Pop was standing over a man on the floor. I could see from the stairs the gun Pop was holding and the blue smoke leaving the barrel.

"Don't shoot Mom!" said Clara, screaming.

"Oh, I fooled you," said Pop to Mom. "I've been smelling this rat ever since he laughed at me when we passed on the river. I just went up to Evans with the boys. I sent them on. I slipped back and waited for the lantern. I saw the boat let a man out. I saw them anchor a boat that they ran in from the log train— ah, yes—and that's why the lantern has been out—a signal that I am not here. I happened to be here tonight! And you, damn you—"

And Pop kicked the man on the floor—kicked him over, and he kind of drew up one of his legs like a swimming frog, moaned, and his head fell over on the floor. His breath sizzled and he lay there perfectly still. We could see the white shirt and the blood down the front. We didn't go all the way up the stairs. Mom there holding to Pop and crying, just bawling on his shoulder, and all us children crying like we'd take fits. All scared to death, too. Lord, that smell of gunpowder and smoke! And Pop there—the big bearded iron-faced man that he was—his shirt torn, his hairy body in the light of the lantern and the moon that hung above the river! Lord, what an awful time it was.

Hilton got on the mule and rode for Sheriff Lakin to come and get the dead man out of the house. Pop told him to. He held Mom in his arms.

"For one cent," Pop said, "I ought to blow out your brains for being with Jim Hailey. Jim Hailey! My God, Jim Hailey with my wife—well, he'll never be any more."

We went upstairs and went to bed. Mom and Pop stood together by the dead man on the floor. Blood had run a big stream and dripped through a knothole in the floor. Mom was holding to Pop and crying, "Bill, spare my life for my children. I'll never do this again. I didn't love Jim Hailey—I love you— you was gone so much. You was always on that river. You never stay with me. You leave me. A woman can't be left so long as you leave me." And Mom sagged to the floor crying, almost into spasms.

Sheriff Lakin came. He put Big-Sandy Jim Hailey in the express, took Pop to Evans, and Uncle Jake went Pop's bond. Pop had to appear in one of the biggest murder trials that there ever was on Big Sandy. People talked about us. They talked about my mother.

When I would go to school the children would say, "Don's mother had a man killed over her. She ain't no good, for my mommie said Don's mother wasn't no good." And the children wouldn't play with Clara, and Grace either. The big boys would say things to Hilton at school and he would fight. They would talk about Mom.

Mom never left the house. She never went to see a neighbor. She would sit out under the oaks and smoke her pipe, her blue eyes gazing steadily at the waters that flowed forever past our door—through drought and freeze, summer, winter, autumn, and spring. The waters of the Big Sandy kept flowing on and on and boats passed and big rafts of logs in the spring and corn in the fall went down by barge loads to the mills at Gate City. Mom would talk to herself and look at the river.

Pop went back to work on the river. Pop went back to the log trains. He kept two guns on him now. Once Pop was shot at from the bushes and the bullet hit Tim Zorns in the arm after it had gone through a bunch of men and just glanced off Pop's spike pole. It left its mark right in front of Pop's heart. And word was sent to Mom: "We are going to kill old Big-Sandy Bill—he ain't died yet but we guess he will."

They took us to the trial for witnesses. They asked me to tell about the light. And I told them I didn't know whether I'd dreamed it or whether I saw a light. But it was one of the two. The whole house was crowded with people and Pop's men that worked on the log train with him was right there with their hands on their guns waiting for Big Jim's men to start something. They were all there and the Law was there but the Law would a had a time if one shot had been fired.

Mom told that she didn't love Big Jim and he didn't love her, that she had told him to get away and stay away and he wouldn't do it. And that he come there that night with a gun and said if Pop ever come while he's around there he'd kill Pop. So Pop beat him to the draw.

And somebody said in the back of the house, "That woman ought to go to a limb. Having men killed over her."

And the tears come into Mom's eyes. She just sat there and waited for the lawyers to ask her questions. And they asked her a God's plenty. They asked her how many times Big Jim had come to see her. And a lot of stuff like that. And Pop just sat there mad as a hornet. He looked like the very devil was in him.

The jury was out awhile—about an hour, I guess—and

when they come in the foreman of the jury said, "Murder in self-defense." Pop come clean of the charge.

There was all kinds of cussing around the courthouse. And one fellow says to Pop, "See that sign up there on the court-house? Reads 'God is not mocked. Whatsoever a man soweth that shall he also reap.' And you, Big-Sandy Bill, will reap a bullet in your own heart. Kill a man over your vile wife. Oh, we are going to get you. I am a Hailey. I have not washed my hands with you yet. I am a second cousin to the man you murdered. There are many of us left yet."

And Pop said, "Bring on all your damned Haileys. There are many Fraziers yet in these mountains. Bring 'em on and shut up— bring 'em on and be damned. I love my wife. Or I would have killed her right there! I would kill another man over her."

Pop walked out down the road to the wagon. Mom never lifted her head out in the crowd. They were all looking at her.

When I would go to school the children would not play with me. They would whisper to each other about me. I would go home and go upstairs to my room and cry and cry. I couldn't help it. They would talk about my mother, and I would hear them say at school, "I'll bet Charlie Hailey gets Big-Sandy Bill. He's a-laying for him. He's going to kill him. He's gone longer now on Big Sandy than any other man has ever gone to kill a good man over a woman. Jim Hailey's men must not have anything to them to let him be killed like this and then not do anything about it."

I would hear all this. And to think Pop was back on the Big Sandy! I would think this: "I can see Pop. He is on the floor. He, too, has on a white shirt. He is bleeding at the heart. A stream of blood runs from his heart to a knothole in the floor. It runs down the knothole. Pop works his leg like a frog that's swim-ming. He turns on his back. He moans. His last breath sizzles. He is dead. Pop is dead. Pop, a mountain of a man, one unafraid of men and the river, but Pop is dead. A bullet went into Pop's heart from the dark. His heart was easy for a bullet as any man's heart. Now Pop is no more than a dry clod of yellow clay in August. Pop is dead."

Mom would turn the coffee cup in the morning after she had drunk her coffee. She would say, "I see the river; I always see the river. I can see a dead man floating down the river." Then Mom would scream. She would get up and go out in the yard. She would sit down in the chair where Hilton sits and fishes. She would sit there and look at the river. It was the valley where we had lived for more than a hundred years, ever since the first white settlers had come to the valley. Now we would have to leave the valley—not that we were afraid to die—we would have to leave. Mom would have to leave. When a woman in the hills meets another man, she and her girls for generations are doomed. We would have to go to a new river.

Pop stopped the john-boat at the willows. He got out and threw the chain around a willow root. He walked up the bank holding to the oak roots to pull his heavy body up the bank. Mom was out in the chair under the oak trees.

Pop said, "Timber is growing scarcer in these mountains than ever before. Things just don't work like they used to. I got the whole river to myself now and I don't want it. Big Jim is gone and God be thanked for the riddance. But we are going to have to leave this river for a new river. Hilton cannot do any good on this river because he is your son. No one will ride his boat. Grace and Clara will have a hard time marrying a respectable man because they are your daughters. We'll have to go to a new river. Let's pack on a barge all the things we have and pass through Gate City and go down the big Ohio and land where there are hills on the Kentucky side. We must have hills coming down to the edge of the blue waters. We will be lost without the hills."

I remember packing things that afternoon and putting them on the barge. We took all we had and put on the barge.

Pop's men helped us load. Big hairy men would carry big loads down the bank. They would sweat and work, their guns in their belts. We got all our belongings and left down the Big Sandy — not anything to pull the barge. It floated down the river that we had known all our lives — the river that had carried Pop so much up and down on its blue bosom — sheltered by the tall mountains and the green timbered slopes, the high jagged cliffs near the tops of the mountains where the mountains shouldered to the skies.

We looked back to our house on the bank. The sun was on the other side of it. We could see the oak trees and the swing between us and the sun. We could see the willows and the well gun and the barn. We could see the sun moving down over the green hills we had seen so many times.

And Pop looked back and said, "Well, old river, it's good-by." Pop steered the boat — it floated along. And Pop would say, "I know this river like a scholar knows a book. I know every shoal in it and almost every snag. It is like a person to me. I know even how its heart beats. I've been over it since I was seven years old. And I've started down the other side of the hill."

Mom would say, "I hate to leave this river. I've loved it all my days. Lived on it since I was a little girl. All my people lived on it in these mountains. I was born here, raised here, and I've never been any place else in my life. I learned to swim in this river. I first dived in this water. Lost a comb from my hair and I jumped down after it. I got it, too. But now we leave."

And Mom looked at the water, blue rippling in the sunlight, water pretty and flecked with little whitecaps. We moved down the river. Night came and a pretty moon and we kept floating, floating to the new river.

The next morning we passed through Gate City and onto a broad river of blue rippling water. One man stood on the bank at Gate City and I heard him say to another man, "Look at them

Big Sandians, won't you, on that barge. Going down the river like a lot of them here lately to find a pot of gold."

We floated down the Ohio all that day and till a moon came up that night. The moon was up in the sky. And Pop said, "Must twist her in to the bank and wait for morning. Here is where we stop. I have been here and found this place. I come on down here after I brought the last log train down the Big Sandy. See these mountains on the Kentucky side. Over there is a town in Ohio. It is Radnor. We can boat between Lowder, Kentucky, and Radnor, Ohio. A lot of Kentuckians work over there in town and they must cross the river."

We moved from the barge to a house overlooking the Ohio. It was a pretty house with maple trees in the yard. There are no mountains in Ohio. We could see the town. Pop started to build a boat. He called it the *Hilton Frazier* for my brother Hilton. He would start it to making trips across the river. My brother Hilton would pilot the *Hilton Frazier*. He was learning to be a pilot now at a boat down the river between Anderson, Ohio, and Vanlear, Kentucky. He was working without pay. He didn't get to fish in the river and swim like he used to when he was free as the wind on the Big Sandy. Now he was a water dog. He had followed our people, the Fraziers.

Mom would turn the coffee cup and she would say, "No women here to talk. I cannot see the Big Sandy in this coffee cup. I see a wider river. I see more money. I see my daughters married to steamboat captains and boatowners. Life looks so much better now."

And then she would go out under the maple tree and watch the boats pass with barges on the Ohio. Great loads of coal and sand and steel. But Mom would look for logs. We never saw the log trains on the Ohio we saw on the Big Sandy and we never saw the men with guns around their belts we'd seen back in the mountains. And the man that got to run a crew of men didn't get his job by being able to holler the loudest either. He got it when the old got too old to do the job if he was of blood kin and next in line. That's the way it works on the Ohio.

Pop built the boat. Pop saved some money on the Big Sandy. "A Frazier is never without money," people would say on Big Sandy. "Them Scotchmen can live on a rock."

Pop said, "Now, this boat will break us or make us. It just depends on how the town on the other side of the Ohio grows. If it does much growing we'll not be able to handle this business in a few years."

First the steel mills came to Radnor, Ohio. Then the shoe factories came. Kentuckians went over the river to work. The days passed and the gold poured into our hands. When a man paid his fare in pennies to brother Hilton, he would throw the pennies in the Ohio right in front of their eyes. Brother Hilton grew to be big like Pop and he was a pilot first and then captain of the *Hilton Frazier*. Pop made a new and bigger boat and we ran two boats across the river.

The years passed. The days passed into months and the months into years. We grew to be men and women. We learned to love the Ohio as Pop loved the Big Sandy. Pop never went back to the Big Sandy. He would say, "Elizabeth, we'll live here together until we die on this river. They can take us back to the Big Sandy and bury us in the old churchyard where we was borned and raised."

When Pop got on the Ohio River he shaved the whiskers off his face. Pop didn't look like he used to look upon Big Sandy. We remember how he worked there. He worked yet. He would swim to the middle of the Ohio River and catch a boat that had broken loose somewhere upon the river. Pop was still a water dog. Gray hair on his head didn't matter. He worked and told the men what to do. Money come in and plenty of it.

Pop built another boat with a dance hall on it—a fancy

boat—and called it the *Elizabeth Frazier*. And Brother Hilton piloted it up the Big Sandy with the calliope playing. He stopped at Gate City and gave a big dance. Had his old-time band right on the boat. No one remembered Elizabeth Frazier. They remembered Big-Sandy Bill Frazier that shot Big Jim Hailey. But a young man in a blue suit with a cap, white cuffs, a black tie, and bright buttons on his suit took the boat up Big Sandy. He went right up Big Sandy with the music, stopping at every town for a dance. He went right in with the music playing "My Old Kentucky Home." People shed tears to see the big boat and to know this nice-looking captain was old Big-Sandy Bill's boy that left the river years ago over killing a man over his wife. People danced on the boat and had a good time. Horses scared at it and broke the tongues out of the wagons. And children ran from the banks of the river afraid of the big boat. People would say, "Big-Sandy Bill's boy, Hilton Frazier, captain of that boat. They say Big-Sandy Bill's made money like dirt since he left here. Made barrels of money and got rich down on the Ohio. Had a bad wife, though. Remember that trial? It's been about twelve years ago—you remember, don't you?"

While brother Hilton was up to the Levisa Fork—the only man to ever put a boat that far up the Big Sandy and the biggest boat that ever plowed the waters of the Big Sandy—a big rain fell and the water raised. It got so high the smokestack on the boat couldn't go under the new bridge that spanned the river right above Evans, Kentucky. Brother Hilton had to lay up twenty-four hours. The Government paid him three hundred dollars. He told the people that spread over the Big Sandy River valley, "W'y, Hilton Frazier is a big enough man that when his big boat is delayed the Government pays him." And the Big-Sandians went on the boat and talked to Hilton and asked about old Big-Sandy Bill Frazier when the boat stopped at the town and the calliope played "Old Kentucky Home."

At home Mom turned the coffee cup after she finished drinking her cup of coffee. And she said, "I can see Hilton. Hilton is dead. Hilton married. Hilton, dead. My first son! I can see the gun. I can see it spitting smoke." And Mom screamed. She said, "I tell you when you sow the seeds of life you reap the seeds of life. When you sow the seeds of death, you reap the seeds of death. Things come home to you on this earth. There is not any getting around it. I'll reap what I sowed on Big Sandy. There is not any escape. I can see it here. I know it is coming regardless of the money we have and the three boats we have."

Hilton told Mom, "Mom, I am going to marry Hilda Thombs. Her people are river people. They've been on the Ohio for three generations. Her grandpa used to run the old Grey Steamer here fifty years ago. I love her. I make the money. I am going to marry her."

Hilton did marry Hilda Thombs. She was a pretty girl. She looked like Mom used to look. She was every bit as pretty as Mom. And when Hilton married her, he started running a boat from Hardin, West Virginia, to Cincinnati, Ohio. It was bigger money for brother Hilton. He ran the *Elizabeth Frazier*—one of the big passenger and freight boats—on the Ohio. We would be out and wave when he passed. He would always whistle and whistle for home. Mom was proud of her boat and Hilton running it on the Ohio.

Old Jink Hammonds tipped Brother Hilton off: "Hilton, do you leave a light hanging on your porch on every Thursday night? Is that a signal you leave?"

One night, I remember, Mom had read the coffee cup that night and she said: "I see a dead man. I see him bleeding. It is Hilton."

And Grace said: "Mom, you think too much of Big Sandy. That is over. Forget about it. Coffee grounds are coffee grounds. They don't mean a thing."

Hilda and Hilton just lived a stone-throw from us. Mom said, "The other night I saw a lantern swinging at Hilton's house. If I did not I was dreaming. It looked to me like a lantern."

The boat whistle never moaned this night on the river. It always whistled before. Hilton slipped to the house.

There was a lantern on the porch. Lester Shy, captain of the Little Ann, beat Brother Hilton to the draw. Mom heard the shot. She screamed. She jumped out of the bed.

"I told you," said Mom, "Hilton is dead. Hilton has been killed."

We jumped out of our beds. We ran over to Hilton's house. Hilton was on the floor. Blood was spurting from his heart onto the floor.

Pop was along. "Oh, my God," said Pop. "Oh, God—I remember."

Mom was screaming. "You will reap what you sow," said Mom. "I was twenty-eight when this happened on Big Sandy. Hilton is twenty-eight."

Mom fell to the floor screaming. She had her hand in the little stream of blood running from Hilton's heart. Lester Shy had gone.

"He'll be brought to justice," said Pop, "Big Sandy justice where each man is his own law. I'll bring him to justice. I still can shoot."

"No, you won't," said Mom. "We have just reaped what we sowed. I've thought this was coming all the time. I have expected it. You'll lay your gun down. You'll not shoot any more. Enough has been done already without any more killings and heartaches in a world where you and I are growing old. We are growing out of the world. It is not leaving us. We are leaving it."

Hilda was down beside of Hilton. She was screaming, "I have caused it all. It has been my fault. Hilton has been away so much. God knows a man on the river is never with his wife. If I'd been on the boat with Hilton." And she would scream.

And Mom took her by the shoulder and said: "Take it easier than that, Hilda. No use to cry now. It is all over. I believe I understand."

I could smell the gunpowder. It smelled like it did that night on Big Sandy, the night I was a lot younger than I am now. I remember the stream of blood that night and how Big Jim moved his leg up like a frog. I saw brother Hilton do the same thing. I wonder why a man shot through the heart always does it. Grace and Clara just having one fit after another over the death of Hilton; they, too, heard his last breath go like a sizzle of wind, and he fell limp. His whole huge body relaxed and would be relaxed forever—Hilton, so much like Pop, his hairy arms, his color of a clay-clod hair, his big body stretched on his own floor in death and the killer gone free to kill again.

The *Elizabeth Frazier* did not make its regular trip on the river. It hauled the clay of its young Captain Hilton Frazier up the Ohio and through Gate City. Pop was piloting the boat. Pop can take a boat anyplace. A flag was floating at half-mast from the boat. We passed through Gate City and onto the waters of the Big Sandy.

"I used to know every snag in this river," said Pop, "but I guess it's changed as my hair has changed in the years I have been away. It seems like home to me, this little river where it takes more work to make money, more skill to pilot a boat."

Mom never spoke. Her eyes were swollen. We stopped at the little house we left. The oak tree in the yard, where we had played, we anchored to one of the oak trees. We carried the casket up the steep bank to the house where the funeral would be preached that night. The old men that used to work for Pop—that used to river-rat with him—would come back. They would be there. They would come from the mountains.

Mom walked into the house. She saw the old stains of blood upon the floor. Mom screamed and started to sink to the floor. Clara caught her.

That night, mountain men, huge men—tall and bony with steel-bearded faces—filed up the path from the river. Women came with them. Women lean and tall, dressed in long flowing dresses and with shawls around their shoulders, came up the bank with their men. I slipped into the room where Hilton was in his coffin. I had played on the river with Hilton, the river whose water washed him to cleanse him for burial; I had talked to him. I knew him as intimately as I know a stalk of corn in the garden.

I went in the room while the crowd was gathering in to hear Brother Ike Strickland preach the funeral. I went up to where Brother Hilton was laying a corpse. And I said, "Speak to me, Brother Hilton. Speak to me about the river. Tell me about the Big Sandy. Did you know you was back at the old house on the Big Sandy? Speak to me—oh, speak to me, brother Hilton—" The wind came through the window and moved his hair and ruffled the window curtain. "Uncle Jake lives here now. Do you know it? You remember him, don't you, Hilton?"

But not a sound came. I could see the moon and the white clouds in the sky. I could see the Big Sandy up between the two mountains, a ribbon of silver fading away between two rows of willows, far up between the mountains.

I could hear them in the other room crying. I could hear them singing, "There's a land beyond the river, that they call the sweet Forever." The moon was high above the Big Sandy and the wind was blowing through the window. Hilton lay there with his lips curved like Pop's, just like he wanted to say something. I could see the tombstones around the church where we used to go to Sunday school and church, the place where all of Pop's people are laid after they left the Big Sandy.

Tomorrow we'll take Hilton there. He'll be laid there among his kin that have followed the river, have been shot and shot others, those who have cut the timber from the mountain slopes and cleared the valley. That is where Hilton will sleep. The Big Sandy will flow not far away; one can hear it murmuring from the church where Hilton sleeps for it is not a stone's throw away. It knows the dreams and holds the dreams of three generations of Fraziers now sleeping in this Big Sandy earth.

RICH MEN

I don't mean to be braggin'," says Pa, "but, Lester, you can ask your Ma there and she can tell you we started from scratch. She can tell you that I've been a sharp trader in livestock. I take it atter my Pap. He ust to be one of the best buyers on Big Sandy. He bought droves of cattle. I remember ridin' a pony and goin' with Pap. We took a big shepherd dog with us. He helped us drive the cattle home. We'd come home sometimes with a hundred head of cattle. When the buyin' in Kentucky got scarce we crossed the Big Sandy and bought cattle in the state of West Virginia."

Pa rocked in his chair in front of the big fireplace. Ma was knittin' Pa a pair of socks. She listened to Pa talk about cattle buyin'. Sister Nell was poppin' corn over the bright flames that leaped up from the forestick. Ma never said a word when Pa was talkin' about cattle-buyin'. She didn't say he was the best trader on Big Sandy. She didn't say he wasn't. Ma only looked at the fire and knitted Pa's socks.

"Lester," says Pa, "I want for you to be a cattle buyer. I've paid for four thousand acres of land. I've got it in grass. I've got one of the finest grass farms on Big Sandy. I ain't sayin' I'm exactly a rich man. And you can judge from the neighbors around us I ain't a poor man. When they haf to sell a cow to get a little needy money, they know where to come. They know old Hen Blaine's got the money. They know when he ain't got it he can mighty quick find it. I'm allus ready to buy and sell cattle. I love the looks of cattle. I allus have a purty drove of cattle around my barn. You know that, son. We ain't been without them since you've been a little shaver and I rocked you on my knee."

Pa knocked the ashes off his big cigar. Sister Nell finished poppin' the capper of corn. She shoved back the lid. She passed it around us. The capper of corn didn't go very far. Nine of us got a handful of corn apiece. "I'll not take any popcorn," says Pa; "can't you young'uns see that I'm smokin'?"

"What do you think about my tradin', Tibithia?" says Pa, looking over at Ma. He was trying to make Ma talk. He wanted Ma to say he was the best trader on Big Sandy.

"I don't think about it," says Ma. "I don't think it's a great thing to skin poor people out'n their cattle. I think there'll come a time when you'll reap what you sow. You sit there and brag, and my Pap allus told me that pride comes before a fall. I think you are headin' for a fall."

Pa took his thumbs down from behind his vest. He looked hard at Ma. Then he turned his head. He looked at the blazin' fire. Pa's black eyes danced in his head. He was riled the way Ma talked to him. He watched Sister Nell shuffle another capper of popcorn over the fire. Ma just kept on knittin' a sock like nothin' had happened. I hated to see Pa mad at Ma. I think she told him the truth. Pa couldn't see himself as others saw him. I didn't know whether he was the greatest livestock trader on Big Sandy or not. No one but Pa had ever told me that he'd swum one hundred head of white-faced cattle from West Virginia across the Big Sandy to Kentucky at one time. After Pa told me this he said the old-timers used to call him Tradin' Hen Blaine. I'd never heard Pa called that in my life.

"I think I'll turn in," says Pa. "Seems like any more I'm not a welcome man around my own fireside. Seems like my wife has turned my children on me. I'm one of the most upstandin' men along the Big Sandy River. If I've not made my family a respectable livin', then who has, I'd like to know?"

Pa looked at Ma for an answer. Ma kept on knittin' socks. She never spoke to Pa. Pa walked out of the room. He went in the back room to bed. We stayed up a long time and popped corn. Ma put her knittin' away. She pulled off her glasses and laid them on the stand table.

"Children, it's bedtime," says Ma. "Lester, you got to get up at four in the mornin' and help your Pa with all this feedin' before you go to school. You ought to be in bed right now."

"Yes, Ma," I says. I went upstairs to bed. I remember I had dreams about cattle. I had dreams about Pa tradin'. I saw whole droves of cattle on the hills. I saw them run away from Kentucky and swim the Big Sandy River to the state of West Virginia. I thought Pa's cattle jumped the fence and run back to West Virginia. I was glad. I wouldn't haf to feed them any longer. Then I thought they come back home and gnawed the bark from the black-oak trees. I thought they were so hungry that their sides caved in. I thought when Pa saw them comin' back he stood by the gate and cried because they were so poor. I was dreamin' about Pa's cattle when I heard him say: "Roll ou'n that bed, Lester. It's feedin' time."

II

When I got dressed and got downstairs Ma had our breakfast ready. Pa, Ma, and I et our breakfasts together. Ma watched when Pa's coffee cup was empty and she would take the biler and pour Pa more coffee. Pa would wipe his mustache after he took a sip of coffee. He would press it out against his red cheeks with his hands. Then Pa would take more honey and hot biscuits and butter. He would drink coffee with his honey and his buttered hot biscuits. I could allus tell when Pa was ready to get up from the table. That was when he had finished eatin' ten biscuits. He would allus drink four cups of strong black coffee. Then Pa would get up and light his cigar. We would go toward the barn. When Pa got near the barn he laid his cigar on a big stump. He'd never go about the barn smokin'.

We had to fork hay for two hundred head of cattle. Pa had one hundred and fifty white-faced cattle. He had fifty pick-ups of all sorts. "Scrub cattle," Pa called them. We kept our cattle on the outside durin' purty winter weather. We didn't have barnroom for all of them. When the snow fell, a lot of our cattle laid in the pine grove around from the barn. We'd carry hay from the stacks and throw it over the fence on patches of briers and brush to keep the cattle from trampin' it under their feet. We'd fork down hay out'n our big barn loft for the cows and cattle we kept in the barn.

Pa walked in front. I could see the fire sparkle on the end of his big cigar when the wind blowed. The frost was white on the ground. The stars were still in the sky. Pa laid his cigar on the big oak stump. He walked in the barn. We climbed the ladder to the barn loft. Pa forked down hay for the stalls on one side of the barn. I forked down hay for the cattle on the other side of the barn. It wasn't daylight yet. We walked out near the pine grove. We had our hay stacked near the fence. We started to fork our hay and pitch it over for the cattle on the other side of the pasture fence. The stars were leavin' the sky now. The wind laid. It was gettin' light enough to see over the pasture fields.

"'Pears like," says Pa, "I hear a rustlin' in that haystack."

"Must be the wind," I says, "shakin' the hay."

"No, it ain't no wind," says a voice. "You gouged me with that fork!"

"What are you doin' sleepin' in my hay nohow?" says Pa.

A man rolled out and shook the straw from his back. His ragged clothes would barely hang on him. His pants were patched until it looked like another patch couldn't be sewed on. He had a long beard over his face. He had long black chin whiskers. Pieces of brown straw were mixed with his black beard.

"You wouldn't scold a old man that found shelter from the ragin' winds of winter in your haystack, would you?" says the stranger.

"Come to think about it," says Pa, "I don't guess I would."

"What is your name?" says the stranger to Pa.

"Tradin' Hen Blaine," says Pa, puttin' his thumbs behind his vest and danglin' the watch fob hangin' to his gold watch chain.

"Oh, you are that rich Hen Blaine, ain't you?" says the stranger.

"Some people think I'm a rich man," says Pa.

"I'm a rich man, too," says the stranger.

"A rich man?" says Pa. "Then what are you doin' sleepin' in people's haystacks?"

"I ain't got no good clothes," he says. "I couldn't ast to stay in your fine house."

He took his hands and raked the straw from his beard. Pa bent over and laughed and laughed. Pa started laughin' again. "A rich man," Pa would say; then he would laugh and laugh. "A rich man sleepin' in my haystack!"

"Why, I own big farms," says the stranger. "I just love to own land. I'm goin' to live my life on this earth. I'm goin' to die. Then in seven years I'll be back on earth doin' my business!"

"The man's off, Les," Pa whispered. "He's a funny old man." Pa bent over and slapped his knees and laughed. I thought Pa would die laughin'.

"No, I ain't off," says the stranger. "I'm in my sound mind. I'm tellin' you the truth. I'll be back here seven years atter I die, takin' care o' my business. People won't believe me, but it's the truth. They won't believe I'm a rich man, either."

"What is your name?" says Pa. "I don't think I ever heard of you."

"I don't guess you have heard of me," says the stranger, "but you will hear o' me someday. You will hear o' me atter I die and come back seven years later to run my farm. My name ain't worth knowin' now, but it will be."

"Man talks crazy," says Pa. "I never heard sich foolish talk."

"No, I ain't crazy," he says. "How many times do I haf to tell you I ain't crazy? I'm just cold from sleepin' all night in your haystack. Why don't you invite me to your house? Why don't you give me a good warm breakfast? That is the way one good neighbor should be with another."

"I would have a dirty tramp like you in my house," says Pa. "Not only dirty, but you ain't all there in the head!"

"You tell a man straight to his face," says the ragged stranger. "You ain't a bit nice. You'll never be back runnin' your purty farm seven years atter you have left this world. You'll be dead as a lizard."

"So will you, too," says Pa. "You look like you have one foot in the grave now and the other one about to slip in!"

"You're so mean to me," says the strange man.

"Don't talk like that," I says to Pa.

"Your father is a very rich man," says the stranger to me. "I am a very rich man, but your Pa won't believe me. He thinks I'm a tramp."

"I don't think any more about you," says Pa. "Clear out'n here now. I've got to finish feedin' my cattle. I ain't got time to be bothered with you. I have work to do."

"Have you got cattle?" says the stranger. "I have cattle. I love cattle. I have big farms filled with cattle. I cheated people to get my cattle. I am a rich man."

"Cheated people?" says Pa.

"Yes," says the stranger, "and you've cheated people. Ain't I heard of you before? You are Tradin' Hen Blaine!"

"Right," says Pa. "I'm Tradin' Hen Blaine."

Pa bristled up. He looked over his frost-covered fields. Pa looked as big as I'd seen him.

"I'd like to walk down to the fence with you and look at your cattle," says the dirty beardy man.

"Just so you don't fall down, you old plug, you," says Pa. "If you do I'll fasten a drag chain around your legs and haul you to the bone yard with the rest of my old plug stock." Pa laughed and laughed. Pa bent over and laughed at what he had said to the strange man.

"I'll make it, all right," he says. "I get happy when I get to look at purty cattle. How many head of cattle do you have?"

"I have two hundred head," says Pa. "I have one hundred and fifty white-faced cattle and fifty scrubs."

"Lord," says the old man. "You've cheated a lot of people buyin' that many. You are a great trader. Didn't anybody ever tell you that you cheated fer to buy all these cattle?"

"Yes," says Pa. "My wife did."

The cattle come to the fence for their hay. There is a big drove of them. The woods are full of cattle.

"Go turn the rest of the herd out'n the barn," says Pa. "I want a tramp just to see my herd all together. Says he's a rich man. I just want him to see a real herd of cattle."

"All right, Pa," I says.

III

I run to the barn to turn the cattle out in the pasture. The frost was goin' up in streaks of fog to the mornin' sun. The air was clean and sweet to smell. I run over the frosty road to the barn. When I come back from the barn I saw Pa talkin' to the man with his hands. The old man was leanin' on his cane. He was noddin' "yes" and "no" to the words Pa said. He was agreein' with all Pa said. Pa felt pleased. I could tell by the way he put his thumbs behind his vest.

"You have a great herd of cattle," says the stranger. "Just what would you take for all that herd of cattle?"

"Oh," says Pa, "I've had three buyers already. I was offered fifty-five hundred dollars by one. Another offered me fifty-seven hundred. The last offer I got was six thousand. I'm holdin' to spring to get my price."

"Then you sell in the spring," says the stranger.

"No," says Pa, "I buy of a spring and sell in the fall. Then I buy in the winter when people's feed gets scarce. I sell in the spring atter I've wintered the cattle. That is the way I make my money."

"You're a smart man," says the old man. I looked at the patches on his pants. I could see the hide through the patches. His flesh was blue. His bowed legs were quiverin' with cold. The cane shook in his tremblin' hands.

"How much would you take fer them cattle?" says the old man.

Pa started laughin'. Pa bent over and laughed and laughed. He lit a new cigar. He puffed smoke and laughed. He pulled at his vest with his thumbs and laughed. "You wantin' to buy all my cattle?" says Pa.

"I thought you might make me a price," says the old man.

"Why, I'd sell them to you, if you'd pay me right now," says Pa, "fer thirty-five hundred dollars."

Pa started laughin' again.

"Just a minute, Tradin' Hen Blaine," says the stranger.

"You've just dealt with 'Ginsang' Tootle from Bruin. Ain't you heard o' me?"

"Lord, yes," says Pa. "I've heard o' Ginsang Tootle. You ain't him, are you?"

The stranger just reached down and started tearin' a patch from the knee of his pants.

"I can give you three one-thousand-dollar bills," says Ginsang, "and a five-hundred-dollar bill – or I can write you a check fer it!"

"You ain't doin' neither," says Pa. "I was just jokin'."

"Oh, yes, you are Tradin' Hen Blaine," says Ginsang. "Men don't back out on you when you deal with them. You ain't backin' out on me. People don't do me that way. You've traded with me. I'm drivin' your cattle off."

Pa's face turned red. His blue eyes got as big as dollars. Pa couldn't speak. Pa had been tricked.

"I've been layin' fer you, Tradin' Hen Blaine," says Ginsang. "I've heard you'd never been cheated. I heard you'd cheated everybody you'd ever traded with. So I've laid fer you. I laid in your haystack! My helpers are waitin' fer me out by the big road. They have the shepherd dogs and the horses. I ain't been in your haystack all night."

"But I'm a ruined man," says Pa. "I'm a ruined man, for all I have is in my cattle."

"You're a rich man," says Ginsang, "and I'm a rich man. We are both rich men. You know how I got my start?"

"No," says Pa, "and I don't care."

"I laid before a man's fire one whole week and carried a little mattock through the woods and dug ginsang. One mornin' I got him to price his cattle. I had the money ready. I took 'em. He tried to back out like you did. But I wouldn't let him no more than I would let you. I got the name of 'Ginsang' atter that. So I'm Ginsang Tootle from Bruin Creek. Remember me by that name?"

"I remember you, Ginsang Tootle," I says. "Don't you bring your cattle to the Grant store at Crossroads and get a load of things every fall before bad weather sets in?"

"I do," he says.

"I was over there when storekeeper Reece Setser made you a present of a hat if you would throw your old one away. You'd bought three hundred dollars' worth of stuff from him and had it loaded on your cattle wagon. When you drove away you stopped your cattle and went over the bank and got your old hat, didn't you?"

"I did," says Ginsang. "I'm the man."

"You didn't have a long beard then," I says.

"No," says Ginsang. "I growed it so your Pa wouldn't know me. I come to cheat him like he has cheated everybody else. Death is goin' to cheat me, but I feel like I can uptrip him. That is why I'm buildin' my house now and havin' furniture put in it. I'll be back in seven years doin' business. I'll be back buyin' cattle on the Big Sandy River. I can't stand to leave this river."

"Then you did mean what you said a while ago," says Pa.

"I ain't told you no lies," says Ginsang. "I own land and cattle and I am a very rich man. It is easier fer me to tell the truth. I can do what I want to do when I tell the truth. It sounds like a lie to everybody. You are one of the best traders on Big Sandy River. But I've uptripped you."

"You don't haf to say it. I'll come again. I'll beat you if my spirit has to trade with your spirit in another land."

"I must get my cattle," says Ginsang. "I must be on my way. Just turn them out'n the pasture and start them down the road. I'll feel big behind them."

I opened the gate. Ginsang walked away with Pa's big herd of cattle. The road was filled with cattle. Ginsang walked behind. His patched pants would hardly stay on his skinny body.

His beard fell to his waist.

IV

"Why, the man fooled me," Pa said to Ma. "He acted crazy. Talked about comin' back to this earth seven years after he dies, to start buyin' cattle again. He worked me into a trap. I thought he was a tramp."

"Ain't you never heard of old Ginsang Tootle?" says Ma. "He had a house built and filled with furniture for him and his wife. He thinks and has her believin' they're comin' back atter they have been dead seven years. He's the one that cheated old Fonse Leadingham out'n all his cattle. Stayed there a week and slept like a dog before the fire. Run over the hills and dug ginsang. Asked Fonse what he would take for his cattle. Got him to set a cheap price. Ripped a patch from his pants leg— shelled out the money and bought 'em right there."

"I'm a poor man tonight," says Pa. "It just took the wind out'n me to lose my cattle like that."

Pa didn't smoke a cigar. Pa didn't brag. Pa looked downhearted.

"You'll haf to be more careful," says Ma. "Watch who sleeps in your haystacks from this on. Everything you've told me that he told you is the truth. How could he fool you that way, Henry?"

"The long beard on his face," says Pa, "or I'd a-knowed him. Then he started talkin' about bein' a rich man—and that he would die and in seven years he'd be back to run his farm. I thought he was crazy. I thought he was a tramp. I didn't know I's talkin' to Ginsang Tootle."

"Wolves will come to you dressed in sheep's clothin'," says Ma.

"Yes," says Pa. "That wolf in sheep's clothin' has made me a poor man. But I'll come again. I can see a hundred head of white-faced cattle swimmin' the Big Sandy River. I'll beat him yet. I'll cheat him if my spirit has to cheat his spirit in another world!"

Ma looked at Pa and laughed. Pa lit his cigar. He put his thumbs behind his vest.

"Tradin' Hen Blaine," says Pa. "Still the best trader on the Big Sandy River."

SYLVANIA IS DEAD

"It's too bad about Sylvania," Bert Pratt said as he caught hold of a sassafras sprout and pulled himself another step. Lonnie Pennix was behind.

"Durn this old coal pick," Lonnie said. "If I didn't have it I could make it all right."

"I got this long-handled shovel and broadax and I'm making it all right," Bert answered from above. "You're a lot younger than I am. You ought'n to be grumbling."

September was here and the leaves were falling from the oaks and beeches. The backbone of the mountain was gray and hard as the bleached bone of a carcass. The buzzards floated in high circles and craned their necks.

"Funny thing about a buzzard," Bert said. "He knows when anything dies in the mountains. I've often wondered if a buzzard could smell."

"Must be a buzzard can smell," Lonnie answered.

"What do you say we blow a minute before we get to the top," Bert said with his breath getting shorter. "I'm about pooped out. We just didn't think about the heat nor the cold when we ust to climb this mountain and get moonshine from Sylvania, did we? I've come over this old mountain many a night, drunk as a biled owl. Come right down here over these rocks

73

with a couple o' big jugs strapped on me. Had a pistol in each hand shooting to hear my pistols crack."

The two men started again to climb the mountain. Their shirts were wet as sweat could make them. They were sticking to their backs.

"I could wring my shirt out and hang it on a grapevine to dry," Lonnie said.

"Take it easy, Lonnie, and get good footholts on the sand rocks," Bert answered.

"Look at the buzzards again," Lonnie said as he pointed to a cloud of circling buzzards.

"Whooie! At the top at last," Bert said. "I'd rather walk twenty miles on level ground as to climb that baby."

"When I see the shack, I have sad thoughts about poor old Sylvania," Lonnie said. "You could trade Sylvania a pistol fer licker when you didn't have the money. You could trade her corn, leather britches, beans and turnips, fer pistols, clothes, butter, eggs, ham meat, sow middlins, lard, flour, and corn meal."

"Look out there, Lonnie, at that crowd, won't you!" Bert said as he stood and looked toward the shack. "How did they ever get up this mountain?"

The mules and horses were tied to the garden palings and to the little blackjack saplings in the front yard. Many of the horses and mules were bareback and many had saddles on them. Overhead the buzzards circled low.

"Shoot into the buzzards, Lonnie, and shoo 'em away."

"Don't reckon the crack of my pistol will disturb the peace of the funeral as much as the buzzards will. Up there in the air pilfering around where they ain't got no business."

Lonnie pulled the pistol from his hip holster. He leveled it toward the turkey buzzards and pow-powed five times.

"Shooting around here and my wife a corpse," Skinny ran

from the door of his shack and shouted. "Getting the mules and horses skeered to death! It ain't good manners, boys!"

"Just shooting away the buzzards, Skinny," Lonnie said. "See 'em taking off the mountain yander. Brought one down fer I saw 'im flopping among the black-oak tops."

"That part is all right, boys," Skinny answered. "Buzzards are a perfect nuisance in a time like this." Skinny walked back inside the shack.

The men had brought their picks, broadaxes, long-handled shovels, and corn scoops to dig the grave. They had brought handsaws, axes, hammers, nails, foot adzes to make the coffin.

"I tell you Sylvania is a big woman," Woodbridge Spears said. "Just six hundred and fifty pounds. She's never been out'n that house since she was a little girl. She married Skinny, a little hundred-pound man, and she has lived all her life in there with him. Her Pap and Ma moved out to let her and Skinny have the house. If they'd moved Sylvania out they'd a had to tear the house down. They didn't bother about doing that."

"But she'll have to come out'n there today," Remus Wolf said. "God knows how we'll get her out. Might haf to tear the house down. Might haf to saw the door out bigger."

"Might just take the floor up and bury her under the floor," Estill Valence said. "We'd just have the furniture and the barrel to move out."

"We can't do that," George Fannin answered. "Skinny might want to jump the broom again. He wouldn't want his first wife buried under the floor."

"You're right, George," Remus said. "It would cause a lot of disturbances atterwards."

"We don't want no disturbances," Bert said with tears in his eyes. "I've come here and got moonshine when the country was dry as a bone. I was right here when the Revenooers was atter Sylvania. They come and bought some from her barrel and

75

then showed her the Badge. She just laughed at them. 'You'll haf to get me out'n the house first,' she said. 'Atter you get me out'n the house, how are you goin' to get me down off the mountain?' All they could do was pour out a barrel of good licker. It wasn't no time until Sylvania had the barrel replenished and we were going back again."

The saws and axes were clicking up at the barn. You could hear the men talking and laughing as they worked.

"I'll bet that coffin is four feet wide across the bottom."

"Looks big enough for a whole family."

"We'll never get it through the door."

"Purty black-oak wood we're makin' this coffin out'n. Some say black-oak ain't as good as wild cherry."

"Just put the two in the ground fer fence posts, gentlemen, and see which lasts the longest."

"Right out under the pine where Pap and Ma are buried is where I want you to dig my wife's grave," Skinny said. "Bert Pratt, you take charge of it. It's the only place up here where there's dirt enough to sink a grave."

"I'll sure attend to it, Skinny," Bert said.

Bert walked in front with a broadax and a long-handled shovel on his shoulder. Men followed him carrying picks, mattocks, long-handled shovels, and short-handled shovels across their shoulders. They followed Bert out the mountaintop, across a little sag where Skinny had a corn patch. They walked over to the tallest pine in the grove. Under the tall pine were two graves with sandstone tombstones hewn out with broadaxes.

Where Skinny had marked the place for the grave, Bert started digging.

"I'd do anything fer old Skinny," Bert said to the men. "He's in bushels o' misery just now."

"I'd do anything fer him too," Rodney Fitch said. "There

76

never was a better woman that Sylvania. When she sold you a gallon of moonshine you got a gallon of unadulterated moonshine and not two quarts of moonshine with a quart of water and a quart of carbide all stirred up well and shook before drinking. I don't know what we'll do without her. We won't have no market fer our corn."

"They say," Tom Hankas said as he let his pick fall against the hard mountain earth, "that you'll never miss your mother until she's gone. I say we'll never miss Sylvania until she's gone. She's been a mother to all of us."

One crew of men worked hard and fast digging the big hole. Then they got out and rested and another crew took their places and worked until they got tired. Then the third crew of men took the tools and worked until they got tired. Then the first crew came back and replaced the third crew.

"We got a lot of dirt to move before high noon," Bert reminded the men as he sat under the pine and fanned his hot face with his cap.

The lazy wind blew over the mountaintop. Leaves swarmed in the wind. Leaves fell into the grave the men were digging for Sylvania. Buzzards flew above the shack while Flora Fitch and Vie Bostick worked in the shack and prepared Sylvania for burial.

"It's getting high noon," Skinny said. "It's time the boys had the grave dug."

"We got Sylvania ready fer burial," Flora Fitch said, standing in the door of the shack. "We dressed 'er in that flowered silk dress she got married in."

"She allus wanted to be put away in that dress," Skinny said.

"I see them coming from the barn now with the coffin," Vie Bostick said.

"Coffin looks like a young house to me," Lonnie Pennix

remarked.

Skinny walked out to the new coffin. He looked at the black-oak wood gleaming in the sun.

"It's a nice job, boys," Skinny said as his bony hand tried to shake it.

"Took six of us to carry that coffin from the barn down there," Amos Chitwood said. "Black-oak wood is powerful heavy."

"It'll take twelve of us to carry Sylvania to the grave, then," Bert Madden said.

"The boys have the grave ready," Lonnie said. "See 'em coming out the ridge path."

"Looks like they've all jumped in a rain barrel," Flora said. "They are all so wet with sweat."

Skinny walked inside the shack.

"The grave's ready," Bert said, wiping sweat from his beardy face with a red bandanna, then squeezing the sweat from the bandanna with his big hands. "Had a time getting through that dry ground. I had to plug five buzzards, too. Hope I didn't skeer you none."

"A little shooting is not goin' to bother us none," Flora answered. "What's a-going to bother us is when we start to take Sylvania out'n the house."

"Can't we saw the door bigger?" Rodney Fitch asked.

"Just as well take one side the house out by the time you make the door big enough to take that coffin out," Vie Bostick answered.

"The chimney nearly kivvers one end of the shack," Bert said. "Why can't we just tear it down? Won't take long."

"Bert, ask Skinny about it," Rodney Fitch said. "Tell 'im that's the only way to get her out."

Bert went inside the shack to speak to Skinny. The crowd of sweaty men waited outside. They held their working tools in

78

their hands. The yard was filled with people. They stood and looked at the new coffin and talked about it. The horses and mules tramped around the blackjack saplings and fought the flies. The mules heehawed and laid back their ears and bit at the horses.

"I tell you men it was a job to get Sylvania ready for burial," Vie said. "It'll take six powerful men to put her in the coffin."

"We'll get 'er in all right," Rodney Fitch said.

Bert came to the door.

"Boys, tear down that chimney," he said.

Bert was the first to climb that wall. Lonnie climbed after him. They stood on the clapboard roof and rolled the rocks off the chimney. Lum Tremble reached Bert up a coal pick. Bert pried the rocks loose from the daubing where they were stuck.

"Soon have it done, boys, the way you're raining the rocks down here," Rodney Fitch said. "Stand in the clear, fellers, and see that the rocks don't roll on your toes."

The chimney was lowered to a flat pile of cornfield rocks. The hole was big enough to take the coffin through.

"All right, boys, let's take the coffin in and get Sylvania," Abraham Pitts commanded.

Three men got on a side and one on each end of the coffin. Over the chimney rocks they tugged it into the shack.

"Set 'er down easy, boys, on these poles now, Abraham Pitts said. "Don't ketch anybody's finger now. Take 'er easy...down ...down...easy...down."

The coffin was placed on three poles. The poles were placed on rocks so the men could get their hands under the poles. Sylvania was upon the bed now, a great heap in a flowered dress.

"About six of you strong men lift her," Bert ordered.

Bert took his handkerchief from his pocket and wiped the tears from his eyes. Many of the men shed tears. The women

79

stood and looked on. They could not begin to lift Sylvania. They strained their backs trying to roll her into the big flowered dress they had spliced so it would fit her.

The men, one ahold of each leg, one ahold of each arm, one at the head and one at each side, lifted her from the bed. "Easy, easy now, boys – easy – easy – easy –" It was a bad place to lift, and hard lifting, but they placed Sylvania in her coffin.

"Couldn't a made a better fit," Lonnie Fitch said.

"It was my wife's dyin' request that she didn't have her funeral preached nor no songs sung," Skinny said. "See that barrel over there! It's the last my wife made. It's all fer you, boys. There's the dipper over there. What you can't finish today you can finish Monday when you come back to hep me make my new chimney."

"Fellers, I'm a little thirsty," Bert said. "Let me to that dipper."

"She kept us wet through the dry season," Rodney Fitch said.

"It just takes another dipper to cool my throat," Lonnie said. "I'm hot as a lizard in a new ground fire."

The thirsty men stood around the barrel and drank like cattle around a water hole.

"I patronized Sylvania in life and I'll patronize 'er in death," Bert said. "Take your last long look at Sylvania, boys, while Lonnie get the nails and the hammer."

The men looked at Sylvania. Strong men, tanned by the sun where their flesh was not hidden by beard on their faces, looked at Sylvania and wept. They pulled handkerchiefs and bandannas from their pockets and wiped their eyes.

"Just a lot o' drunk men crying," Rodney said. "It'll be awful before we get her to the grave. They'll all be crying. Ought to a had the licker last."

"Who is conducting this funeral, me or you, Rodney?"

Skinny asked. "I'm doing what Sylvania requested. I'm going through with it if they all get down drunk."

"Ouch, whooie, that damn big-headed hammer," Lonnie yelled. "I couldn't hit the side of a barn with it. Lord, I nearly mashed the end of my finger off trying to drive that nail."

"Let me have that hammer," Rodney requested. "I can still drive nails. Hit some people with a sour apple and they get drunk. They can't take their licker."

Rodney shaped the coffin lid and spiked it down while the men looked on.

"My poor Sylvania is gone forever," Skinny cried.

"Come away from that barrel," Bert demanded. "Do you fellers want to get down drunk and leave the corpse in a shack that has the end out'n it? Get under these poles! What do you think today is, your birthday?"

Two men got under each end of the three poles. "Get in front, Rodney," Bert ordered. "I'll get behind and tail the coffin."

Fourteen men were around the black-oak coffin. They walked slowly out at the end of the house where they tore the chimney down.

"Just like picking up a house with the family in it," Rodney groaned as they walked across the yard and out the ridge path toward the pine. The crowd was noisy now. The men were laughing, talking, and crying. The women walked behind as the men carried Sylvania to her grave. Before they reached the fresh heap of dirt under the tall pine tree, Bert pulled his pistol from his hip holster and shot into a cloud of buzzards.

"Easy—easy—easy—take 'er easy, boys," Bert said. "Don't mash no fingers."

They lowered Sylvania's coffin by the big pine where the dirt was piled high.

"You got the plowlines, ain't you, Oggle?" Skinny asked.

"I got five pair of plowlines," Oggle Fox answered.

"Put two big poles across the grave," Bert ordered. "There they lay already cut."

The men carried the green hickory poles and laid them across the grave.

"All the rest of you back to your places now," Bert ordered. "Let's lift the coffin onto the poles."

"Let's wind a minute," Eif Turnstile said. "I'm about gone."

"Wish I was planted by 'er side," Skinny screamed.

"No use to feel that way, Skinny," Lonnie consoled him.

"Take it easy, Skinny," Bert said.

"Wish I could," Skinny answered.

"Eif, you've had time to get your wind now," Lonnie said. "What do you say we lower this coffin, men? Get the plowlines under it. Two get hold of the end of each line."

The men placed ten plowlines under the coffin.

"Ready now, boys!" Lonnie said. "Heave ho! Heave ho! Heave ho!"

"Let's pull these poles from under the coffin," Bert ordered. "Four men to each pole."

The men took the poles from under the coffin while twenty men held it up with the plowlines.

"Let 'er down," Bert ordered.

The big coffin dropped slowly while two men strained at each end of ten ropes. They pulled the ropes from under the coffin. It was all over.

"May God rest Sylvania's soul," Bert said, wiping tears from his eyes with his red bandanna.

Two men took Skinny toward the shack while clouds of gray dust swirled above the busy shovels. There were words of condolence in the lazy wind's molesting the dry flaming leaves on the mountain.

THE WIND BLEW EAST

"Mom, I don't want to stay with Uncle Egbert and Aunt Viddie," I said. "I'd rather not go to school if I have to stay with 'em."

"It's the only chance we have to send you to school," Mom said. "You know that it works well. They need your help in the store before and after school and on Saturdays, since help is scarce. And you know we live too far away from the high school, and we're not able to pay your expenses in town."

"But town folks are too particular about their houses," I said. "You know how Aunt Viddie is about her house. Uncle Egbert has lived with her so long he's as cranky as she is."

"It's better they're cranky about cleanliness than it is to keep a dirty house."

I knew there wasn't any way out unless I ran away from home. I didn't want to do that. I wanted to go to Greenwood High School since I'd seen the Greenwood Tigers play basketball. I wanted to be a basketball player. And if I went to Greenwood High School, I'd have to stay with Uncle Egbert and Aunt Viddie.

"I hate to stay with 'em," I said to Pa and Mom as I carried my suitcase to the express wagon.

"Son, it's your only chance to get an education," Pa said.

"It's better to stay with 'em and get an education than it is to go through life without one. You'll never know the worth of an education until you have to go through life without one like I have. It's better to stay in a barn and sleep in the manger than it is to go without book learning."

Pa slapped our mule, Barney, with the rope lines and we were off down the road toward Greenwood. I waved good-by to Mom as we left home, down the winding dusty road bordered on one side with maturing corn and on the other by queen's lace and wild phlox.

"You see what I have to do to make a livin'," Pa said as he nodded back to the express wagon filled with a load of truck, two crates of young chicken, two cans of cream, and a big willow basket of eggs.

As the mule trotted toward Greenwood, Pa talked to me about how to behave myself and how to work hard to get learning in my head.

"Learning is something you can't see," Pa said. "But it's powerful stuff. It's dynamite."

Then Pa would rein Barney to one side of the road to miss a terrapin trying to crawl across the road.

"I like to go to school," I told Pa, "but I don't like to stay in a house where I have to pull my shoes off before I go in to keep from getting grains of sand on the rugs."

"It's better than we have, son," Pa said. "Wish we had carpets on our floors. Your Uncle Egbert and Aunt Viddie've done well with their store. But they don't have a family of young'uns to clothe and feed and educate like I have. It's might nice of 'em to try to help me with my young'uns."

It was a big two-story house with a porch below and one above. The house was painted white and trimmed in green. Tall elms grew around the house and the lawn was shaved almost as close as a man shaves his face. It was shaved closer than some men shave their faces. There were flowers blooming all over the yard and small chairs with striped backs were sitting under the elm shades. And near the big house was the big storehouse where everything was sold from axes to sugar and liniment. And the post office was inside the store. Just above the storehouse, not more than a hundred yards, was the big brick schoolhouse where I would go to school.

"This is a fine place for you, Hester," Pa said.

Pa sold Uncle Egbert some of his young chickens, potatoes, and beans. Then he took Uncle Egbert to one side where I couldn't hear them talk. I knew that he was telling Uncle Egbert to take care of me like I was his own son, to make me behave and work hard in the store, and to work hard in school.

Aunt Viddie came out and shook my hand and said, "Glad to see you here, Hester. Come on over to the house and let me show you your room."

I followed Aunt Viddie to the door wagging my suitcase.

"Your shoes have mud on 'em," Aunt Viddie said, carefully examining my shoes. "You'd better take 'em off before you walk over my floors. I know how that country clay sticks to your shoes! You just can't get it off."

"Yep, it's hard to get off," I said.

"You won't get so much mud on your feet here," Aunt Viddie said. "You'll have streets to walk on."

"Yes, ma'am," I said as I followed her in my sock feet with my suitcase up the long flight of carpeted stairsteps. We passed the doors of many rooms, doors that were closed, until we came to a door in the far end of the upstairs hall.

"This will be your room, Hester," she said. "You can unpack your belongings and get into your work clothes and come to the store. We've never needed help so much in our lives as right now."

"I'll be over in a few minutes," I said.

I put on my faded-blue clean overalls and clean blue work shirt and hurried down to the front door where I put my shoes on; then I hurried to the store and started to work.

"Stack the boxes like this," Uncle Egbert showed me. "You'll have to learn this work. It'll take time."

Uncle Egbert had to have everything done "just so" in the store. It didn't matter how many customers he had waiting to be waited on. Often there would be nine people lined up in front of the post-office window waiting to get their post. And if Uncle Egbert was putting boxes upon the shelves, he would get down from the stepladder and stand and look at them to see if he had stacked them neatly. He would let people wait before the window for their post. The storehouse was almost like the dwelling house but not quite – I'd never seen a house, had never been in one in my lifetime, as spick-and-span as Uncle Egbert and Aunt Viddie's.

When I ate at the table I used silverware that hurt my eyes when it shone in the soft light from the chandelier. It was quite different from our old knives and forks and from our oil lamp that sits midway of our table on a faded oilcloth. I had to watch how Uncle Egbert and Aunt Viddie used their knives and forks and spoons; I had to learn table manners by watching them. Even when I used the soap, I had to wash the lather from it and place it back in the soap box just like I'd found it. I'd been used to a washpan, and soap my mother had made. I had to throw a towel down the clothes chute to the basement after I'd used it once. Clothes were taken from the basement and washed every day.

When I went to bed, I couldn't go to sleep, for the bed was so soft. I laid and thought about how folks in town lived as compared to the way we lived. Uncle Egbert had grown up in the country and he had lived like I'd always lived; but Aunt Viddie had grown up in Greenwood and she had had her way about the house and Uncle Egbert had gone her way instead of her going his way. I wondered if something wouldn't happen to a house where people kept it almost too clean to live in and where they wouldn't use a lot of furniture, but kept it covered over, and where they had patterns of silver put away they never used. I'd heard Aunt Viddie talking about her silver, how beautiful it was and too expensive to use on the table. She kept it in the chest drawers. They had enough beautiful dishes for ten families stacked in three-cornered cupboards for display. I'd heard Mom say that pride came before a fall and I'd heard her say when people got too good, something always happened to them. It made me wonder, as I rolled and tossed in this soft bed trying to go to sleep, what would happen to Aunt Viddie and Uncle Egbert's house. They wouldn't let me raise the window blind to my room. They didn't want the sun to shine on the furniture. As I lay wide awake, I thought it was better to sleep in a barn manger with the mules to get an education than it was to live in this house. And I thought, if Pa and Mom only had to stand what I have to stand, I wonder if they'd try to get an education if they were younger and had the chance. I never came inside with shoes on. I left house slippers by the door and when I came to the house, I pulled off my shoes and put on my house slippers. I knew Pa wouldn't want to do this.

I liked the work in the store. And I like going to school. Even the students respected me more because I lived with Uncle Egbert and Aunt Viddie. Everybody in town envied them and women tried to keep their houses like Aunt Viddie kept hers, but many weren't able to have two people working in the house every day like Aunt Viddie was. Uncle Egbert wouldn't approve of the clothes that I had brought from home to wear to school; he bought new clothes for me. I went to school dressed as spick-and-span as the house where I lived was furnished; I went to school as clean as the house where I lived was kept. And the clothes that I had brought to wear to school, I worked in them in the store, and the clothes I brought to wear when I worked in the store, I put back in my suitcase for future use when I'd be back home on the farm. And even in school, teachers seemed to pay me respect because I lived with Uncle Egbert and Aunt Viddie Tremble. Girls tried to talk to me; I knew it wasn't because I was good-looking or smart—it was because I wore good clothes and I was somebody because I was akin to and lived with the Trembles.

Each night I'd go to sleep thinking I'd climbed to the top of a willow in our pasture field down beside a little winding creek and the wind swayed the willow in the wind and it was soft to stretch out on a willow top and bend up and down in the soft wind—sway, sway, sway—until it was nothingness and then morning and awakening again. I knew it was the soft mattress and the willowy springs caused it for I'd been used to a corn-shuck bed on slats. It was hard for me to sleep in such a soft bed— pillowed and tucked and scented down—to blitheful sleep. But one night was different. I heard something over-head—a noise in the attic I couldn't figure out. It kept me awake.

Next morning at the breakfast table I told Aunt Viddie and Uncle Egbert about hearing something in the attic.

"I'm afraid you didn't hear anything, Hester," Uncle Egbert said.

"And if you did hear anything it's been a mouse," Aunt Viddie said. "Probably a rat," Uncle Egbert said.

"But don't mention it to anybody," Aunt Viddie said. "I wouldn't have people to know we had rats in our house for anything."

"I won't mention it," I said. "I wouldn't mention it to you but it kept me awake half of the night."

"Maybe you were dreaming," Aunt Viddie said.

"No, I was wide awake," I said.

I could tell that Aunt Viddie didn't believe me for she laughed.

"And I know it wasn't a mouse," I said. "Its steps were too heavy for a rat."

"May be it was a ghost of some departed dead that once lived and died in this house," Uncle Egbert said with a laugh. "When you hear it again, come to my room and knock and let me hear it too."

I hadn't more than gone to bed when I heard the noise again. I got out of bed and walked down the corridor, and knocked on Uncle Egbert's door. In a few minutes he came down to my room in his pajamas, lounge robe, and house slippers. I was sitting on the side of my bed barefooted.

"Any time you get out of bed," Uncle Egbert warned me, "always put on your house slippers. Never go traipsing over the house barefooted. It's not good manners."

"But listen to that noise up there, won't you?"

Uncle Egbert listened a minute; then he said, "It's a mouse."

"It's too much noise for a mouse," I said.

"Believe you're right," he said. "It must be a rat. But this house is too tight for a rat to get in."

"Too much noise for a rat," I said.

"I'm thinking the same thing," Uncle Egbert said. "Sounds like a cat walking up there. But that attic is sealed tight."

Uncle Egbert listened awhile and then he said, "That noise worries me." But he left my room and went back to bed and I went to bed.

Next day Aunt Viddie's sisters came. They were women as precise about everything as Aunt Viddie. But unlike Aunt Viddie, they had never married. Each had her room in Aunt Viddie's house when they came to visit which was pretty often.

Aunt Viddie told them, as they walked over the house admiring the beauty of the furniture and the cleanliness of the rooms, that I had been hearing something in the attic. And they laughed when Aunt Viddie told them Egbert had told me it was a ghost of some departed dead.

"It's Uncle Dave come back," Aunt Cindy said. "Dave was a man who hated to leave this world and I'll bet he's back here."

"No, it's not Uncle Dave," Aunt Arabella said. "It's Aunt Mary. Mother said she left some old corsets in the attic – and she was such a dear about corsets – I'll bet she's back to get them."

They all laughed like it was funny. I had hopes it would be a big house-snake twenty feet long in the attic and it would take twenty men to get it out and they'd have to tear half the top of the house off to get it.

Next day they teased me about the ghost above my room. And after they'd say something, they'd laugh at their own words. But that night when I went back to bed, I heard two somethings walking over the floor. And I got up, put on my house slippers and my new lounge robe Aunt Viddie'd bought for me, walked down the hall, and knocked on Uncle Egbert's door.

When he came to my room, he looked sour until he saw me in my pajamas, house slippers, and lounge robe. Then his face looked pleasant. "More noise?" he asked me.

"Two noises," I said.

Uncle Egbert said, "That's strange."

He listened awhile, yawned a few times, and went back to bed.

"Did you hear any noise last night?" Aunt Viddie asked me at the breakfast table.

"Two noises," I said. "I got Uncle Egbert up. He heard 'em."

"It's Uncle Dave and Aunt Mary," Aunt Cindy said, laughing. "She brought Uncle Dave back to help her find her corsets."

Then Aunt Viddie, Aunt Cindy, and Aunt Arabella laughed until they jostled coffee from their cups on the clean starched linen tablecloth. But that was all right, for we used a clean tablecloth for each meal.

"It's hard to tell what it is in the garret," Uncle Egbert said. "It's got me worried. Hester does hear something; I know he does for I've heard it two nights now."

Morning, noon, and night at the table, my aunts laughed about the spirits of Uncle Dave and Aunt Mary being back in the garret pilfering around, hunting through rubbage of the long ago. I didn't know Uncle Dave and Aunt Mary but I knew they never married either. And I'd heard my aunts brag about how clean Aunt Mary was about the house. And it made me want to live in a house like my own home again, a house used to live in and not to keep as an ornament.

I didn't feel like I was riding wind-swayed willow branches again when I went to bed. I heard three noises and then I heard an awful fight over my room. I didn't take time to put on my lounge robe and house slippers. I ran down the corridor to Uncle Egbert's room, knocked, and told him to come to my room. And before he reached my room, I knew what the spirits were in the attic for they sent their perfume all over the house. Polecats.

"Oh, it's beastly," Uncle Egbert said, whiffing the scent. "Just how could this awful thing happen to us?"

Then Aunt Viddie came from the room with a handkerchief to her nose. About the same time Aunt Cindy came from her room into the corridor.

"Oh, mercy," Aunt Cindy said.

"Uncle Dave and Aunt Mary and another one of the departed dead are in a fight in the garret," I said.

"Oh, oh, how dreadful," Aunt Arabella said, rushing from

her room. "This lovely old house and all your fine furniture and linens, Viddie! How dreadful! How could it've happened!"

My aunts are not too nice to know the scent of polecats, I thought. And then I thought about what had happened. One polecat had got up in the garret and he had brought his lover, and his rival had followed them and they'd all got into a fight. So there were polecats still in town even though the people walked so they got rain in their noses when it rained. Now we were all getting back to earth again.

But that was one of the most dreadful nights I ever put over my head. We got our clothes, though the scent had settled on them, went downstairs, to get as far away as we could get from the scent, and yet it drifted down to us. In our night clothes we waited for morning to come. My aunts talked about "how dreadful" it was until I couldn't stand to hear them mention these words. Almost before daylight Uncle Egbert went after Tom Hedley, an old trapper, to come and get the polecats from the garret. While he was gone, I had to leave my aunts and get out of the model home for a breath of fresh air. Their talking and the scent were about to finish me.

When Tom Hedley came, just a bit after daylight, he crawled under the floor and found a hole rats, polecats—something—had eaten, big enough to let the polecats go between the weatherboarding and storm sheeting up to the garret.

"How can you get 'em out, Tom?" Uncle Egbert asked.

"Can't git 'em out unless I tear a hole in the roof or the ceiling out beneath the garret," he said.

"Don't do that," Aunt Viddie said.

"Will it leave more scent in the house if you take them out like that?" Aunt Cindy asked.

"Yes, ma'am, it will," he said.

"Then don't do that," Aunt Arabella protested.

"But we got to get 'em out someway," Uncle Egbert said.

"We can starve 'em down," Tom said. "It might take two or three days."

"How dreadful," Aunt Arabella said.

"My furniture," Aunt Viddie said.

"I know it's bad," Tom Hedley said.

"Don't you say anything about this, Tom," Aunt Viddie said. "I don't want people in Greenwood to know about it. I'm embarrassed."

"Say anything about it, ma'am?" Tom Hedley said. "Everybody will know it. If the wind blows east, neighbors in the east will know about it; if the wind blows south, neighbors in the south will know it. The way the wind blows, all the neighbors will know it."

"Hope the wind doesn't blow east," I said. "The whole school will know it."

"That'll be our luck," Aunt Viddie said.

I went outside again while they argued how to get rid of the polecats, to see how the wind was blowing. It was a soft mist-laden scent-carrying morning wind blowing east.

"Oh, the schoolhouse today," I thought.

"We'll have to starve 'em down," Aunt Viddie told Uncle Egbert. "I'm not going to have my house completely ruined."

"All right, Viddie," Uncle Egbert said. "You won't listen to reason. It's best to go through the roof or cut through the ceiling to get 'em. Anyway to get 'em and get the job over with."

But my aunts won over Uncle Egbert. Tom Hedley watched the hole with a gun while Aunt Viddie, Aunt Cindy, Aunt Arabella, and the two women that worked the house, and two men they hired carried furniture out into the back yard. It was the first time the sun had hit it in years and the first time a fresh wind had struck it. And they had to take silverware from the chest drawers and pull each piece from the tiny sheath of close-

fitting cloth it was kept in and give it the sun and air.
Everything had to come from the house.

And I knew it couldn't be kept a secret when I went to
school late. Teachers were taking boys from the rooms into the
corridors, smelling of them and asking them if they had
brought a polecat to school. I think they called it "skunk." Miss
Potter whiffed loudly when I entered the schoolhouse.

"Why don't you smell of Hester Tremble, Miss Potter?"
Tom Stevens asked her.

"He's not been around a skunk," she told him.

I hurried on to my room. Had it not been for the thick wall
of green hedge they could have seen the furniture carried out
of Uncle Egbert and Aunt Viddie's house. They didn't know
where the scent was coming from but they would know before
the day was over. Each boy accused the other of his having the
scent on him and the teachers accused this boy and that boy of
his having brought a skunk to school. The teachers wanted to
dismiss school but Mr. Lawton said school would go on and the
guilty boy would be found and brought to justice. I didn't want
to break the news. It was good news and I knew someone would
break it.

That night we had to go to the Horton Hotel, the only hotel
in Greenwood, and it was a small hotel. Tom Hedley had waited
all day with a gun and the polecats hadn't come down from the
garret. They were sleeping after their night's carousal of
fighting, frolicking, and fun. Aunt Cindy and Aunt Arabella
didn't go with us. They were too embarrassed. They went back
to Gatton to stay with Uncle Bill. And Aunt Viddie was
embarrassed when people passed us in the lobby of the hotel and
laughed. Everybody laughed. Aunt Viddie didn't know where
they got the news until she looked at the Times. There was a
big piece on the front page how the "smelly imps of nature" had
slipped into the city and "picked the model Greenwood home"

for their "residence."

"Wonder how that got in there," Aunt Viddie said, showing Uncle Egbert the paper.

He looked at the paper while Aunt Viddie looked at the *Enquirer*.

"Look," she said, showing Uncle Egbert the write-up. "It's in this paper, too."

I wanted to laugh but I was afraid.

"It'll be in more papers than these two," Uncle Egbert said. "It'll be in a hundred papers if we don't chop in there and get them."

On Tuesday, Tom Hedley killed a pappie polecat; on Wednesday, he shot a mama polecat, and on Thursday, the last old papa polecat came down to earth and he shot him and stopped the hole. Then the house was cleaned, washed from top to bottom, and rescrubbed and fumigated, and the sun-kissed wind-caressed furniture was carried inside and placed just like it had been before the polecats came. Everybody in the school was laughing. Boys, accused of bringing a skunk to school, were pleased when the teachers apologized to them—first apologies they'd ever had from teachers. And people smiled at us when we went down the street. Uncle Egbert's trade fell off fifty per cent. The model home had lost its prestige. And I was allowed to enter the house without taking my shoes off.

SUNDAY AFTERNOON HANGING

Boy, you don't know anything about it. Let yer grandpa tell you a little about this hanging business in Kentucky. You set around here and talk about the hot seat for a man that kills another man in cold blood. Hot seat ain't nothing. People can't go and see a body killed in the hot seat. Just a little bunch allowed in to write up a few of the poor devil's last words. When they used to kill a man everybody got to see it and laugh and faint, cuss or cry, do just as he damn pleased about it. It used to be that way here in Kentucky. Now let me tell you, there's no fun to giving a man the hot seat or giving him gas or a lot of stuff like that, giving him the pen for life. Didn't keep 'em up there and feed 'em for life when I was a boy. They took 'em out and swung 'em to a limb and people from all over the country came to see 'em swing.

Let me tell you how it was. That was before the days of baseball. People came for forty miles to see a hanging. We had one every weekend in Blakesburg for the people to come and see. You know that's how Blakesburg got the name Hang-Town. God, I remember well as if it was yesterday. Used to be an old elm in the lower end of town where they hung 'em. It was upon a little hill where everybody could get an eyeful of the man they swung to the elm limb. Pa and Ma and me, we used to go every

96

Sunday of the world after church was out. We could hardly wait
to get to the hanging. It was as much fun to see a hanging them
days as it is to see a baseball game nowadays here in Kentucky.
God, do I remember the old days. I was just a boy then but I remember it just like it was yesterday. I can see the crowd yet that
gathered at the hangings, and all the hollering you ever heard
in your life it was put up at one of them hangings when a poor
devil was swung up to the old elm limb.

That old tree just fell three years ago. God Almighty got rid
of it. Must a been some of them innocent men they swung up
there and in Heaven they got after God Almighty to do
something about that tree. And God Almight got rid of it. He
looks after his people. He'll do a lot too, I guess, of what his
angels in Heaven wants him to do. Son, I am an old man and I
believe I know. Well, of all the trees in the lower end of
Blakesburg, the old elm where they hung all them men was the
only one the lightnin' hit and split from limb to roots. Tree must
have been five feet through the middle, too. And don't you
know the people wouldn't burn a stick of that wood in their
stoves and fireplaces. They just rolled it over the bank into the
Ohio River and let it float away. People was afraid that if they
burnt it they would be haunted the rest of their days.

You've heard about poor old Jim Murphy and his wife
gettin' killed that time. I know you've seen the hickory club
they've got over there in the Blakesburg Courthouse with poor
old Jim's tooth stuck in it—that hard white hickory club—no,
don't guess you did see it. The 1913 flood got up in the
courthouse and carried it off. Had poor old Jim's tooth in it. See,
here is the way it was. It happened up there in Sand Bottom.
Right up there where that foul murder happened two years ago
when that old strollop and that man tortured the little girl to
death with a red-hot poker. Foulest things that have ever
happened in this country have happened right up there in Sand

Bottom. To go on with my story. A bunch of Sixeymores up there then. God, they's rotten eggs too. Well, there was two Sixeymore brothers well as I remember, a Dudley Toms, a Winslow, and a Grubb into that scrape. The Sixeymore brothers planned the murder of these two old people for their money. They had heard by a woman that went there and cooked for them that they had eleven hundred dollars hid in a old teakettle in the pantry. Well, the Sixeymore brothers–Tim and Jake–promised Freed Winslow Jim Murphy's mules if he would help kill him and his wife. They promised Dudley Toms the two cows and Work Grubb his thirty acres of land if he would help kill them.

They went to the little log house down by the Sandy River one dark rainy night when there was no moon. It was in the dark of the moon. They had the whole thing planned. They thought that if they killed the old people and throwed them in Sandy in the dark of the moon the bodies would never come to the top of the water. So they cut a hickory club; Tim Sixeymore cut it with a poleax up on Flint Sneed's pint, up where the old furnace used to be. People used to go there and see the stump. It all come out in Tim's confession before they swung him. They cut the club– all went there that dark night. Jim made a chicken squall and old man Murphy–game man as ever drawed a breath of wind– run out against his old lady's will. She said: "Somebody to kill us, Jim. Don't go out there." You know how a woman can just about tell things; God gives 'em the power to pertect themselves just like he does a possum or a horse. They can almost smell danger. Old Jim run out and–whack–Sixeymore hit him in the mouth with the hickory club. Killed him dead as a mackrel. That one lick finished him. He just walled his eyes back and died. Then all five of the men went in where old Lizzie Murphy was a settin' before the fire smokin' her pipe and she said: "Give me time to pray once more to God Almighty." She begged to pray but they didn't give her time. Dudley Toms said the hardest thing he ever tried to do was to kill that old woman and her a-beggin' to just get to pray to God Almighty just one more time. He hit her over the head with a fire shovel, and to make sure she was dead he beat out her brains with the shovel. Then they carried them down and throwed them in the dark waters of Little Sandy on that dark night. But nature don't hold things and uphold dirty work. That water give up the dead bodies down at Cedar Riffles. Some fishermen caught them there. And Dudley Toms didn't know that there was a speck of blood left on his hatband. But there was. See, there's always a clue. Can't do a thing like that and get by with it, not even if the law is on your side. Boy, you suffer for what you do in this old world. Talk about men suffering before they died. I was right there at the hanging. Everybody in the county came to it. It was the biggest hanging we ever had. Had a hanging of five that Sunday. Hung these five and they was the kind of fellows the people liked to see swing to a limb. Was a lot better than just going out and getting somebody for stealing a horse and hanging him, or a man for abusing his wife; somebody like that hardly had enough against him to hang. I've seen many a poor devil hang over almost nothing. Today he wouldn't have to go to jail for it. Used to hang him for the same thing. The people wanted a hanging every week and the sheriff and judge had better have a hanging at least once a month or they would never get elected again. If they didn't have hangings often enough the people would go to them and say, "Look here, you'll not get my vote next time if this is the way you intend to do. Lay down on the job, never have a hanging. Damn poor Law. You'll never be elected again."

Well, the day these five men was hung I was just a boy. I remember it just like it was yesterday. I was up to the jail that morning after the confusion and saw them getting their breakfast. Jailer Wurt Hammons said: "Boys, eat hearty. This will be your last grub here on this earth. The devil will serve your breakfast tomorrow morning. You have the chance to have anything that you want to eat that I can get for you."

Well, the Sixeymore boys took a stewed turkey apiece and a biler of black coffee without sugar or cream. Dudley Toms wouldn't eat a bite. Tim said to him: "Hell, take your hanging like a man. Go to the gallows on a full stummick. Get that much off the county before you die." Work Grubb took twelve hard-fried eggs and a pint of licker to wash 'em down with. Winslow took fried eggs and licker—don't remember how many eggs and how much licker. But that is what they had for breakfast. Well, the county carpenter, Jake·Tillman, had the county make coffins for them. He was hired to make the coffins for the men the county hung. He had five good county coffins made—took their measurements and made them to fit. Had one awfully big for Tim Sixeymore. He was six feet and seven inches tall and weighed some over three hundred pounds. Biggest man I believe I ever saw. He wasn't dough-bellied either. Weighed a lot and was hard as the butt of a shell-barked hickory. His brother was about as big and powerful. God, old Tim was a man and not afraid of God Almighty hisself. God would have to watch him at the jedgment bar. If he got half a chance he'd do something to God Almighty.

I remember the two excursion boats that come down the river that day to the hanging and the one that come up the river. They was loaded with people hollering and waving handkerchiefs around the deck. There was a double-decker come up the river with a load of people. And of all the people that ever come to Blakesburg they were there that day. Mules tied to the trees along the streets—not many houses in Blakesburg them days but there was a thicket of trees through the town. Wagons of all descriptions. Hug-me-tight buggies—them things had just come out then—people looked at the new contraption and quarreled about the indecency of men and women riding in them little narrow seats all loved up. Said they ought to be hung for an example for doing it. And there was a lot of two-horse surreys and rubber-tired hacks and jolt wagons there that day. Jolt wagons with whole families riding in wagon beds full of straw. People and people everywhere you looked. Never was such a crowd in Blakesburg as there was that day. Little children crying and dogs that followed the wagons to town out fighting in the streets and the horses neighing to each other and rearing up in the collar, mules biting and kicking each other! It was the awfulest time I ever saw. If a dark cloud would a riz over that town I would a swore the world was coming to an end. But it was a pretty day for a crowd and for a hanging. Sun in the sky. June wind blowing. Roses in bloom. One of the prettiest days I believe I ever saw. The reason that I remember it so well was that they hung 'em at sunup. Some of the people had come all night to be there in time to see the hanging in the morning.

Well, the band got there. You know they always had a band at the hangings to furnish the music. Had a seven-piece band at this hanging. Always before we just had a drummer, a pot beater, and a fifer. About everybody likes a fife. It puts madness in their bones and bodies and helps down the screams of the women and the fighting of the dogs and the whinnying of the horses. The band had on the gayest suits you ever saw for this occasion. Just like a political rally where they used to butcher five or six steers to feed the people. These band players had on bright yaller pants and red sashes and peagreen jackets and them old three-cornered hats. God, but they did look nifty.

Well as I remember the band struck up a tune that day. It was "Dixie." Some of the horses broke loose and took down through the town but the people let 'em go. They stayed still for the hanging. It was the biggest thing we'd had in many a day. Horses broke loose without riders on them and took out through the crowd among the barking dogs, running over them and the children. People didn't pay any attention to that. It was a hanging and people wanted to see every bit of it. They didn't care if a child did get run over so it wasn't their own. And it took five or six sheriffs; they had big guns on 'em to keep any fights from starting and they wore bright yaller jackets. Lord, all the people there. And you could always tell a mountaineer them days from the back country. He always had the smell of wood smoke on him and barnyard manure. Big bony devils! Hairy as all get out! Never would shave their bony faces!

I remember seeing the first horse and express come into sight. Dudley Toms was sitting on his coffin with a rope around his neck, the hangman's knot already tied. Bert Blevins always did that for the county. One of his knots never did slip. It always flew up in the right place and hit 'em one of the jaw and broke their necks. Bert was a whiz on this hanging business. And when the horse come in sight and Dudley was a sittin' up there on the coffin—God, the people nearly tore the limbs out of the trees with their jumpin' and screamin' and they had that big shell-bark hickory club that Tim hit Jim Murphy with back there the night he made the chicken squall. That had just been three weeks before. They really brought men to justice back in them days when they had to have someone to hang every Sunday after church. Screams was so loud that you had to hold your fingers in your ears. Here was that big shell-bark hickory club held up in the air by a big man while Dudley stood on his coffin and made his confession. They wanted to hear it. They wanted all out of a hanging that there was in one.

At first Dudley Toms wouldn't talk. The jailer said, "Tell them, Dudley. They want your confession before you give it to the devil. We want it first-handed here. You can give it second-handed to the devil." And Dudley he stood up there on his coffin while that horse—a new one they was breakin' in to haul men to the gallows—he just ripped and snorted.

And Dudley said, "First time I ever killed anybody. Was hard to kill Lizzie Murphy with that shovel. But I had to do it. No use to cry over spilt milk. I hate like hell to hang. I do. But I'd rather do it right now and see what all this after death is that I've heard so much about. I hate to die. But take me out of all this—take me out!" And he kinda broke down.

Well, they unfastened his hands from behind him so they could see him kick and pull on the rope with his tongue turnin' black and hangin' out of his mouth. They just made him stand on the coffin and they tied the rope that went around his neck to the rope that was already fastened to the old-hangin'-tree and just drove the wagon out from under him while the band struck up a tune. I'll never forget seein' him swing there and kick— that expression on the dyin' man's face. The band was a-playin', the children a-screamin' because it was the first hangin' a lot of them had ever seen. Some of the women started shouting. Never saw anything like it in my life. But Dudley's kinsfolk was there to get him. Some of the women fainted and they just had a couple of barrels of water there so they could throw cold water in the faces of the fainting women. That's what they done. Had boys hired right ready to throw water on the faces of the fainting women or the fighting dogs when they got in the way of the hangin'.

The next to ride up was Freed Winslow. He was up on top of his coffin and the horse that hauled him wasn't so afraid of the suits that the bandmen wore. The horse had been to many a hangin'. Well, while the kinsfolk was claimin' the body of Dudley Toms, Freed Winslow was standing on top of his coffin making his confession. It was a fine confession, too, if there was ever a good hangin' confession made. Said Freed Winslow: "Ladies and gentlemen, I have made peace with my God. I am not afraid to die. I prayed all night last night. I been prayin' ever since I got in this mess. That very first night after I helped do

103

this killing I saw so many devils around my bed that I had to get up and light the lamp. They was cuttin' all kinds of shines. They even run across my stummick. God, it was awful. I hope to meet you all in Heaven where there ain't no devils to run across your stummick and grin at you. Good-by, folks. Sorry for what I have done and I hope you won't hold it against me. I ought to die."

So they put the knot over his head and drove the wagon out from under him and he fell off his own coffin and the band struck up a tune. While he was in the air struggling for breath and glomming at the wind with his hands, the band players kept pumping harder. That fife kept screaming above the cries of the women. Talking of fainting of pretty girls. They sure did faint. Freed Winslow was a handsome man. There his tongue went out of his mouth. His face black. His curly hair flying in the wind, black as a frostbit pawpaw in the early fall, and he died strugglin' just like a possum struggles for breath after its neck has been broke under a mattock handle.

The next to come up to the hang-tree was Work Grubb. He was thought to be a fine man in the neighborhood. He was a-ridin' on his coffin, hairiest man you ever saw. Looked like one of them men in the days of old with all the beard on his face. He looked kindly like he was ashamed when the wagon rolled up under the tree. I never can forget all them knotholes in his coffin. Bet he wasn't more than under the ground till the water started seepin' and the dirt and these worms started crumbling through these knotholes. Well, the band struck up a tune and the people screamed. Just like a man when he makes a score nowdays in baseball. It was a score with death then. The band had to play while the people screamed and waited for his confession. He waited calmly as I ever saw a man waiting for death. He wasn't scared, not one iotum. He just waited and when the people screamed till they were hoarse he stood up on his coffin and said, "What I got to say to you is: Go on and kill

104

me. Remember the killer pays. I was guilty and I deserve to die but you don't deserve to kill me."

One old fat snaggle-toothed woman up and hollered, "You won't get pore old Uncle Jim Murphy's thirty acres of land, will ye? Might get some hot land to farm in hell. Say they've got a lot of desert land down there!" And she just hollered and laughed at the condemned man going to the elm limb.

Well, the band struck up "Dixie." And the wagon drove out from under him soon as the rope was fastened. And Work swung there with his thin legs dangling in the air. Didn't use a cap on their faces in them days. People wanted to see their faces while they was dyin'. The band played while he dangled at the end of the rope and clutched for thin air. Of all the cries that ever went up from the people it did there. Then Doc Turner went up and stopped the swinging body and put his hand on the heart. He said, "He's dead. He's gone to the other world."

The next they brought up on the wagon was Jake Sixey-more. He was a-laughing. They asked him if he wanted to make any confession. And he laughed and said, "All I want is a pint of Rock and Rye to stick in my hip pocket for old Satan and a good homemade twist. He's going to have hell, with me and my brother Tim both with him. We'll both want jobs and we'll get into it. I want to get on the good side of him first. I'm not a damn bit sorry over anything I've done. Just one life to live, one death to die, something beyond or nothing beyond and I'll hold my own any goddam place they put me. So, swing your goddam rope to me soon as you give me that half-pint of Rock and Rye and that twist of Kentucky-burley terbacker."

"Sure thing," said the sheriff. "Give it to him. I'm afraid it's the last he'll ever get."

So the fellow just give one of them big horse-pints with just one little dram taken out of it. He give him a twist that looked as big as my arm at the elbow. He took it, thanked the fellow in the gray with the long handle-bar mustache and dough-belly that shook as he walked, and then he said, "I'm ready, gentlemen. Pull your goddam rope."

Well, the crowd was kindly quiet for a few minutes, then the band struck up a tune. And he was riding on the highest wagon and the highest coffin. The rope broke his neck the first crack. Of all the screams! His tongue just come out of his mouth, a twisted tongue, and where he bit it, it was bleeding. God, what a sight. And his face black as a pawpaw leaf. He swung there low against the ground, the limb sagging and the rope swinging. Doc Smith run out and put his ear to his heart. He said, "Dead man. He is in the other world by now or gettin' mighty close."

Well, people—just his old dad and mammy there in their rags. God, I felt sorry for them. I couldn't help it. Had two boys there that day to hang. They took him off in the coffin and carried him a little ways and put him down in the grass. They waited for Tim to die so they could haul them both to the same double grave on the same wagon. Her gray hair flying in the wind, him a mountain man with the smell of wood smoke and cow manure on him. He had shed tears. He was a man stout as a rock. His sons were no stronger-looking than their old white-haired father.

Well, the last wagon come up there that day. It had one of the biggest coffins I ever saw on it. The biggest man I ever saw was riding on top of that box. His big hands looked like shovels folded up there on his chest. He looked mean as the devil out of his eyes. They were black eyes and they had beads of fire shining from them. You could see them from the crowd. His hair looked like briers around a stump: a big mop of it, and it looked like a comb had never been run through it in his life. Clay still on his knuckles where he had worked in the mines. He'd kill and he'd mob and he'd work. He was a great worker. Could do as

106

much work as four ordinary men and lift more than any two men in the mines. Lord, he was a sight to look at. He looked like a mountain man. He could eat the side of a hog's ribs at one meal and a whole pone of corn bread and drink a gallon of buttermilk. He could eat three dozen fried eggs and drink a whole biler of strong coffee. Now he was facing the gallows. He just set there like a rock. I heard one old whiskered man with a willow cane say: "Now, if he confesses all his guilt we'll get a good confession."

The band struck up a tune. "Dixie," I believe. Nearly played it and "Old Kentucky Home" to death that day. It was one of the songs. And the people started screaming. It was the last one of the five and they just tried to see how much noise they could make. God, it was awful to hear. I remember his pore old mother fainting and how they dashed two buckets of cold water in her face. I remember the tears that come from his pore old pap's wrinkled eye...it was a sight to see! I have often wished I'd never seen it. God, it was awful to think about.

When the band stopped the sheriff said, "Let's hear you confession, Tim Sixeymore."

Well, that great big man got up and stood on his coffin. And he looked like a giant to me. Great big devil, unafraid of the whole crowd.

And he said, "Yes, I've got a big confession to make. I got plenty to tell you bastard men and wench women, goddam you!"

You could a heard a pin drop there that day till some strange dogs started fighting and then the babies started crying. Well, they throwed water on the dogs and got them stopped and the women started nursing the babies and got them stopped. If they didn't want to nurse, the women just made 'em nurse. And they soon stopped crying. They wanted to get the whole confession.

"Gentlemen bastards and sonofabitches. Women wenches and hussies and goddam you all. Get this, the whole crowd of you that's come here to see me hang. I've done a whole hell of a sight more than I ought to hang for than this. But you—you come here to laugh at a man that meets death. All I got to say is goddam every blessed one of you and I hope to hand every one of you a cup of water in hell. You low-down brindle house-cats, come here to hang a man when he ain't done a single damn thing to you. I've killed seventeen men, raped five women, stole more than I can tell you about. Got a good mother and a good father. Don't hold a thing against them, you lousy bastards and wenches and young babies that nurse your mother's milk. This will be something for you to tell the generations about yet to come. And that is not all. I planned to kill Jim Murphy and Lizzie Murphy. It was all my work and yet all these fellows had to die. I hope God Almighty burns this sonofabitchen tree with lightning before another hundred years roll by. Poor devils without a chance. Die for you to laugh at and see struggle on the scaffold. Die for you to laugh at as you would a chicken fight. You low-down cowardly sonofabitches. Now laugh at me. I'll show you, by God, how a man can die. I'm not a bit afraid of whatever is to come. I'll be ready soon as I get one more good drink of Kentucky whisky and a chaw of terbacker in my jaw. Then you can give me the rope, goddam you. Strike up your goddam band. You people whoop and holler as much as you damn please, you low-lifed lousy bastards. I can whip any four fair-fisted in the crowd. Will fight you right up here on top of my coffin. Want to try it, any of you? None—"

There was silence in the crowd. Not a voice was lifted.

"Well, then, give me a drink of licker and a chaw of terbacker and I'm ready for the Happy Hunting Ground."

The sheriff stepped up and give him a drink out of a full horse-pint and give him a chaw of his own twist of terbacker. I'll

108

bet twenty men offered him a drink of licker but the sheriff took charge because it was his duty under the sharp eyes of the Law.

When he got the rope around his neck I remember he said, "Look here, you bunch of wenches. Let me show you how to die. I'll hope to give your tail a couple of kicks in hell. I'll just get there first. So long, you goddam bellering crowd."

Well, a lot of the old men held their heads. The women sniffed and the band struck up the last tune, they thought, for the day. But it wasn't the last tune. They put the rope around his neck and tied it to the rope in the tree, and drove the wagon out from under him. Well, he just snapped that rope like it was twine and laughed till you could a heared him for a mile. The limb swayed with him, too. No well rope would hold him after it was wore the way it was, hanging so many people. Somebody went and got another rope. It was a brand new rope. And they fixed a new rope up in the elm and caught another limb so the two of them wouldn't give. And the seventh time, the rope held him. Well, the sheriff had to arrest his father and mother. They started fighting in the crowd. They's lots of people started talking it up for them and if they hadn't got him hung when they did it would have been a pitched battle by three o'clock. People started taking sides. You know what the meant in them days.

It wasn't long before the band started playing a retreat. It must have been Napoleon Bonaparte's retreat or some big general's—maybe George Washington's. That was what happened at the end of the hangings. Had to have some soft music to soften the people up a little bit. God, it had been an awful day. Women pulling hair and shouting and praying, singing, screaming till you couldn't hear your ears. God, Kentucky used to have her hangings. And that was the biggest one I ever saw in Kentucky. Lauria and Kent Sixeymore riding on their sons' coffins. Lauria was a-setting on the end of one and Kent was a-setting on the end of the other. It was a sad thing to see. Pore old man and woman! Their hair white as cotton fleece flyin' in the spring wind, the dogs a-barking and a-fighting. And the band, just about petered out on fast music, started playing that slow soft kind. People almost in tears! Big day was over. People getting at the little restaurant where it said, "Good lodging for a man and brute and a glass of licker and a night's lodging for a quarter." People trying to get something to eat. Women and children hungry and old skinny hounds running up to the back porches to the slop barrels and fighting over them. People fighting in the streets. Wagons going out of Blakesburg with the dead. No wonder they call that place Hang-Town! It was a hang-town. If you could just a seen, son, that crowd a-breaking up and leaving. It was a sight. People getting acquainted and talking about the hanging, talking about their crops and the cattle and the doings of the Lord to the wicked people for their sins. That was the biggest hanging I ever saw. Used all them two barrels of cold water on the fighting dogs and the fainting women. When the crowd left, all the gardens and flowers had been tromped under. Town looked awful and limbs broke out of the trees where people couldn't see out of the crowd and climbed the trees and got up in them like birds! God, but it was awful!

Then a little later on they got to building a scaffold an' just letting a body see their bodies before they dropped down into a trap door and a sawdust bottom. They even put a cap over their face till people couldn't see their faces. Just kept a-gettin' it easier and easier till they didn't hang 'em at all. Got to having baseball games instead and then people got bad in these parts. Law got to be a joke! Something like it is now. Give 'em just as easy a death as possible, like the hot seat. They used to let 'em hang in Kentucky!

THE REAPER AND THE FLOWERS

As I walked up the dusty Academy Branch road with my books, I found Pa. He was lying half in the road and half on the grass. Pa's feet and legs were lying in the road and his brogan-shoe toes were turned up. The slick-worn hobnails in the shoe soles were shining like clean-polished silver in the slanting rays of the setting September sun. Pa's beardy face was turned up to the sun, too. And he'd closed his eyes against the sun's rays. His big arms and hands lay limp beside his huge body on the wilted ragweeds. His mattock, shovel, and sickle lay beside him.

I knew my sisters, Etta and Claris, had passed Pa up. They'd come from the Blakesburg Grade School and had beaten me home. Brother Estil, an eighth-grader, had come home with them, too. Claris and Etta couldn't help Pa. But Estil could. Estil could have pulled his legs around out of the road for when Pa got like this he was always limber at the knees. The trouble was, they were ashamed of our father.

"Pa," I said, as I walked over to him, "wake up!"

Pa grunted and groaned like a man in a deep sleep. But I took hold of his overall jacket and shook him. I knew how to wake him. I shook him and I rolled his head from side to side in his loose black hat.

"Alex," Pa groaned as he tried to rise.

111

"It's not old Alex, Pa," I said. "It's Melvin."

"Oh, it's you, Mel," he mumbled as he tried to get up. "You've come after me."

"No, I just happened to find you."

Then Pa pulled with all his might under his own power and I lifted. We got him up to a sitting position. I put his arm around my shoulder and he used all the power in his body. After three tries, we got him to a standing position. He steadied himself by putting his hand on my back until I reached over and got his mattock, shovel, and sickle. Pa put his arm around my shoulder, and held the sickle in his hand. I carried the mattock, shovel, and books, and a lot of his weight. He was a big man, too. My father weighed two hundred forty pounds.

We walked slowly up the dusty road and turned up Left Academy Branch. I bore up well with my load until we reached the little hill where our shack sat upon the steep bank. Then it was work getting Pa up the hill. Streams of sweat ran down my face. But I wasn't going to leave my father beside the road with his legs half across it for a wagon wheel to run over. Maybe it would be an automobile, for a few of them came up Academy. I was in high school, too, and I had a lot of pride. I didn't want everybody seein' Pa in this condition.

When we got to the front porch we saw Etta, Claris, and Estil sitting there.

"Come, Mom, see what Mel's bringin' home," Estil shouted.

"I'd be ashamed if I's you, Estil," I said. "You'd let him lay down there half in the road and half out and lose his legs. You don't have no pride. Wait until next year when you get into high school, you'll change your mind. You're like Claris and Etta, you're ashamed of Pa!"

"We are ashamed of 'im!" Etta was quick with her words.

"If he gets in that condition let 'im lay there until he gets out," Estil said.

Then Mom came running onto the porch.

"Oh, it's Uglybird," she said. "Where did you find 'im?"

"Beside the road," I said. "His body on the grass and his legs across the road. Why didn't Etta, Claris, or Estil tell you about 'im?"

"We didn't want Mom liftin' on 'im," Claris said. "We knew Mom would go down there and try to fetch 'im to the house!"

"It's that old Alex Troxler," Mom shouted. "He's the cause of Uglybird's downfall. Every time somebody dies and he digs the grave and gets paid, here's that old bootlegger to get Uglybird's money. Hauls him down there and dumps him out beside the road! I'd love to choke old Alex until his tongue lolls out."

"But help me get him in the house," I said.

I was standing there holding the shovel and mattock. And Pa's arm around my shoulder was as heavy as lead.

"Leave 'im on the outside," Mom shouted. "I can't bear 'im."

Then Pa looked up at Mom. When he looked at her he grinned.

"Now, you're talkin' to 'im, Mom," Estil said. "I'm glad to hear you talk like that. He's treated you bad enough! Remember the time he came home on a big bender and sickled your flowers down?"

"I hate for my classmates to know Uglybird Skinner is my father," Claris said. "When his name is mentioned everybody starts laughing and I bow my head in shame."

"If it wasn't for you, Mom, we'd starve to death," Etta said. "Everybody in Blakesburg thinks Pa beats you up."

Then I looked at my father's ugly face. Everybody thought he was ugly but Mom. Pa was still looking at Mom with a grin on his face.

"Shut up! Every last one of you," Mom shouted. "He's your

father and you should respect him!"

Mom, who was as slender as a beanpole, and she was as fast in her movements as Pa was slow, ran down the front steps like a sparrow. She took the mattock and shovel from me and the sickle from Pa and ran to the tool shed. Mom was a woman that didn't want anything lying in the front yard. She kept the house clean and neat and the yard as clean and pretty as the house. Then Mom was back in a jiffy and she put Pa's other limp arm around her shoulder and we started up the steps with him. Pa did his best to hug Mom as we went up the steps.

"None of your foolishness now, Uglybird," Mom said.

"I love you, Mollie," Pa mumbled.

"Shut your mouth, Uglybird," Mom snapped like a turtle.

When we got him in the house, Mom put him on the best bed. Mom didn't mind his dusty clothes on her clean bed. Then she took his shoes off and spread a clean sheet over Pa so he wouldn't be uncovered in a draft. She put a feather pillow under his head.

"I wouldn't do it, Mom," Claris said. "You've got more patience than I'll ever have with a man."

"Shut up, Claris," Mom scolded her. "You don't know how much patience you'll have with a man. It's old Alex Troxler who causes all our trouble!"

Pa looked up at Mom and grinned again.

"I love you, Mollie," he mumbled. "I could about squeeze you in two right now if I could lift my hands up to you!"

Then Mom had me kill a chicken and she made Pa some broth that night. She fed him with a big spoon.

"Mel is the only child I have with the right respect for his father," Mom said as we watched her feeding Pa broth with a tablespoon. "I want the rest of you to get respect for 'im. He's a good father. Alex Troxler, that old bootlegger, lives too close to Lonesome Hill! I could choke his tongue out! And the Law

114

that lets old Alex get by with his bootleggin' I could pour scaldin' water from a teakettle spout on the last one of 'em!"

"If he only loved you like you love him," Claris said, "he wouldn't act like this. It's not Alex Troxler's fault. It's Pa's fault."

"Don't let me hear you say that again, Claris," Mom snapped as she gave Pa another spoonful of broth. "He'll drink the broth tonight and be ready to eat the chicken tomorrow."

The next morning Pa was all right. And as usual he never mentioned what had happened the day before. Pa never bragged about the benders he got on. He wasn't exactly ashamed of 'em. He just didn't talk about 'em.

Pa ate chicken for breakfast and drank a lot of black coffee. He sat across the table from Mom and when he looked at her, he smiled and there was a light in his eyes. As we walked down Academy Branch to school, Pa walked along with us. He was dressed in clean blue overalls, jumper, blue workshirt, and a pin-striped cap.

"Now, let's all stay together, young'uns," he told us when Claris and Etta tried to run ahead. "I'm proud of my young'uns. I like to be seen with you!"

Claris, Etta, and Estil were glad when they left us to go to the Blakesburg Grade School. Pa and I went on together.

"Mel, your ma is a great woman," Pa said as we walked along. "There was never another one like 'er!"

"Do you really love Mom?" I asked.

"Love her," he said, with a big smile spreading over his face, "I could squeeze her in two!"

"How do all the big tales get started about your beatin' Mom?" I asked him.

"I'll show you one of these days," he said.

"How can you talk the way you do and love my mother?" I asked him.

"See, I was called Uglybird from the time I was a baby because I was so ugly," he told me. "I know I've got a head the shape of a pear turned upside down. And I've got a big mouth, teeth that a dentist can't pull, big moose jaws, and shoulders as broad as a corncrib door. Got eyes that slant and everybody who looks at me thinks I'm awfully ugly. Now, your mother was a skinny homely girl when she was growing up. No boy only me ever noticed her. And she's the only girl who'd look at me. So we got married and the longer we looked at each other, the more beautiful she was to me and the more handsome I was to her. We got better-lookin' to each other all the time. And two people actually as ugly as we are have two handsome boys, and two of the best-lookin' gals in these parts!"

Then Pa laughed as I'd never heard him laugh before.

"Stop here on the courthouse square with me a minute, Mel," he said. "I'll show you how tales get started."

There was a group of strange men standing on the courthouse square talking. Pa walked over where they were. They looked at him and at each other and smiled.

"Do any of you fellers have any troubles with your wives?" Pa asked.

"Well, yes," one muttered, since Pa had asked him so suddenly.

"I guess every man and his wife have a few words now and then," said another, very seriously.

"I've been married twenty years," Pa said. "I've got a remedy for getting rid of all that trouble. Give your wife a good beating twice a week!"

Pa didn't laugh at his own words. He rolled up his jumper and shirt sleeves, and contracted a knot of muscles on his great arm which was as large as a goose egg.

"Twice a week I shake my little skinny wife until she screams," Pa told them as the men looked strangely at each other. "I shake her until her teeth rattle. And they're not false ivories either. I'm boss at my home. Every man should be. Fellows, my name is Uglybird Skinner."

And then Pa walked away while the men looked at him and at each other. After Pa and I had gone, they started laughing. We heard them laughing as Pa went on his way to dig the well and I went on to high school.

Pa's tales about his beating my mother had spread everywhere. He would tell them how he made Mom milk four cows night and morning, feed five fattening hogs, carry water from a spring, feed the chickens, and gather eggs. How he made her do these things in addition to keeping a clean house and an orderly yard filled with pretty flowers. He never told these strangers any better.

And when Pa walked down the road with us, on our way to school, he'd say, "September sixteenth. This was the day Tom Jason was caught and hanged for pizening his wife! Have to sickle the briers from old Tom's roof today." Or, Pa'd say, "November nineteenth. On November 19, 1902, old Mort Hanners dropped dead after he'd danced a jig on the street. Wonder where he's dancing now? Got to straighten his marker today."

Pa knew everybody buried on Lonesome Hill, the day he departed life, and the cause. Each week in the year, he would always mention one's name and say something about him. Pa had worked on Lonesome Hill helping his father, Grandpa Tobbie Skinner, when he was a boy. Grandpa Skinner had been the first sexton and he had told Pa about everybody buried there. And Pa, from the time he took over, never failed to get the history of each inmate on Lonesome Hill. And when he said something about one each day, my sisters were ashamed. But Pa didn't mind.

And on a hot July day when we were sitting peacefully under the sweet-gum shade in our front yard, John Cantwell and Wilburn Collins came down the Left Academy Branch with eight yoke of cattle hitched to a log wagon. They were pulling a yellow-poplar log fifty feet long to a sawmill. Wilburn was walking beside the leaders when they came down below our house.

"Stop the cattle, Wilburn," Pa shouted. "Let 'em wind. It's a hot day to pull a log like that!"

Wilburn stopped the cattle and started talking to Pa. While Wilburn talked, Pa looked over the oxen until he came to the wheel cattle, a yoke of big Red Pole bulls. They were butting each other while John Cantwell punched with a sharp stalk to quiet them.

"Go fetch me a bucket, Mollie," Pa told Mom.

"What kind of a bucket, Uglybird?" Mom asked.

"Water bucket," he said.

Mom jumped up and ran to the kitchen and brought back a water bucket in a jiffy.

"Here's the bucket," she said, giving it to Pa.

"I don't want it," he said. "You do the milking. Go down there and milk them cows there against the cart Uncle John's a-havin' such a time with!"

And then Pa screamed with laughter. Mom threw the bucket over the hill and took off. Claris got up and left too. Wilburn turned his face the other way and laughed louder than the slow-moving wind among the sweet-gum leaves. Etta looked hard at Pa when she got up and left. I sat beside Pa and watched Wilburn and John drive the oxen down the road with the long log, barely making curves since they were laughing until they couldn't speak to their oxen.

Pa did another thing, too. Once when he was in Blakesburg where they were paving the streets, he looked at some empty cement sacks.

"I like the looks of these cement sacks," Pa said.

They were cloth sacks, dusty with cement and piled in a heap near a large concrete mixer.

"Like the looks of 'em?" said a stranger, who was overseeing the road job. "If you'd like to have 'em I'd be glad to give 'em to you!"

"I shore would," Pa said. "Oh, thank you, thank you!"

My father thanked the man as if he'd given him a fortune.

"Say, fellow," the man said, "I never like to be inquisitive about a man's business, but I'd like to know what you want with 'em!"

"Take a guess," Pa said as he started to gather the big pile of sacks into his arms.

"I'd think you'd want them to cover a lettuce or a tobacco bed," he said.

"I'm not a farmer," Pa told him. "I'm a gravedigger. I want these sacks to make me a suit of clothes!"

Pa never cracked a smile. The man looked at Pa and then he burst into explosive laughter. He didn't believe Pa. And when we went away, this man walked over and was telling one of the men who worked for him something. And when I looked back, he was telling another man and they were laughing until we could hear them two hundred yards away.

When Pa took the sacks home, Mom wanted to know what he was going to do with them. When Pa told her, she started laughing.

"Uglybird, everybody thinks you're so ugly already," she said between spasms of laughter. "What will they think when you wear a suit made of cement sacks?"

"I'll make 'em laugh," Pa said. "I'll be a better-lookin' man than I've ever been. I'll make everybody laugh. What the world needs is a little more laughter. I'll even wear my suit on Lonesome Hill! Too much grief out there nohow."

But Mom was still laughing at Pa's idea.

119

"If you'll wash these sacks, I'll make the suit for you," Mom said.

Pa washed and dried the sacks. Mom made him a jumper and overalls. She made Pa a little cap out of a cement sack, shaped like the pin-striped caps he wore. When Pa put on his suit and cap and walked down Main Street in Blakesburg in his slow gait, his arms swinging like big heavy pistons, everybody he met couldn't speak to Pa for laughing. They laughed after he'd passed them. They'd stand on the street and look at Pa as he walked on and roar with laughter. The men working on the street stopped pouring concrete as Pa walked by. They looked at him and their laughter was explosive. Everybody in Blakesburg laughed.

At the first funeral on Lonesome Hill after Mom had made him his suit, Pa stood by the grave he'd dug with a shovel in his hand. Across the broad shoulder on his jacket and across the seat of his pants was the brand of cement and the name of the company. And when Pa moved around, several people had to hold their laughter. One evening Pa told Mom that the Dawson Hardware owner, Henson Cauldwell, told him the brand of cement Pa was advertising on his suit had sold better than any other brand.

I had finished high school and sister Claris was a senior. She was elected May Queen of the Blakesburg High School. Pa was proud of sister Claris. He told everybody she took her beauty after him. There was a picture of Claris on the front page of the Blakesburg *Weekly News*. And, the following week, there was a picture of Pa on the front page. It was the first and only time Pa ever got his picture in the paper. And here is how he did it.

Blakesburg was putting on a charity drive. Pa thought of a way to make some money. Since he had only one fight in his life, and had lifted a man over a fence with his fist for calling him a liar, he challenged Jason Whiteapple to fight him. Pa was now forty-five and Jason was forty-five. But Jason weighed three hundred and forty pounds. Jason Whiteapple was the only man in our county who could kill a beef with his fist. He never shot one but broke its neck with his fist. Pa had the editor to write up how he felt the fight should be conducted. Everybody must pay admission and the fight would be held in the high school gym. They were not to use any gloves and might fight, without intermission, until one knocked the other out. And Pa concluded he wanted to do this for charity for he knew what it was to be poor since he had been a poor man once himself. Here was a picture of Pa, stripped to the waist, showing his woolly expanded chest and the goose-egg knots of muscles on his arms. The lower half of Pa's body was dressed in his cement-sack pants. When people saw the picture of Pa they laughed again. But Jason Whiteapple refused to fight "Uglybird the Undaunted."

Pa continued to dig graves on Lonesome Hill as the years passed. And he continued to tell each day of the man that had passed on. Pa wouldn't let him be dead. He kept the sleepers on Lonesome Hill alive. They were his companions since he kept their last homes in order.

Pa found new angles for his stories on how he treated my mother. He told the reason he tolerated Mollie was because she'd get up at midnight and make him a pot of black coffee if he asked her. He tolerated her because she saddled and bridled his horse when he wanted to ride. She split kindling with a double-bitted ax and made fires on early winter mornings and warmed his socks. The women on Academy Branch who had seen Pa lying beside the road where Alex had dumped him many times also spread tales on Pa. Down in Blakesburg, women believed Pa had done all the things he said he had to my mother. They talked about how he didn't love her. They knew poor Mollie Skinner had held on because of her fine family.

In late May after Etta, the youngest, had finished Blakesburg High School my mother complained of not feeling too well. As she sat in her rocking chair one evening while my sisters went ahead with the work, she didn't answer when Etta spoke to her. She was sitting with her eyes half open. Her breath had stopped. Mom was dead.

Her grave was the first one my father or my grandfather didn't dig on Lonesome Hill. And on the day of her death, Pa didn't tell us his character sketch of an inmate on Lonesome Hill. Pa's big lips weren't spread in smile and he didn't give us his words of cheer. There wasn't any light in his squinty blue eyes.

And this time the man who had seen so much grief on Lonesome Hill, and had tried to cheer other people, felt some of that same grief. Even in the funeral crowd when Mom was laid to rest, women looked at Pa and whispered softly to each other. I heard one whisper, "If that old brute had been better to her and hadn't beaten the poor thing she might have been on top of the ground today instead of under it. He didn't love her." Not more than a half-dozen women in that funeral crowd went up to Pa and extended to him their sympathies. This hurt me. I knew my father better. I used to think the same way they thought until Pa told me how he loved my mother until he could squeeze her in two. I never forgot how homely he said she was and how no man would look at her and no woman would look at him when they were young. But they noticed each other, and as the years passed she became more beautiful to him.

After Mom was gone, Pa never went back to Blakesburg. And he never put on one of his cement-sack suits Mom had made for him. He gave up being sexton of Lonesome Hill. Estil and I took over Pa's job. In early June, Pa took a little basket of Mom's flowers from the yard and went up on Lonesome Hill. He took his sickle along with him. It was the first time I'd ever seen

122

my big father carry a little basket of flowers. Then, every day through June, he took a basket of her flowers back to her.

"Pa, don't take it so hard," Claris told him one morning. "You have us with you and I'll try to take Mom's place here at the house."

"No one can ever take her place, Claris," Pa said. "More than half of me is dead."

Every day in July, rain or shine, Pa carried a small basket of Mom's flowers to her on Lonesome Hill.

"You look sick, Pa," I said. "Is there something wrong with you?"

"Sick in the head as well as the heart," he said. "I've got a burnin' in my head."

Then my father started losing weight. In early August it was hard for him to climb Lonesome Hill with his basket of flowers which he took each morning before sunup. By middle August, Estil and I took Pa to Doctor Torris in Blakesburg.

"That burnin' in your head is worry!" Doctor Torris looked at Pa and smiled. "You've got to pull out of it, Uglybird!"

As we walked back up the street, Pa's old friends stopped him. Each one asked what was wrong. Pa's answer was that he had a burning in his head. And they laughed at Pa like they laughed when he wore the cement-sack suits. Anything Pa said to them was funny.

During the last two weeks of August, Pa managed to get to Lonesome Hill by walking with a cane. On the last day of August, three months after my mother's death, Pa collapsed at our front doorstep with his cane in one hand and his empty flower basket in the other. Estil ran to Blakesburg for Doctor Torris. But before Doctor Torris arrived, Pa had breathed his last. It took only three months of grief to kill one of the most powerful men I had ever known.

HOW SPORTSMANSHIP CAME
TO CARVER COLLEGE

"**W**e must be like other colleges," Professor Dixon said. "We can't let a thing like this go on. We must have better sportsmanship between the lower and upperclassmen!"

Professor Dixon pulled the neatly folded handkerchief from the pocket near his coat lapel and carefully ran it over his mouth and his shoebrush mustache as he looked us over with his black beady eyes. We upperclassmen sat on one side of the auditorium while the lowerclassmen sat on the other. Not one of us dared cross the broad aisle. The feeling between our groups was high.

Only an hour before, President Poore had called a special chapel at Carver College. He gave a long talk, pleading for "harmony between the upper-and lowerclassmen." Then he prayed for "divine guidance in this time of trouble," since all he and his faculty members had done toward ironing out our differences had been fruitless.

It had begun two weeks before when three seniors started to "initiate" Bullie Sneed who had been brought to Carver from a mountain school to play football. Bullie couldn't understand why three seniors would "get funny" with him, and since he was big, powerful, and handy with his dukes, he whipped all three. Then the upperclassmen came to their classmates' aid and

Bullie's friends started gathering to help him. This was where the first troubled started.

On the afternoon this fracas occurred, we gathered at the dining-room door for supper. Most of us worked all or part of our way and we were usually hungry and gathered at the dining-room entrance fifteen or twenty minutes before it opened.

On this evening, soon as Bullie jumped on one of the three seniors who had tried to "initiate him into the Carver fold" the fight was on. Everybody joined in and it was a free-for-all such as old men and women had never seen before. We knocked windows from the dining room, crashed doors, tramped shrubbery and flowers into the ground.

Faculty members came and couldn't stop the fight. President Poore came and he couldn't do anything with us. The town marshal and his deputies were called and they couldn't do anything about our fighting. The Clayton County sheriff, a big red-faced robust man, and his deputies were called and they rushed to the scene but couldn't stop us. We fought until we got so tired we couldn't fight. Then everybody quit and took care of his fellow buddies who had been knocked cold and trampled on and those with closed eyes. We upperclassmen weren't whipped and we knew it. And the lowerclassmen said they weren't whipped.

But I do know it was the first time in the history of our school where we had such a big crop of lowerclassmen that we upperclassmen were afraid of them. I know that we were afraid, though we wouldn't admit it, for we took baseball bats and clubs into our rooms so if we were attacked we'd have something harder than our fists to strike back with.

After we'd had this fight, President Poore met with his faculty and decided to do something about it. That night a meeting was called in Republican Hollow in an apple orchard where we were supplied with wieners, buns, and marshmallows. A bonfire was built for us and someone brought a brand-new hatchet. After we ate, only a few men from each side testified how well they liked their fellow students on the other side. Then we sang songs together, but the singing was very weak, and after the singing we buried the hatchet.

But only a few of the more peaceful mountain boys from each side participated in this affair. On that very night strong young upperclassmen stood back under the apple trees whose autumn leaves glowed in the soft bright firelight. They whispered to each other while the singing went on and looked beyond the bonfire at another group of larger boys and more of them, known as lowerclassmen. We could hear their voices and a few cuss words as they looked and pointed at us. We knew the trouble was not at an end, that we would meet sometime somewhere and fight it out even if on this night we had buried the hatchet.

"Now back East we had good sportsmanship at all the colleges and universities," Professor Dixon said, as he put his handkerchief back. "And I don't see any reason why we can't have it here. Of course, this is my first experience in a mountain college. But I think we can initiate a few games between the upper and lowerclassmen that will promote a spirit of friendly rivalry."

Then Professor Dixon looked us over. Not a man on either side smiled. One could hear a person breathe.

"I have a little game in mind," Professor Dixon said, "that we used to do back East. And it's fun. We'll put flag in the top of a big tree and let forty-five of you upperclassmen defend the flag and let fifty lowerclassmen try to take it from the tree."

"Why let them have fifty men and us only forty-five?" Big Dick Donley, president of the senior class, asked.

"But you see, Mr. Donley," Professor Dixon persuaded, "the lowerclassmen have an uphill fight. They have to climb the tree to get the flag and you can put as many men around the tree as you want to guard the tree and as many men up in the tree as you think is necessary to keep the freshmen down! They have the odds against them!"

"Looks all right to me," Paul Sykes said, his face reddening.

"What do you think about it?" Professor Dixon asked, looking toward the big lowerclassmen.

"What do you say, Bullie?" a tall freckled-faced boy said.

"I say we can take that flag," Bullie said.

"Maybe," someone on our side said.

"Where is the tree?" I asked, wondering if we had a tree big enough on the campus.

"We've got the tree selected and the flag in it," Dixon said.

"Then what are we waiting on?" Big Dick said.

"We're ready," Bullie said.

When we left the auditorium, our side went out together. We followed Big Dick. The freshmen followed Bullie. Not one of our men got mixed up with their crowd and not one of their men got mixed up with us.

"Now you can call your men off to themselves and plan your strategy," Professor Dixon told Big Dick.

"That's just what I aim to do," Big Dick said. "We know that gang we're up against."

"As soon as you're through talking it over," Professor Dixon said, "let me know and I'll take you to the tree."

We knew that Big Dick, who was the most powerful among us, would go to the very top of the tree to protect our flag. And below him we would put our best tree climbers, tall men who could swing on limbs and could kick with their long legs.

"Step on their hands when they start climbing up," Big Dick told us; "kick 'em down any way you can even if you have to ram the toe of your shoes in their mouths. That's the tough-

127

est crop that's ever come to Carver. We'll have a time with 'em. Let's go keep our flag flying at any cost."

"Ready, Professor," Big Dick shouted.

Big Dick arranged for himself and eleven more of his most active men to go up into the tree. He selected twelve more men, the heavy powerful men, to guard the trunk of the tree, and the remaining twenty-one to meet Bullie and his gang as they came uphill toward the tree. Big Dick called us his "assault troops" and he put me with this group. When he selected me, I shook like a leaf, for I knew what was coming. I'd seen too many fights between the lower-and upperclassmen already. I'd seen Big Dick hit Stanley Graff, knock him clean through a window, taking out sashes and windowpanes, when we were working in the shoe shop.

But this freshman came around the house and back in at the door for some more. He was tough. They were all tough. Big Dick, two-hundred-and-twenty-five pounder, was a man. He could run the hundred in nine and four-fifths seconds. He'd taken as many as seven first places in track meets; he was fullback on our football team, a guard on our basketball team, and an outfielder in baseball. And he was handy with his dukes. He did a lot of boxing but he couldn't hurt Graff.

Professor Dixon led the way and Big Dick followed him and we followed Big Dick. The men to follow Big Dick up the tree, mostly our basketball squad, were up near Dick. And the tree guards, which were mostly the linemen on our Bulldogs, followed the tree climbers. And we "assault troops" followed the tree guards.

I don't know what Bullie said to his men or how he arranged them. They followed us, hollering like a pack of wolves. When Professor Dixon showed us the tree, we looked to the top and saw our flag, a big white cloth, flying from the topmost twig above the copper-colored leaves.

128

It was a big elm tree, the biggest and prettiest tree on the campus, where many of us had sat with our sweethearts on Sunday afternoons. Many of us who had been more interested in the course of "love" than any other subject in our happy years at Carver had an affection for this tree. But now it was just another tree.

Big Dick put his powerful arms around its trunk and went up its stalwart body like a cat until he reached the first limbs. Then the climbing was easier. Behind Big Dick were Big Nick Darter, Amos Smelcher, Tim Evans, Johnnie Dowling, Enic Pratt, Charlie Fugate, like ants following each other up the tree. While down below us at the foot of the hill was Bullie Sneed in front of his men, waiting until the signal was given to battle us. Our tree guards gathered around the tree trunk and waited while we, the assault men, grouped together, each one trembling like a leaf in the wind, and waited for the signal to meet Bullie and his fifty men. There were twenty-one of us. We knew we wouldn't be able to stop Bullie and all his men but we could slow them.

"Ready, everybody," Big Dick shouted to his men from the top.

"Have been ready and waiting for some time," Bullie Sneed yelled.

"All right, let's go," Professor Dixon commanded.

"Let's meet 'em with full force, fellows," Ickie Porter shouted, running downhill to meet Bullie.

When we met Bullie and his men we hit body to body, head on and every way that men could hit. I was never hit harder in line practice in football.

Men were knocked down and they groaned when others fell upon them or over them. Fists flew and men kicked. We knew it was a fight to a finish. As I went around and around with some freshman, I looked below me and saw some big man had

Ickie down sitting on him, resting as he fanned his hot face. And then as we whirled around in a tussle, I saw Bullie, with a pack of big men, shoving our men aside and making it toward our guards.

"Take 'em, men," Bullie screamed as they fought their way to the tree. "Knock 'em out! Knock their teeth down their throats!"

And I saw our men upend Bullie's men as they approached, but not for long. Bullie and his men would reach up and get one of our guards by the hand or pants leg or sleeve and jerk him down the hill over the slick grass, stripping his clothes as they went.

"Fight 'em, men," Big Dick yelled as he observed the fight from the treetop. "Stand your ground! They're closin' in!"

"Stand, hell," someone shouted.

We were a battered lot. Many of us hardly had on enough clothes to hide our nakedness. Noses were bleeding, teeth were knocked loose, hands were hurt, and men were lying senseless upon the grass but the fight went on. Bullie was trying to go up the butt of the tree while his men, who had overpowered our guards by numbers and not strength, guarded him. Bullie got up to the first limbs when Tim Evans dropped down low enough to kick Bullie until he had to let loose and drop to the ground. All our men in the tree laughed to see Bullie knocked from the tree. But it didn't hurt Bullie. He got up and started up the tree again while his men pounded our tree guards and "assault men" until we were all nearly knocked out, lying helpless upon the grass. Often three of his men would polish off one of ours. Not until now did we know Bullie's tactics. When he got us out of the way on the ground he could concentrate on the tree.

Finally I got my man down and he was willing to lie down for awhile. He had had enough. I went to rescue Ickie for three of Bullie's men were sitting on him, resting while he groaned beneath the load. When I approached, one of the men jumped up, grabbed me at the neck, stripped my shirt clean, and slung me twenty feet or more down the hill where I whirled and spun before I finally hit headfirst on the grass.

"Hold that tree, men," Big Dick shouted as he directed the fight from his safe perch.

Now Bullie and several of his men had places up in the elm. And our men had dropped down to kick them, but they caught their feet and legs and were trying to pull them from the tree. One of their men was holding to Big Nick Darter's legs and swinging like he was on a grapevine swing while Big Nick held to the limb above with all his strength.

Girls could no longer be held in their dormitories. They broke out and came to see the fight. The upper-class girls were on our side yelling for us while the others were yelling for the lowerclassmen. Faculty members came too, and though they had preached sportsmanship to us, they started yelling for one side or the other. Someone called the town marshal and his deputies and the county sheriff and his deputies. It was one of the women teachers or maybe the president who had got scared again. And they came, but they couldn't do anything with the ninety-five men who were determined to fight to the finish.

Three of Bullie's men let Ickie up and grabbed me. They threw me down and sat on me while they rested. And their load was something to bear up. From where they sat on me, I could look up and see the fight in the tree and I could hear the screams from the men in the tree above the roar of the crowds.

"Get that man in the top," Stanley Graff yelled. "Then we'll haul down their dirty rag."

The lowerclassmen didn't pull Big Nick Darter down but when another one swung on his legs to pull him loose, they broke the limb from the tree and Big Nick came down holding it in his hands with two men holding his legs. They hit the

131

ground with a thump. No one bothered about them in the thickest of the fight. I saw Bullie and his men getting higher and higher in the tree. I saw limbs coming down with men holding them and two or three men holding to their legs.

In twenty minutes there wasn't a lower limb left. A few limbs remained in the top where Big Dick was still safe for he was guarded by three men below him. But Bullie must have had twelve men left. We wondered how long it would be before they got Big Dick and our flag. Bullie was the highest of all his men but one of our men stepped down and put a foot on each of Bullie's shoulders and jumped up and down. Though Bullie hugged the tree like a bear he couldn't take this. He dropped down without a limb to catch him but he fell on a soft pile of men.

"Stop the fight, Sheriff," some faculty member yelled.

"Here goes my football team!" Coach Powers yelled. "Who planned a thing like this anyway?"

"My basketball team," Coach Charlie Andrews yelled. "Sheriff, can't you do something?"

But the sheriff couldn't climb that tree where the fight was raging. There wasn't any more fighting on the ground for no one there was able to fight. There wasn't anything that a sheriff could do. When Amos Smelcher came down he brought a freshman with him and Tim Evans and Johnnie Dowling brought two each. But six men were up in the tree.

The fight was up among the last limbs where the elm top rocked in the wind. Every time a man started up, Big Dick kicked him down. He kicked Bullie's men until they fell out or had to come down. Just one man stayed. He wouldn't leave. That was Stanley Graff. He would reach up to get Big Dick by the leg. But Big Dick would kick at his hand and he'd jerk it back while everybody yelled like at a basketball overtime period when the score was tied.

132

Big Dick got mad at Stanley's tactics. He dropped down a step to put his feet on Stanley's shoulders to shove him from the tree. But Stanley got him by the legs and started swinging and since Big Dick was so heavy and the top limb was so small, with Stanley's extra weight the limb slivered and down they came, bringing all the treetop but the one twig that held our flag.

"There goes my track team," Coach Speed Mullins yelled as Big Dick dropped through the air still clinging to the elm limb and with Stanley Graff holding to his legs.

Then the crowds rushed in to help care for their wounded. Someone pulled the three lowerclassmen from me. I wasn't hurt like many of the others but I had escaped only in my undershirt, shorts, socks, and shoes. Since Carver College didn't have an ambulance, they rushed the college truck to the scene. I saw them carry Big Nick Darter, our best baseball player, and the two lowerclassmen that had swung on his legs to the truck. They were knocked cuckoo.

Then they picked up Bullie Sneed and carried him to the truck. He yelled, cussed, kicked with one leg, and screamed, and his words sounded funny for he had lost his front teeth and one leg was broken. Next they carried Big Dick and Stanley, who were knocked cold as icicles, and laid them side by side in the truck bed. The driver gunned the truck and was away, rushing them to Natesboro General Hospital, across the mountain. The rest of us could nurse our own bruises.

"Come on, pal," Ickie Porter, my roommate, said to me. "You've got on more clothes than I have."

Ickie only had on his shorts. He held my arm for I was wobbly, and we walked past where the coaches had surrounded Professor Dixon and a great argument was going on. But we'd had all we wanted and we didn't stop to listen. We didn't want to listen any longer to the moans coming from men stretched out on the grass where their sweethearts, friends, and faculty

133

members administered sympathy.

"Look," Ickie said, stopping to point back at our flag. "It's safe now! Not anybody on this campus that can climb that tree now."

Ickie was right for there wasn't a limb except the topmost twig where our flag waved. And there wasn't a piece of bark left on it big as a matchbox.

LOVE IN THE SPRING

It was last April when I met Effie. It was over at the Put-Off Ford at the Baptis foot-washing. Effie is a Slab Baptis. She was there having her feet washed. And I can't forget that day in April. It is always work in the spring. Fence to fix. Plowing to do. Cattle to tend to. Seems like everything is to do in the spring on the place. Planting crops is the big job. We don't have no place to go only to church and we don't feel like going there only on Sunday. That is the day we have off and we don't have that day off until we've milked seven cows and slopped the hogs and got in wood and got up water for the day. I can't forget that Sunday in last spring when I met Effie. I just packed in the last load of wood and Mom says to me, "Elster, you are going to fall for a woman sometime so hard that it's going to hurt you. Run around and talk about Mort Anderson being in love and how silly he is. Wait till you fall in love once. The love bug is going to bite you right over the heart."

I went to the baptizing with a clean white starched shirt on and a blue necktie and blue serge pants and black slippers. I looked about as good in them as I can look. I felt good just to get off to the foot-washing. I remember that row of elms along Little Sandy River had just started to leaf out. The rest of the hills just had a few sycamores and poplars down along the creeks that had leafed a little. It was a pretty morning. And down by the ford I never saw as many people in my life gathered at that one place. And I've seen a lot of baptizings there. Horses hitched to the trees with ropes and bridle reins. Wagons here and there with washing-tubs of grub in them and chears where whole families rid miles in them to the foot-washing. And horses eating yaller corn out'n the wagon beds of a lot of the wagons. I just walked down where they's singing "Where the Healing Waters Flow." It was soft music and I wished I was a child of the Lord's then. Good people, the Baptis is; we live neighbors to them. Ain't no better people to help you out in a time of sickness or weedy crops in the spring. Come right in and help you out. Now on this bank and washing feet. I walked down along the edge of the river where the horseweeds had been tromped down. I just wanted to look the crowd over. A whole row up and a whole row down. The row standing up was a-washing the feet of them on the ground. Just setting there on the ground as unconcerned and washing feet. Then they would sing another verse of "Where the Healing Waters Flow."

I looked up in front of me. I couldn't believe my eyes. I saw the prettiest woman I ever saw in my life. She was prettier than a speckled pup. Honest I never saw anything like her. Eyes that just looked at you and melted like yellow butter on hot corn bread, blue kind of eyes, and a face that was smooth as silk and cheeks the color of the peeling on a Roman Beauty apple in September. Her hair was the color of golden corn silks in August hanging from the shooting corn. Hair pretty and curly waving in the wind. I never saw a woman so pretty in my life. Her hands didn't look to me like no hands that had held to the hoe handle like my mother's hands and my sisters'. Her hands were pretty and soft. Her teeth were white as a bubble of foam in the Sandy River. She was an angel among the sinners trying to come clean. My heart beat faster when I saw her. Some man had his back to

136

me. He was washing her foot. He had an old chipped washpan and a big towel and a bar of homemade soap made from oak-tree ashes. He'd put it on her foot like he was putting axle grease on a wagon hub. Then he would smear it with his hands and rub. Then he would take the towel and dry her foot till it would look pink as a wild crab-apple blossom. I just stood there and looked at her. She looked at me. He saw her looking and he looked around. Of all the big ugly devils I ever saw in my life it was this fellow, Jonas Pratt's boy, Tawa Pratt. Lived down on Little Sandy on that big farm in the bend by the grove of cedars.

When he turned around and saw me looking he said, "Ain't you a Baptis?"

And I said, "No, I ain't no Slab Baptis. I'm a Methodist and I go to Plum Grove to church."

"Go on about your business then," he said, "and leave us Baptis alone. This ain't no side show. We are here worshiping the Lord."

I could see he just didn't want me to see the girl. He didn't like me. I didn't like him. I don't care if he was worshiping the Lord. And I says to him, "If that's the way you feel about it, all right. But I want to know the name of the girl here with you and where she lives."

That burnt him up. His lips just spread out and he showed them big yaller horse-teeth in front. I just thinks to myself, "What woman could kiss that awful mouth behind them big horse-teeth?" He looked at me with them black polecat eyes and his hair was right down over his eyes. He was a sorry-looking devil.

The girl says to me, "I'm Effie Long. I live up on Duck Puddle." I never said a word. I'd go to Duck Puddle. That's just down on Little Sandy four miles and up a hollow that comes into Little Sandy not far from the riffles. I knowed right then and there I'd see that woman again. I said to myself as I walked back

137

from the riverbank over through horseweeds, "That's my wife if I can get her. Pretty as a angel right out of Heaven."

I thought of what Mom told me. I would fall for a skirt. I did like the looks of that woman. I went home. I remember it like it was just one hour ago. The daisies looked good to me. First time flowers ever did look good to me. I pulled off the top of a Sweet William and smelt it. It smelt sweet as sugar.

"The love bug's got me right over the heart," I said to Mom soon as I got in at the door. "I saw my wife at the foot-washing – over there among the Baptis today at the Put-Off Ford."

And Mom she says, "Elster, you ain't fell for no Slab Baptis, have you? No Slab Baptis woman can ever come under this Methodist roof until she's been converted into the Methodist faith. That bunch all running around and drinking licker. Won't see no licker in Heaven nor no spittoons for that old terbacker."

That's how women are. Right half of the time. When a man is in love, what does he care for spittoons in Heaven and bad licker or good licker? What does he care who a Methodist is or a Slab Baptis is? He wants his woman. That's the way I felt. Mom married Pop fifty years ago and she don't know what it is to be young and be in love. I just never said a word.

A week hadn't passed till I heard about church down on Duck Puddle. Slab Baptis holding a pertracted meeting down there. I put on a white starched shirt, a blue necktie and blue serge pants and my black slippers and I went down there. It was a awful walk through the brush and over them ridges. But I followed the fox hunters' paths for more than two miles across through the brush. I walked across the rocks at the riffle and hit the big wagon road up to the church. Meeting was a-going on when I got there. I had to stop and ask four or five times before I found the place. A pretty place after a body gets there but a devil of a time getting to it. I never went inside the house till

I peeped in at the winders and looked over the house to see if I could see Effie. I looked and looked. And one time when I looked with my eyes up agin the winderpanes the Slab Baptis preacher said, "A lot of pilferers on the outside of the house tonight. The devil in sheep's clothing is out there. Methodists are snooping around." When I heard this I slipped back in the dark. I'm a Methodist and couldn't be nothing else. Methodist church is good enough for Pa and Mom and Grandpa and Grandma and it's good enough for me. Even if they don't want me, for I bet on chicken fights and play cards once in a while.

I slipped back to the winder. I had looked every place but the amen corner. I looked up there and saw the angel I had seen over at the ford. She was in a mighty good place to be. Me a Methodist and out in the dark. I picked up courage and just walked up and bolted in at the door. I found an empty seat and I saw Effie start looking at me. I started looking at her. And I looked up there and saw old Tawa too. He was in the amen corner. He started showing them teeth soon as he saw me. And I thinks to myself, "Old boy, one of these days I'm going to get me a rock and knock them ugly teeth down your throat. Running around here with a set of horse-teeth in your mouth."

The crowd looked at me. A lot of them had seen me at the Methodist church. A lot of them had seen me at the foot-washing. They all knowed I was a Methodist. They know the Harkreaders are all Methodist, every last devil of them!

I just waited till church was out. I was going to take Effie home. And I had my mind made up. If that horse-toothed thing of a Tawa should come around me and started anything, it would just be too bad. I was going to use my fists long as they would stand it. I got bad bones in my little fingers. And after my fists I was going to knife it with him and after that if he whopped me I was going to use the balance of power. I carried it right in my pocket. The prettiest little twenty-two you ever saw in your life – could put five balls between your eyes before you could say "Jack Robinson." I don't go into no strange territory unless I go prepared for the worst. That's the way we got to do here. I don't care if we are Baptis and Methodist.

The preacher was saying, "Men and women, since you got to work in your crops tomorrow and I got to work in mine, we'll call the meeting tomorrow night at seven. All of you be here and bring your songbooks. Sing 'Almost Persuaded,' folks, and all who wants to come up and jine us just come right on." I never saw so many people fall at the altar.

Church was out and the people already saved. The young people went home and the old people stayed to pray with the people at the "mourners' bench." They was just a-going on something awful. A lot of them were sheep that had left the Methodist flock too. A bunch that wanted to stay in our church and drink licker and play cards and we just wouldn't have it in Plum Grove.

Effie come right down the aisle and I said, "Honey, how about seeing you home tonight?"

I know my face got red when she said, "All right." Here was old Tawa right behind her with that crazy grin showing that big set of yaller horse-teeth. I thought if he wanted anything he could get it on this night. I didn't speak to him. No use to hide it. He didn't like me and I didn't like him.

I got Effie by the arm, and I held it like a leech. We didn't speak. We just walked out of the house and past a bunch of boys at the door waiting for their girls and the other fellow's girl. People just looked at us. Boys lit up their cigarettes and pipes and the old men started spitting their ambeer. A lot of the women lit up their pipes too: old long-stemmed clay pipes. Something you don't see around our church at Plum Grove among them already saved. If they done it they went home or out behind the brush.

I hadn't got out from under the oak trees by the church house till I had Effie by the hand. And I said, "Honey, I can't eat, drink, work, nor sleep for thinking about you."

And I reached down and got her by the little soft hand, and she looked up at me and said, "Ain't it funny? I feel the same way about you. I have felt that way ever since I saw you at the foot-washing. I can't forget you. I keep thinking about you. When I saw you tonight I was thinking about you."

I just squeezed her hand a little harder and I said, "Was you, honey?" Then we went on out the path without speaking.

We went out past the Duck Puddle graveyard. White tombstones gleaming there in the moonlight. Lord, it was a sad thing to think about. I wondered what had become of old Tawa. It was a little dark even if the moon was shining. I didn't care, though. I had Effie. I didn't blame him for loving her, but I just didn't want him to get her.

I guess we went through twenty pairs of drawbars before we come to Effie's place. It was a little log house upon the side of a bank, pretty with flowers in the yard. I'd always thought flowers was for the womenfolks. I told Effie I'd never liked flowers till I met her. I told her everything like that. We just went up to her door. I said a lot about the crops. Before I started to leave we was standing out at the well gum. The moon come down upon her old log house there among all them roses and flowers. It was a mighty pretty place.

Effie said, "Guess I'd better get in the house and get to bed. Got to work tomorrow."

And I said, "Where, honey?"

"In the terbacker field," she said.

And then I said, "W'y, you don't work in no terbacker and stay as white as you are."

She said, "That's all you know about it, Elster. I use stocking legs on my arms and a sunbonnet."

And I says, "Honey, I love you. I want to marry you." I just pulled her up to me and kissed her there in the moonlight.

Soon I left her there and run over the hill like a dog. Tears come into my eyes. Just to think about that. I used to laugh at such stuff. Now, I had six or seven miles to walk home and blue Monday and the plow before me the next day. But seeing Effie was worth a dozen trips like this. When a man is in love he just don't care.

I went to bed that night—must have been morning. It was after the roosters crowed for midnight. Lord, but I was tired. I just could see Effie. I could pull her up to me and kiss her. I could see her eyes, I could see her teeth. I could see her log house in the moonlight. I just couldn't forget it all.

I got up and et my breakfast. Drunk two cups of black coffee and went out to milk the cows. I'd just stop at the barn and look off into the wind.

Pa come up to me and he said, "Elster, what in the devil and Tom Walker's got into you here lately? Just go around with your head up in the air dreaming. W'y, you even stop when you are shaving your face. If I didn't see you the other day shave half of your face and put the razor up I'm a liar."

I never said anything, for it was the truth. I just couldn't help it for thinking about Effie.

I went out to plow corn. I took the mule and the double-shovel plow and went down the path by the barn. I didn't pay any attention but I started to plow on the wrong side of the field and was plowing up the corn. I couldn't think about anything but Effie and how I run away and left that night with my eyes filled with tears.

Then I thought, "W'y, I must be crazy to act like this. I'm forgetting everything. I'm not happy as I was. I can't laugh like I did. She didn't say she would marry me. That's it. That's what's the matter."

I just couldn't get back to see Effie that week. I had too much to do. Too much corn to plow and seven cows to milk.

Well, I went out to work Tuesday morning. I couldn't work. I thought I'd go up and see Uncle Tid Porter. He lives right on the bank above us. He gives us boys a lot of advice. Uncle Tid was in the woodyard whacking off a few sticks of stovewood.

I walked up and I said, "Uncle Tid, I'm in love with a girl. I can't sleep. I can't work. I can't do anything. I'm going crazy."

You ought to have seen Uncle Tid sling his ax agin the ground and laugh. You know Uncle Tid is a pretty good doctor when we can't get one from town. He uses the yarb remedies and he does pretty well. Used to be the only doctor in this section. Now, he give us advice along with spring tonics of slippery-elm bark, shoe-make bark, and ginsang and snakeroot.

"Well," said Uncle Tid, shaking his long thin chin whiskers stained with a little terbacker juice—his blue walled eye squinted a little—"when did you meet this girl and where is she from?"

"I met her last month at the Slab Baptis foot-washing at the Put-Off Ford. She's from Duck Puddle. She's a beauty, too, Uncle Tid. W'y, Uncle Tid, to tell you the truth, I never loved a flower till I met her. Now I notice them. See the wild rose in bloom in the woods. I noticed them this morning. She is with me everywhere I go. I can't sleep. I can't eat."

"It's love in the spring," said Uncle Tid. "Love in the spring is so uncertain I wouldn't trust it. Don't be too sure of yourself and jump in and try to marry. Wait a while. Just go out and watch life in the spring. Go to the house and put the mule in the pasture. Take the afternoon off and go to the pond and watch the frogs. Go find some blacksnakes in love and watch them. Watch the terrapins and the turtles. Everything is in love now. Listen to the songs of the birds. Listen how they sing to each other. It is time to be in love. All the earth is in love now. And

143

love is so uncertain in the spring."

I just got on the mule and went back home. I took the harness off old Barnie and put it on the stall in the barn and I slapped him with the bridle and made him skiddoo to the pasture. I laid up the drawbars and I made for the pond. There's a lot of bull grass there and about a foot of water. It's a regular frog and water-snake hangout. Lord, of all the noise! I slipped up by the pond. They all hushed. I never heard another noise only I heard some plump-plumps into the water. I saw that I'd scared them. So I laid down on my belly behind a bunch of bull grass out of sight from the frogs. It wasn't two minutes before they all started singing. The old frogs didn't do much singing. They'd get up on a log and jump off and chase each other. I crawled up to the edge of the pond and watched them. If you don't believe young frogs love in the spring when they are doing all of that hollering you just go around the pond and see for yourself.

When I got up to leave there, I heard the birds singing. They sung their love songs to each other and it seemed like I could understand some of the words. But the prettiest thing I saw was two snakes entwined upon the bank in the sun. They were blacksnakes and very much in love. If it had been before I met Effie I would have picked me up a rock and killed them because Pa says they kill all the birds and young rabbits. I saw two turtles out in the pond on a log. They were bathing in the sun. I just watched them a while. No wonder I fell in love with Effie, pretty a girl as she is. No wonder I dream of her at night and plan a house to take her to. My mother's bread don't taste as good to me as it used to taste. My bed at home don't look as good as it used to look and home and Mom and Pa don't seem the same. I just can't help feeling that way. I dream of the way Effie is going to bake my bread and fix my bed and clean my shirts and patch my pants. Life is great; and to be in love, love is so much greater. It's about one of the greatest things in the world – to be in love till you can cry. I just went to bed thinking about the house I had in mind and it was altogether different to the house here where we live. Just to see Effie with a blue dress and a little white apron on, lifting big white fluffy biscuits out of the pan, white biscuits with brown tops, and good hot gravy made out of milk, and butter yaller as a daisy eye, and steam off my coffee hot as hell and strong as love!

I just thought, "Well, I'm going to tell Pa and Ma that I am leaving them. That I am going to marry that little Slab Baptis and hunt me a home and help to replenish the earth with a good stock. A body can look at her and tell that she is of good stock and I ain't of such bad stock."

I went to the house. I never got the mule back out of the pasture. I was through. Of course I knowed Pa would hate to see me go and it would break Mom's heart when I told her. Mom is a Shouting Methodist and it would kill her to see me marry one of them Slab Baptis that drink licker and bet on chicken fights and play cards. But no use to lie to Mom about it. I would go today and fix everything up. Frogs could fall in love and the birds and snakes and terrapins and lizards – well, why didn't I have the same right? And if Pa put his jib in I would tell him to stay out of my love affair and Uncle Tid Porter too. It may be love in the spring but I loved in the spring.

I'll never forget going into the house. Mom was making biscuit dough. I heard Pa telling her I put the mule up and knocked off for half a day. Pa didn't like it and he was worried.

"Well," I says to Mom, "I got news for you."

And Mom says, "What kind of news, Elster?"

And I says, "I am going to leave you. Going to get married."

"Who are you going to marry?" says Pa, his neck and face red as a hen's comb in the spring.

"I am going to marry Effie Long, that little girl I met over

145

at the foot-washing last month," I said to Pa.

"One of them Slab Baptis?" said Pa.

"Yes, one of them Slab Baptis," I said.

"And you been raised under a roof like this one," Mom said, "under a Methodist roof, and then go and marry a Slab Baptis, one that has a religion that believes in drinking and playing poker and betting on rooster fights and spitting at cracks in the crib floor. Then you going to marry one of them kind. Remember, Elster, if you get burnt you got to set on the blister. You are brought up to believe a certain way it is hard to break away from. Elster, your people have been Methodist for nearly a hundred years. And you go marry that infidel. Don't you ever let her darken my door. You can come back when you want to but you be sure you keep her away."

The tears come from Mom's eyes. Pa put his hands up over his eyes.

And I said to Mom, "Home here ain't the same any more since I met Effie. Life ain't the same. I tell you. My bed ain't the same upstairs and the good biscuits ain't the same."

"Your Ma's bread is the same. Good as it was twenty years ago. Best cook in the country. Then you talk about the bread and even your bed upstairs. Son, I'm not going to stand for anything like that. You can get out of this house if that is the way you feel about things around here. Get your clothes and go." Pa said it and his voice kinda quivered.

I went upstairs and got my clothes. It didn't take me long, for I don't have many. Lord, it burnt me up to think about the whole thing. Life with Effie and I'd never come home to see the boys and Mom and Pa. I'd stay away till they would be glad to see me. That's what I'd do. They'd have to send to Duck Puddle to get me.

I put my clothes into the newspaper and got my work clothes—my heavy shoes and my Sunday shoes and my twenty-two pistol. I thought it might come in handy about a home of my own. I went down through the front room. Mom was crying.

"Ain't you going to eat a bite before you leave?" Mom said.

And I said, "Nope, I don't believe I care for anything to eat."

"Take a piece of hot corn bread and butter it and eat a piece of smoked ham as you go."

I took it. Lord, but it tasted good. I had et Mom's cooking for eighteen years and it was good. But I went out of the house. I wasn't going to wait till fall. Couldn't plant any ground that late. I was going to marry early enough to rent some ground and get out a late crop and pray for a late fall so they would ripen. I could make it all right.

I walked out into the sunlight. It was a pretty day in May. I never felt so good in all my life. Had my clothes under my arm and going to get my sweet Effie – sweeter than the wind red rose. I went down past the barn and I said farewell to the milk cows, Boss, Fern, Star, Daisy, Little Bitty, Roan, and Blacky. I waved my hands to them and to Pete and Barnie in the pasture, mules I'd worked many a day. Barnie nickered at me. He walked along the pasture fence far as he could follow me. I'd been his master ever since he was a colt. Now he would get another master. I said good-by to the trees, the barn, to everything. I was going to a new country.

Sky was pretty above me. The birds never sung any sweeter for me. The wind had music in it. Flowers bloomed so pretty by the road, whole hillsides covered with wild roses. Well, when I got to the riffles the sun was getting pretty low on the other hill. I knowed it would soon be time for them to come from the fields. I'd just get in there a little after suppertime. Lord, but I was hungry. I got across the rocks at the riffle all right, and I went right up the creek till I come to the church house. I was moving fast to get there before dark. A little moon in the sky already.

I crossed the ditch by the church and took out toward the first pair of bars. If I ever go over a road once I never forget it. I soon came to the second pair of bars. The moon was a little bigger in the sky. One of them quarter moons. And a dry moon at that. One edge kinda turned up. Darkness had come at last but here was the house. Light in the front room. So I goes up and looks in. There was old Tawa. He was setting on the couch beside of my Effie. I knocked on the door. Effie come to the door.

I said, "How are you, honey?" and I just closed her in my arms.

Old Tawa showed them big horse-teeth with that funny grin, them polecat eyes just a-snapping.

"Come here, Mart Long," Tawa hollered.

"Come where?" said a voice from upstairs. I heard him getting out of bed. Sounded like the whole loft was coming in. Must a been a big feller. "What are you coming here for?" said Tawa.

"If it's any your business," I said, "I'm coming here to marry Effie. That's why I've come."

"You ain't getting Effie," said Tawa. "She belongs to me. I'm one of her kind. I am a Slab Baptis. I ain't no damned infidental."

I thought I'd take my twenty-two out and blow his lights out. Calling me a infidental. I never did like the Methodists so much as I did now.

And I said, "Who in the hell are you calling a infidental? You polecat, you. I'll clean this floor with you."

I started to turn Effie loose and get him. Just then in stepped Sourwood Long, Effie's pap.

"There's our infidental Methodist," said Tawa to Sourwood.

And Sourwood said, "W'y, he just looks like the rest of us. Got eyes like us and a mouth and talks. W'y, he's like the rest of us; only I don't want Effie marrying you until you repent and get into our church."

"I have come after Effie right now," I said. "Besides, I am a Methodist. I don't intend to repent neither. Why can't she get into the Methodist church? What's wrong with us?"

"And what's wrong with us?" said Sourwood. Black beard covering his face. His arms were big as fence posts and hairy as a brier thicket around a old fence row. He kept them folded upon his big hairy chest. He didn't have many teeth. Had a lot of snags in his mouth, a big nose, and he was dark as a wet piece of chestnut bark.

"Nothing ain't wrong with us," said Tawa. "We are the only people right. You know we got a lot of them Methodists in our church when the pertracted meeting was going on. Left your church for ours."

"You got a lot that couldn't stay in our church," I said. I was ready to fight. I still had Effie in my arms. I hadn't turned her loose yet.

"You ain't going to marry Effie. I wouldn't have one of you fellers in my house for dinner let alone in my family to put up with you a lifetime. Get out of here right now."

Another voice from upstairs. "Sourwood, what's going on down there?"

"Malinda, what are you doing up there? A Methodist has come to get Effie. Come on down here."

"Better let a Methodist have her than that thing down there. That Tawa. Get 'em both out of here. Get 'em out quick."

I never saw Effie's mother. I don't know how it was done. It was done so quick. Old Tawa must a come around the back side of the house and upon the front porch and hit me over the head with something. I remember I waked up out in the yard. My clothes were under my head for a piller. The moon was in the sky. It just seemed like I'd been asleep and had slept a little too long. Seemed like a dream. Lights all out of the house just like nothing had ever happened. They's all in bed, I guess. Don't know what ever become of Tawa. Have never seen him from that day to this. I can hardly tell you how I got home. I was about half-crazy from that lick. I remember I was so hungry. I remember, too, the chickens were crowing for the daylight. I didn't have my twenty-two on me. It was gone.

Mom was getting breakfast. I went in and I said, "Mom, your biscuits are all right. Lord, I can eat twenty-two this morning. I'm so hungry."

"Where's your wife?" Mom said.

"I took another notion," I said. "I remembered what you said. I didn't want one of them infidentals after we've been Methodists so long. I thought it over and changed my mind."

"I thought you would," said Mom. "A boy with your raising and get into a mix-up like that. Couldn't bring her home. You'll do better marrying one of your own kind. I'm making you some good strong coffee."

"Good strong coffee is what I need. Strong as love but not love in the spring. Love in the fall. Coffee hot as hell, too."

Lord, but Mom did look good to me in that apron. She just looked the best I ever saw her. And her biscuits tasted right, too.

"Mom, you are the best girl I've ever had," I said and I kinda give Mom a bear hug and she says to this day I cracked a couple of her ribs. She says she can hardly get her breath at times ever since I hugged her.

This has been a day in September. Uncle Tid Porter was down today. He said to me, "Now is the kind of weather to fall in love, now while the chill winds blow and the leaves fly, now while the frost has come. The spring is the time to marry and go on a gay carousal like the frog. Like the snakes and the flowers and all living things. Spring is the time to marry, not the time to fall in love. Love in the spring is fickle as the wind."

Love in the Spring

"I have often wondered what has become of Tawa," I said to Uncle Tid, "the fellow that loved the girl I loved last spring. W'y, he's the ugliest human being I ever saw for to love as pretty a woman as Effie—"

"She's married him, I guess," said Uncle Tid. "That's the way of a woman. They do the unexpected thing, not knowing which way the wind will blow and if there will be snow or rain tomorrow. That's what a man likes; he likes the unexpected thing."

The wind blows outside. The wind is cool. Pa is out at the barn putting a roof over the fattening hog pen. Mom is still complaining of her ribs. "I never heard of that but once before in my life. A teacher came to this deestrict to teach school and he hugged one of Mort Giggin's girls—it was Ester, I believe—and he broke three of her ribs. I tell you he never got another school in this deestrict."

SETTIN'-UP WITH GRANDMA

When Grandma Shelton left this world, I was standing beside her bed. Doc Braiden, who had long been her doctor, turned to Mom and said, "Her breath is getting shorter, Martha. It won't be long."

Then Mom walked away, wringing her hands and crying. And I started crying too. Pa wiped the tears from his suntanned face with a big bandanna. Uncle Mel walked back and forth across the floor. Cousin Grace Shelton ran out on the porch, leaned against the log wall with her face hidden in her arms, and cried like her heart would break. Uncle Jason sat in a big rocking chair with his elbows resting on the chair arms and his face resting in his hands. He didn't cry. He looked silently at the floor and didn't say anything.

"I think Ma will meet all her loved ones that's gone before but one," Uncle Mel said as the tears streamed down his face. "That's Brother Jeff. For I know where my mother is going. She's going to a place of eternal rest away from the troubles of this world. Ma'll see Pap and she'll meet her father and mother and our little sister that left this world at four years old. But Brother Jeff," Uncle Mel said. "It's enough to make all of us want to be better men when we think of the way he acted."

"That's just what I'm thinkin'," Uncle Jason said. "I'm a-settin' here now a-thinkin' as much about Brother Jeff and the way he acted as I am about poor old Ma's leavin' this world. It brings something home to me," Uncle Jason talked on, shaking his head sadly, "and makes me want to be a better man. Brother Jeff is the one that hurried Ma's death along."

Doc Braiden's lips twitched like he wanted to say something. But he didn't. Maybe he thought it was a family affair and he'd better stay out of it lest he might be accused since he'd been Grandma Shelton's doctor for the last thirty years of her life. But I thought he wanted to say that Grandma had lived a very long time. This was in August and if Grandma had lived until October she would have been ninety years old. She had lived nineteen years beyond the Good Book's allotted time of three-score-years-and-ten. Grandma had been here a long time.

After Uncle Jeff had left this world three years ago when he was sixty-seven, Cousin Grace and I had gone to live with Grandma. I cut the stovewood, milked the cow, kept the yard cut and a garden tended, and did the chores that Uncle Jeff had done. Cousin Grace did the housework and the cooking. She had more help than I had, for Grandma was very active up until she had taken sick three weeks ago.

Since Grandma wouldn't live with her only living daughter or either of her two surviving sons, Cousin Grace and I had to stay with her. She selected us from her twenty-seven grandchildren. Mom, Uncle Jason, and Uncle Mel wanted to send all of their children, let each of them have a stay with Grandma and know her better, but Grandma didn't want that. She had her own ideas about things and she still told her children what to do. Grandma's little three-room shack, where she had lived all her life, was home to me since I'd been away from my home three years. It was home to Cousin Grace too. And now I thought of all this, as Grandma lay dying. This home would be no more for us. The shack where Grandma was born, where she went to housekeeping, where she had raised her family, would be deserted now.

"Brother Jeff caused Ma more worries than all the other three children put together," Uncle Mel said to Pa. Pa didn't answer him. He just sat there looking at the floor. Pa had been in two or three rows with Mom's brothers and he didn't say anything for or against Uncle Jeff, though Pa had always liked him and he said he was the best Shelton of the name with the exception of the one he had married. "Ma will see all her loved ones but Brother Jeff."

Pa wanted to say something. He twitched his lips. Then he tightened his lips to hold back his tongue. Pa just sat there and watched and listened.

"That was it," Doc Braiden said to Mom who was standing beside him at Grandma's bedside. "That hissing little sound was the last breath."

Mom, Uncle Mel, and Uncle Jason took on something awful. Only Uncle Jason didn't carry on like Mom and Uncle Mel. Cousin Grace cried harder than ever on the front porch when she heard Doc Braiden say that was Grandma's last breath. I cried harder too when I saw Doc Braiden pull the quilt, one that Grandma had pieced and quilted years ago, up over her face, in the little half-bed by the window.

"When the Savior calls, there's not anything a doctor can do," Doc Braiden said, as he picked up his medicine kit and started for the front door. "But if I can be of any more help to you, let me know."

"I know you've done all you could for Ma," Mom wept as Doc Braiden went out the front door. "But her time has come to go. And not any doctor could save her."

"Not when the Master calls," Uncle Mel said.

Doc Braiden got in his car that was muddy halfway up the body and drove slowly around the curves and through the mudholes down Big Lost Creek.

"We'd better have somebody here besides the family," Pa said as he listened to all of us crying. Uncle Jason was crying now. "I'll go norrate Mother's death to the neighbors. We'll have to have a settin'-up here tonight and we'll have to make plans for the burial."

Then Pa got up and left the shack.

That afternoon, our neighbors kept dropping in until the shack was filled with people. Mallie and John Howard came. Murtie and Uglybird Skinner, Peg and Arn Sparks came. Bertie and Cief Welch came. Sina and Jim Young walked from Plum Grove soon as they heard. These were the older couples that knew my grandma and had lived close to her one time or another. Pa was riding over the hills and up and down the hollers letting the people know of Grandma's death.

Just before suppertime, the young couples came from Lost Creek and Plum Grove. They came and took the kitchen over. They didn't bother to ask Cousin Grace where the food and cooking utensils were. They found everything for themselves and started cooking. Tom Hackless brought his guitar along and he sat beside Maxine Kilgore on the front porch and sang the old hymns and songs, and those that were not weeping or working joined in singing. That was the way it was at a settin'-up. I had been to them before. I had seen them before. The settin'-up Grandma had for Uncle Jeff was one we didn't talk about but a lot of people did. They'd never stopped talking about it. For Uncle Jeff's friends came and many had a time leaving. They had tried to drown their cares and grief about Uncle Jeff's passing.

Everybody knew about Uncle Jeff, and I heard John Howard whisper to Cief Welch that it was Uncle Jeff, Grandma's wayward son, who had helped wreck Grandma's health and bring her to her death. I heard Bertie Welch whisper something to Sina Young about it too. They were all talking about Uncle Jeff, except Mom, Uncle Jason, and Uncle Mel. They were hanging their heads in grief and wiping their tear-stained eyes. I thought Uncle Jeff was gone and forgotten except by his own people. But Grandma's death had revived everybody's memory of Uncle Jeff.

While we sat in the room with a kerosene lamp on the mantel and one on the stand-table dimly burning, with wick flames fluttering when the wind came in at the open window, I could see a big harvest moon high in the blue sky, flooding the little valley between the hills Grandma had once owned, a farm that had been owned by her people since the beginning of Greenwood County in 1802. This was the land she loved and her father had loved, but they had left this land for a better land. Uncle Jeff loved this land, too, I thought as I sat there looking through the window at the moon. I wondered if he loved the place where he was now. Then I remembered I didn't have the right to judge. But I heard the people in the room talking about Uncle Jeff and it brought back memories.

For Uncle Jeff was the child growing up that Grandma had relied on most. He was always trusty and a good worker and Grandma had often bragged on his "good judgment" when he was a boy. Then Uncle Jeff got married when he was nineteen years old. He married Minnie Weston. When Uncle Jeff got married and got a home of his own, he put into practice some of the ideas he suggested to his father, my grandpa Silas Shelton. Uncle Jeff bought a sawmill on credit and a tract of timber. He sawed the timber on the farm, paid for the land and timber and sawmill on his first adventure. Then he rented this land for tobacco and paid for the land and made a nice profit. Uncle Jeff went on and on buying more land and cutting more timber and renting his land and raising more tobacco until he bought all of Culp Creek and started buying the land on Big

White Oak. People got afraid of Uncle Jeff. Said if he lived long enough he'd own all of Greenwood County. People got to the place they wouldn't sell him land. Then Uncle Jeff would get a trusted friend to buy for him and turn the land over. People got afraid to sell a piece of land to anybody, afraid it would get to Uncle Jeff.

Then something happened. Uncle Jeff took a nip from a bottle one cold frosty morning at the sawmill to warm him up. He kept on taking nips from the bottle to warm him up. And as time passed and his eight children grew, he kept taking more nips. Uncle Jeff, the wealthiest man in Greenwood County, started selling his land piece by piece. Soon as one of his six sons or his two daughters was eighteen, he married and left the big house that Uncle Jeff owned. For Uncle Jeff's sons were tired of riding mules over the country to find him. Once he was gone four years. That was after he had sold a Sandy River bottom farm for eleven times as much as he gave for it. That was when Uglybird Skinner said that when a man got too big for his pants something would always happen to him. He said either the devil or the Savior got him and it was usually the devil. That's when everybody said Uncle Jeff had gone to the devil and all his people but his mother and my father lost faith in him.

When all his children had left their home but two, Aunt Minnie left and went to live with her oldest son, Elbert. When Uncle Jeff had sold all his forty-three hundred acres of land and houses down to the house he lived in and six acres of ground, he started selling his livestock, then his sawmill and farming tools, even his scythes, cradles, tobacco knives, and garden hoes. The last two children, Estille and Essie, left him and went to their mother and oldest brother. Uncle Jeff was left alone and he sold his house and slept in the mouth of a deserted coal mine until Grandma brought him home to her.

This was when I got to know Uncle Jeff better. I had to go

to Grandma's when Uncle Jeff went away. He had a mule and an express wagon and he'd start to Blakesburg when he got a little money and he wouldn't get back. Sometimes the mule would bring him home. Uncle Jeff would be lying in the express bed asleep and dead to the world. Grandma and I would always run down to the barn-lot gate and stop under the tall windows. When we couldn't see any driver on the seat, we knew Uncle Jeff was laying in the express bed. Then Grandma and I would pull at Uncle Jeff (and he'd do all he could under his own power) to try to get him out and to the shack and put him to bed. Grandma would cry and I would cry as we worked with Uncle Jeff. Many a time he fell from the express bed like a barrel of salt or sugar and hit the ground with a thump. Sometimes that helped him and he stirred more under his own power. But Uncle Jeff was a big man, two hundred and ninety pounds, six feet three inches tall, with big hands, big feet, and a big fine-looking head and a handsome face with a pair of black eyes that shone like embers in the dark.

When Uncle Jeff sold his mule, old Moll, and his express wagon he used up the money over one weekend. After this, Uncle Jeff, though he said he couldn't stand on a hillside and cut sprouts and plow, would walk five miles to Blakesburg faster than I could when he got some money. Once while he was in this condition he got in a church house in the night when the moderator and his congregation was praying to the Savior to tear off the shingles and come down through the roof. Uncle Jeff was sitting quietly in the back corner of the house and listening to the service, when the moderator asked for testimonies. Then Uncle Jeff got up and testified. He said it wasn't practical for the Savior to come down through the roof and tear off the shingles when there was a door and windows and besides there would be an added expense for fixing the roof. Uncle Jeff was arrested and fined for this and he was laying out a fifty-dollar fine at a dollar a day in Greenwood County Jail when Grandma paid his fine.

Once in January I went one cold morning to hunt Uncle Jeff. I found him near a filling station where he had slept all night. There was an eight-inch snow on the ground, but it was melted all around Uncle Jeff and four or five feet away from him in all directions. Uncle Jeff was wet and steaming and I gave him hot coffee and he was able to get home under his own power. I walked along and held his big hand so he wouldn't slip and fall on the snow and ice. Everybody, especially Grandma, thought he would take pneumonia and die. But he never had a cold.

But the worst danger for Uncle Jeff that I remembered before the real thing happened was when he came from Blakesburg and would think he was home and just go to one of the shacks beside the road, open the door, and walk in in the night. This big man was very quiet. When he was like that, he never could talk. He'd clap his big hands and go "Woo-woo!" Once he got beside Choppie Thomas's bed. Choppie was sleeping beside his wife and they heard "Woo-woo" in the night. Gracie Thomas heard it first and told Choppie and he told her she didn't hear anything, to go back to sleep and let him sleep. But she heard it again and Choppie heard it. Choppie lit the lamp and there Uncle Jeff stood at the head of their bed, wearing his dark suit, a rose in his coat lapel, and a big black umbrella hat. Choppie reached for his pistol and then recognized Uncle Jeff.

Uncle Jeff got in Spittie Jackson's shack once. He got in Buffalo Darby's shack one night. And Fonse Keeney found him in a spare bed in his shack one morning. Then Grandma had to norrate it to the people that Uncle Jeff was harmless when he was like this. That he couldn't stand tobacco smoke, cigarette, pipe or cigar, that he didn't chew tobacco, and he didn't drink

159

coffee but he drank milk for breakfast, and that she had never heard him sweat an oath in her life. I told County Sheriff Bill Atkinson, too. And I told Blakesburg's marshal, Ellis Cantwell, the same thing. Because Ellis Cantwell would use a billy club and I didn't want him to billy Uncle Jeff.

When Dink Callihan, the short red-headed sexton at Plum Grove, and Wilburn Clifton walked into the room, Wilburn had a rule in his hand. They had come to measure Grandma to make the coffin. Then Bertie Welch and Arn Sparks took the rule and measured Grandma under the cover. There was a lot of crying and grief in the front room where Grandma lay dead, but in the kitchen where people were eating and drinking there was a lot of noise. There was the rattle of dishes and cups and saucers. There was the clanking of knives, forks, and spoons. While out on the porch there was the sweet music of a guitar and soft voices under the moonlight. Though Grandma was dead, there was more life in her shack than I had ever seen. As soon as Wilburn had the measurements so he could know how big to make her wild-cherry coffin and Dink would know how big to dig the grave, they left the shack very quietly as I had seen them leave many shacks before. They knew just how to do it in a very sad way.

At nine o'clock, Clara Braiden, who was blue-eyed with blond hair and very pretty, brought food and hot coffee into the room and passed it around among the grief-stricken who were sitting up with Grandma. As soon as she had left the room Sina Young whispered: "Clara's in love with Tom Hackless. Too bad she can't sit beside him in Maxine Kilgore's place and listen to that sweet music. If she could," Sina whispered hoarsely in Bertie Welch's ear, "she wouldn't be in the kitchen a-cookin' and waitin' on us."

At about ten o'clock Mallie Howard, who was looking at Grandma's bed, said, "I thought I saw the quilt move."

"You're gettin' afraid," Uglybird Skinner said.

Then Uglybird laughed a wild laugh like he thought it was funny. This was the first time anybody had laughed in this room on this night.

"When you stare at something, Mallie, as I've watched you a-starin' at Grandma Shelton's deathbed," John Howard, her husband explained, "you'll think you see something move whether it does or not. Your eyes will play tricks on you, especially in the night at a time like this when everybody is upset."

Then all was very quiet in the room and everybody looked at one another. They have stopped talking about Uncle Jeff for one time tonight, I thought.

When the hand on Grandma's old Seth Thomas clock on the mantel was just about at ten-thirty, Mallie Howard let out a scream.

"What's the matter with you, Mallie?" John Howard asked. "Are you a-gettin' nervous? Will I have to take you home?"

"I guess it's just in my head," she answered, looking at the floor. "But I thought I saw that quilt move again, just about where Grandma Shelton's hands ought to be!"

Uglybird Skinner put his hand over his mouth to keep from laughing.

"Don't be afeard, Mallie," Sina Young said. "Rejoice at the death and grieve at the birth. When you come to think of all the grief, sin, and misery in the world, these are the words for a body to remember."

Just when the clock was striking eleven, there was louder talking, laughing, and clanking of dishes in the kitchen and faster music and louder singing on the porch. Clara Braiden entered the front room with a pot of hot coffee and a tray of teacups and saucers. But she didn't get to the center of the room when she walled her eyes, let out a scream, and dropped the

161

coffeepot and the tray of cups and saucers. She stood there and trembled like a leaf in the wind while she screamed. Then she got control of herself, left the room screaming out onto the porch and into the road which was flooded with moonlight.

"She's alive," she screamed as she left, running down the road for home.

There was silence in the room as everybody looked at the bed and at each other. I looked at the bed and I didn't see the quilt move. But the talking and laughing stopped in the kitchen and the young couples on the porch were thrown into disorder. The guitar-strumming and the singing stopped when Clara Braiden ran among them screaming and off down the road. A few of the young people took off too, for I saw them running down the road from the window.

"Maybe it's our dead ancestors back in this room," Uncle Mel said.

"Speak to us if you are," Uncle Jason said.

"It's something," Mallie Howard said. "I don't believe my eyes deceived me."

"Let's be practical about this," my father said. "If Mother Shelton is still alive, there is a way to tell. And if she is," he added as an afterthought while the silent faces stared at him, "don't anybody get scared."

"How can we tell?" Mom asked.

"Hold a mirror before her and tell whether she's breathing or not," Pa said.

Not one of the women would do it. Pa got Grandpa Silas Shelton's little shaving mirror, where Grandpa had kept it years ago and Grandma had never moved it, and he turned back the quilt and held it before her. Pa wasn't afraid but the women turned their heads and they certainly didn't talk about Uncle Jeff and Clara Braiden now. When Flossie Flyman came into the room she threw up her hands, ran back to the kitchen screaming, and everybody started taking off.

"She hath risen from the dead," Flossie screamed, nearly causing panic among the people at the settin'-up. Jackie Bowlen left the road and ran into a swamp beside the big sycamore and mired up to his waist. Young people were running in all directions.

"She's breathing," Pa said. "She's alive!"

Then Mallie Howard ran out at the door with John Howard after her. Sina Young jumped from her chair to go and Jim Young grabbed her. Arn Sparks filled her pipe with tobacco and puffed one cloud of smoke after another. Cousin Grace fell to her knees and started praying. Mom shook until I thought she'd fall. Uncle Mel couldn't speak. Uncle Jason trembled until he couldn't speak and had to hold onto the mantel, his long legs were trembling so.

"She's moving more," Pa announced so everybody could hear. "I've got this quilt from over her head so she can get more air!"

Pa stripped the quilt down to her waist. There lay Grandma in her flowered nightgown. I saw her hand move. She was trying to lift it.

"No use to hold this mirror to her now," Pa said. "Mother Shelton is alive. She's getting more alive all the time."

I looked over the room and there were not many left. Not anyone in the kitchen or on the porch. Sina and Jim Young had gone. Peg and Arn Sparks had slipped out. Murtie Skinner jumped up to go but Uglybird wouldn't let her. He grabbed her by the arm. "Stay, Murtie," he said. "Let's see where she has been and who she's seen."

"Water," Grandma whispered to Pa.

Then Cousin Grace ran into the kitchen and fetched a glass of water. Pa held it to Grandma's mouth and she sipped a few drops. Then more life came and she raised her hand.

"More water," she whispered. "My mouth is dry."

Pa gave her more water to sip. Then Grandma moved her body.

"More water," she whispered a little louder, "and I'll tell you where I've been and who I've seen."

Pa lifted her head a little higher with one hand and held the glass with the other and let Grandma sip.

"My throat is so dry," she whispered between sips.

Now Grandma was beginning to move like I had seen her move before. Pa put a pillow behind her and lifted her up some. A little color was coming back to her face.

"I've been to Heaven," Grandma whispered, but we could hear for the shack was quiet now. "I've been on a long journey."

Then Pa held the glass and Grandma sipped more water. Uncle Mel, Uncle Jason, and Mom stood beside Grandma's bed, looked on, and trembled. Bertie and Cief Welch stood beside them. Uglybird and Murtie Skinner stood close. Pa, Cousin Grace, and I stood beside Mom.

"The Savior smiled at me after I stumbled up a long dark path and entered the gates of Heaven," Grandma said. "He beckoned me through where my friends and loved ones were waiting!"

Then Grandma took a bigger sip of water.

"Did Pap meet you, Mother?" Uncle Mel asked.

"No, your father was not there," Grandma said. "I'm sorry."

Then Grandma was silent and Pa gave her more water. Uncle Mel, Uncle Jason, and Mom looked at each other with tear-stained eyes in red sockets.

"But you'll get a surprise when I tell you your brother Jeff met me," Grandma said with light in her dimmed eyes. "Jeff is there and you wouldn't know him. He's a fine-looking man and all straightened up. My mother and father were there. Looked just the way they used to look. Mother wearing a little checked apron with a pocket in the corner."

I wanted to ask Grandma more about Uncle Jeff, but words came hard for her and she wanted to tell so much about where she had been and who she had seen but she had to rest and sip water.

"I told you about your brother Jeff," Pa said to Mom. "Everything Jeff teched turned to gold but it wasn't Jeff's fault. He couldn't help it. People squeezed him when he done a little better than they did and drove Jeff to one thing. Not Jeff but the people will pay for what they done to him. Jeff was a square man. He just traded with people. Jeff never wronged a woman, never lied, stole as much as a hen egg, swore an oath, or hurt an animal. Jeff Shelton was a good man. I'm not as surprised as you are," Pa talked on, looking directly at Uncle Mel and Uncle Jason, the two of Mom's brothers he'd never cared for. "Jeff had a heart. Something good about Jeff. He fooled you, didn't he?" "Well," Pa added with a smile, "he didn't fool me. He didn't pretend. He wasn't a hypocrite!"

"I saw little Helen, too," Grandma said. "I would have never knowed her. She's a woman now. Children grow in Heaven. She had to tell me who she was."

"Tell me more about Jeff," Pa asked Grandma.

"I was proud to see him," Grandma said. "I'm so happy. But I expected to see Silas. But he wasn't there. That's what hurts."

Murtie Skinner doddled her head until Uglybird had to put his arm around her shoulder and hold her.

"Did you see my father and mother?" Uglybird asked.

"I saw Maude but I didn't see Little Jack," Grandma said. "I saw so many of my old neighbors. But I didn't have time to talk with them."

Little Jack Skinner had been a great land-grabber. He'd stolen hundreds of acres of land. I remembered when he died how glad everybody was that he had left this world. For people were afraid of him. But I didn't know about Grandpa Shelton for I was a child when he left the world and I'd not heard much said about him one way or another.

"Did you see my pap and mother?" Cief Welch asked.

"Saw both of them," Grandma whispered. "They look just like they always did."

Then Grandma sipped more water and she said, as she looked toward Murtie Skinner, "I saw your sister Kate there and your father Les and your mother Agnes. I used to know 'em a long time ago. They wanted to ask me questions but I didn't have time. For the Savior beckoned again." "It was to go," Grandma whispered sadly.

"I even saw my grandpa and grandma, Mary and Kennealas Wright, there," Grandma whispered. "They looked like people from a different world the way they were dressed so old-fashioned. Saw horsetrader Jim Lyons there. Everybody said he was a lost sinner and sich a bad man. I saw him in Heaven. Saw John Pratt and Leanie Skaggs. So many I can remember just now of old neighbors and friends who came with Mother, Jeff and Little Helen, Grandpa and Grandma Wright to meet me. But the Savior, sitting upon his Great Throne, beckoned me back. He said, 'Go back and come again.' He sent me back for a purpose," Grandma whispered in little breaths, looking at Uncle Mel and Uncle Jason. "I hated to leave Heaven and come back here."

Then we stood in silence and looked at Grandma.

"But I'll just be here on the footstool a few more years," Grandma said.

Uglybird looked at Cief and they looked at Uncle Jason and Uncle Mel. Mom looked at me and Cousin Grace and then she looked at her mother there on the bed talking in her right mind, for she had always had a right mind.

"This is something," Uglybird Skinner said. "It makes a

166

man think."

"You'd better go see Dink and Wilburn," Pa said to Ugly-bird. "Tell them before they start work."

"Go tell Dink and Wilburn I'd want them to go ahead if it would take me back where I've been and to them I've seen," Grandma whispered.

"Mother, you're goin' to be all right," Pa said. "You need rest. You can tell us more tomorrow. We don't want you to talk too much tonight. Soon as you are able you'll have a lot of people to tell your story. But now," Pa added, "what you need is rest."

Then Pa removed the pillow and let her lie back down. He pulled up the quilt over Grandma. Mom, Uncle Mel, and Uncle Jason, Cousin Grace, and I stayed at Grandma's and Murtie and Uglybird Skinner walked quietly from the shack out into the night. We knew they would norrate the news Grandma had risen from the dead, that there would not be any more settin'-up with her another night nor a big funeral at Plum Grove.

I was glad that the news about Uncle Jeff from now on would be better.

BIRD-NECK

It was last spring when Bird-Neck worked on one side the holler and I worked on th' other. The crick run right down below us. It separated Bird-Neck's cornfield from mine. We'd holler to each other across the crick.

"Eb, if you don't hurry up you're goin' to haf to snake your corn. Weeds and sprouts are goin' to whop you before you get to the top!" Bird-Neck would say.

Then Bird-Neck would jist laugh and lean against that little crosspiece between the handles o' his plow. I can jist see old Bird-Neck yet, the way he'd laugh. Big tall man with iron jaws. He'd wear big heavy brogan shoes with his toes a-stickin' out, old overalls with the patches sewed on from th' outside, a old blue faded work shirt, and a slouched black hat that had gone to seed at the top like a doodle o' hay.

I'd holler to Bird-Neck, "I won't haf to snake my corn. I'll be at the top o' my hill before you're to the top o' yourn."

Bird-Neck would laugh. Then he'd say, "You ought to beat me, Eb. I'm forty years nearer the last hill that you are. But in my day and time it took a man to beat me at my work." Then Bird-Neck would laugh and say, "Get up, Moll. Go along, old gal!"

Bird-Neck was seventy-nine years old. His white hair come

down long on the back o' his neck below the brim o' his slouched hat. Moll was twenty-nine years old. Her hair was nearly as white as Bird-Neck's hair. Bird-Neck plowed her without a line. He jist had to tell 'er when to start and stop.

I'd say, "Bird-Neck, you shore to God got a good mule."

Bird-Neck would say, "Yes, old Moll's a good'n. She knows more about plowin' than half the men in this country."

My ground was a lot better. My corn was higher, too. "W'y, your corn ought to be better than mine, Eb. I plowed this same old hill when you was a little shaver a-settin' on your pappie's knee. That was thirty-nine years ago. That was when Jane was alive. You don't remember her. Atter she died I let this hill take a rest. It growed up in sprouts and briers again. Then I jumped the broom with Lan Moore's widder Jenny. Had more young'uns, you know. I had to come back and clear this hill again. I've purt' nigh wore our four hundred acres o' these old hills in my day."

Then I'd see Bird-Neck unhitch the trace chains. He'd wrap 'em around the back straps on Moll's britchin'. He'd jist turn 'er loose by herself. She'd go up the hill and around the ridge road to the house. Bird Neck would call Shep. "W'y, he's so deef," Bird-Neck would say, "sometimes I jist haf to go out there under the shade o' that big shell-barked hickory and shake 'im to let 'im know it's quittin' time. A dog, like a body, gets old atter a while. Ust to be as good a possum and squirrel dog as there was in the hills. Too old to smell a track now. Jist keep 'em."

Shep would follow Bird-Neck up the hill. Bird-Neck would push down a dead sassafras pole or a dead locust pole fer stovewood. He'd put it on his shoulder and walk up the hill to the ridge road home. He'd follow the way old Moll went. Shep would follow Bird-Neck up the hill, waggin' his gray tail.

It was in July, I'd plowed and hoed my corn three times. I was right at the top o' the hill workin' on my last row. Bird-Neck had plowed and hoed his corn three times. He was workin' on the top row. I hollered across to Bird-Neck and says, "You might be forty years nearer the last hill but you've finished layin' by your corn the same time I have."

"Yep, I'm don layin' by my corn now," says Bird-Neck. "I want you to come over tonight. I've got a drap in the jug fer both o' us."

"I'll be right over, Bird-Neck," says I. "You know when they's a drap in the jug you can't hold me away. I ain't had a drap in a long time now. Now that the work is all done, I'll be right over." I saw Bird-Neck follow old Moll up the hill. Moll drug the plow home. Old Shep followed at his heels waggin' his bushy gray tail. Below 'em was his big twenty-acre field o' corn around the slope jist as clean as a pawpaw whistle; stumps standin' there without a sprout growin' around 'em; rocks gray and bare layin' in the corn balks. The corn looked so purty and clean.

I put my plow in the shed. I unharnessed the mule and turned 'im loose on the pasture. I et my supper and started out to Bird-Neck's shack.

Jist to tell you the truth about his shack, it's run down a lot in late years. The clapboards on the roof are green with moss. Horseweeds grow up high as the winders. W'y, it was jist like a groundhog path through the high weeds to get in at the front door. It jist looked to me like the weeds, briers, and the weather had nearly taken Bird-Neck's shack. I found my way in and knocked on the door.

"Come in, Eb, old boy," says Bird-Neck. He unlatched the door. I walked in the room. Bird-Neck didn't have a oil lamp like we got. He had a pine torch. Didn't make much light but a body could see the room purty well. It was a big room. Jist Bird-Neck and old Shep in the house.

"Bird-Neck," I says, "you know what you need?"

"I know what you are goin' to say, from the looks o' this dirty

170

house," says Bird-Neck. "But I don't need a wife, Eb. Not any more. I've had three."

"You ain't too old," I says, "to get you a spouse in your old days to keep you company."

"No more wimmen," says Bird-Neck. "It's all over. Here's my woman now. See 'er right over there in the corner? Two gallons there fer us tonight."

"It's a lot o' licker," I says, "and I ain't ust to it."

"Ah," says Bird-Neck, "fer some o' you young bucks all you got to do is hit you with a sour apple and you're drunk. Us old boys could take our licker and take it straight. I've drunk a gallon a-many a day and done all the plowin' the mule could stand. Atter the day was over I'd go to a square dance and dance all night. That was when I was younger. I got a little older and I could still drink my gallon a day. But I didn't go to dances. J'ints got a little stiffer. I'd fox-hunt all night. Jist run the ridges and listen to the hounds. Then atter I passed the three-score years and seven I started possum huntin'. Got old Shep here. It warn't as much runnin' uphill and downhill as fox huntin'. Then old Shep got too old to smell, so I jist haf to drink my licker now."

"I can't take a gallon in a night's time," I says. "What is it, that fightin' kind o' moonshine?"

"Nope," says Bird-Neck, "it's the best old Steve Howard can make. It's the kind o' licker old friends ought to drink on special occasions."

Bird-Neck walked over and picked up the jug. It was a big two-gallon white jug with a brown neck. Bird-Neck set it on the stand table. He pulled me up a chear. He pulled himself up a chear on th' other side o' the stand table. The pine torch burned from a tin pan on the middle o' the table. Shep laid on th' old plaited rag rug and snored jist over in front o' the big empty fireplace.

"Well, here it is," says Bird-Neck, "good old life in the jug before I climb my last hill. Eighty years old tomorrow. I've reached my four-score."

Bird-Neck takes out the stopper. "We'll drink from the same jug, my good neighbor and friend!" he says.

I held the jug up. It was a little heavy to hold. It run down my gullet like sand through a sieve. "Bird-Neck," I says, "that's the real stuff. It's as good as I ever tasted. It's the real yarbs."

"All right," says Bird-Neck, "I'll taste o' th' old blood o' my life before I climb my last hill." Bird-Neck holds the jug to his lips. The neck o' the jug is hid in his snow-white beard and mustache. *Gurgle-gurgle-gurgle-gurgle-gurgle-gurgle.*

The wind blowed through the open winder and sorty made the sparks fly from the torch. The blaze would shoot out long; then it would draw back again. The black smoke would go off in little streams o' clouds across the half-lighted room. The lightin' bugs would come in at th' open winders and fiddle around in the room and dab their heads against the ceilin' where the spiders had spinned their webs and the waspers had built their nests.

"I'm ready fer another swig, Bird-Neck," says I. "It's the real stuff and I might be able to kill three quarts before mornin'." I held the jug up to my lips. It was a lot lighter to hold now, atter we'd taken a dram apiece. I jist let 'er slide down my throat. The croppin' was done and tomorrow would be Sunday and no place to go. Jist as well be gettin' over a little celebration with old Bird-Neck.

"Now you're drinkin', my friend," says Bird-Neck, "jist like your pap ust to do. Your pap could hold his licker. I remember the drunkest I ever was in my life was with your pap. We had two gallons and a half o' moonshine licker. We's a-comin' from th' old Dysard place. He bantered me drinkin' half o' it with 'im. Had it in quart self-sealer jars. Durned if he didn't drink five o' 'em. I drinked th' other five. Bill, my oldest boy by my first wife,

found us in the corner o' th' old rail fence that runs up from that
sulphur spring by th' old Dysard house. We's layin' right out in
the hot July sun. The lizards was a-runnin' over us and playin'.
We's limber as two dishrags."

Bird-Neck put the jug to his mouth. *Gurgle-gurgle-gurgle-
gurgle-gurgle-gurgle-gurgle-gurgle.* I've never seen a man that
could drink like Bird-Neck.

"The more I drink the better it tastes," says Bird-Neck.
"That's enough to sorty put the fire in these old j'ints. Enough
to put new blood in this old carcass." Bird-Neck shoved the jug
over my way.

"It's like this, Eb," says Bird-Neck. "I'm a lone man in the
world. I married Jane, old Alex Hix's gal. She's seventeen. I's
eighteen. We had twelve young'uns. All o' 'em lived, half a
dozen gals and a half a dozen boys. But Jane got 'er feet wet one
January. She wasn't forty then. She took the quick consumption
and passed on to the Better World. Then I married Lan Moore's
widder Jenny. She jist had two young'uns. But they's spiled'ns.
My young'uns didn't like their young brother and sister and
their new ma. So Bill went first to th' onion fields in Ohio. He
soon had all my first-nest young'uns up there. Left the nest like
young birds. But I raised me another litter and filled the nest.
I had eight young'uns by Widder Jenny.

"She hadn't had the measles. When she got 'em, w'y the
Lord called 'er home. I was left a-holdin' a nest o' ten young'uns.
I's jist sixty then. So I wanted me a helpmate. I married Melvin
Sprouse's old mail gal, Martha, ugly in 'er young days and
couldn't get a man, but turned out to be purty at forty. We jist
had one boy, young Bird-Neck. All the last nest went to
Oklahoma. Heard about all that land out there. Jist flew off like
a covey o' quails. I's in hopes little Bird-Neck wouldn't go, but
when his ma drapped dead nine years ago he said he couldn't
stay among the hills no longer. So he follered the batch o'

young'uns he's the most ust to, the batch that Widder Jenny bore me. So I'm jist here with old Moll and old Shep and all these old hills I know better'n a book, because I ain't never read a book."

Bird-Neck put the jug to his lips and gurgled and gurgled. He put the jug back on the table.

"I'm ready fer another little swig," I says. I put the jug to my lips and I drinked a good swig. "It's a lot lighter, Bird-Neck. We're dreanin' the jug."

"Let 'er drean," says Bird-Neck. "I jist want to tell you now while I'm in my right mind. I might get drunk and not remember before in the mornin', Eb. But the licker in that jug is my blood."

"Your blood?" I says, "W'y, Bird-Neck, you're gettin' drunk shore as God made little green apples."

"No, I ain't drunk," says Bird-Neck. "I sold myself and bought that licker."

"How much did you get fer yourself?" I asks.

"I got twenty-five dollars," says Bird-Neck. "Enough to pay my taxes fer another year, two or three little debts I owed, and enough left to buy this two-gallon jug o' licker."

"Where in the world did you get it?" I asks. "You ain't kiddin' me, are you, Bird-Neck?"

"No," says Bird-Neck, "I ain't kiddin' you. Here's the way I done it. I heard about the hospital at Goodland where they took bodies and worked on 'em atter they's dead."

"What made you do that, Bird-Neck?" I says. "Lord, you ain't no right to traffic in human bodies; they are the creation o' God's handiwork."

"I got the right," says Bird-Neck, "to trade and traffic on my own body, ain't I? It belongs to me. I've had it ever since I's twenty-one."

"Now at eighty the hospital owns you," I says, "to stand you up with a pipe in your mouth and shoot you atter you're dead and then probe fer the bullet."

"Not until I've climb th' last hill," says Bird-Neck. "Jist to tell you th' truth, Eb, I am sick o' the bargain. But twenty-five dollars is twenty-five dollars. Got my debts and taxes paid, my corn laid by, got my jug o' licker."

"I hate to drink your blood," I says, "but Lord, Bird-Neck, it's good. It's jist so lonesome out here by ourselves. So many birds a-hollerin' and insects a-moanin' their songs and the wind a-blowin'. Makes me feel sorty bad to set here and drink your blood."

"Don't mind that, Eb," says Bird-Neck. "I don't think the contract is lawful. I never broke a contract in my life. I've allus paid my just and honest debts. But I'll be dad-durned if they're goin' to get me. I jist laid here in the bed last night and thought it all over. They ain't goin' to get me, Eb. I ain't goin' to give myself to 'em. I want the birds o' th' air and th' ants on the ground to get my flesh, and the hills to get my bones. I want the winds o' the mountains to bleach 'em white. That's the way I feel, Eb."

Lord, I couldn't stand that sort o' talk. It was gettin' me on one o' them cryin' drunks. So I jist turned the jug up and took a big swig. "I feel better now," I says. Bird-Neck turned the jug up and he jist about dreaned it dry.

"He's drunk," I thought. "He ain't sold hisself. He jist thinks he has. Before I get so lonesome here that I start cryin', I'm goin' home."

"Good night, Bird-Neck," I says, "I'm goin' home. I'm drunk. I'm goin' home to Effie and the young'uns."

"Good night ferever," says Bird-Neck. "Good night ferever. You've been a good neighbor and a good friend." I left Bird-Neck standin' there a-holt o' the table. The mornin' wind was comin' in at the winder and tryin' to blow the torch out. Old

175

Shep was lookin' up in Bird-Neck's dimmin' eyes and waggin' his tail.

All day Sunday I was in misery. I kept thinkin' about it all. I jist thought, "Might be somethin' in it. Old Bird-Neck is a man to laugh and a man fer a lot o' fun, but he's allus as good as his word. He might a sold hisself."

It bore on my mind all day Monday. I's cuttin' the wheat on the flat between Bird-Neck's shack and mine. I saw old Moll over in the pasture jist across from me. She looked like a heap o' skin and bones. She got about and nibbled the tender grass. I could see Bird-Neck's wheat field from the flat I's workin' on. But I didn't see Bird-Neck that Monday mornin'.

It was on Tuesday mornin' when I went to work that old Shep started howlin'. He jist howled and howled. He'd never done that before. He howled as lonesome as a whippoorwill hollers. "Oh, he's jist old and lonesome," I thought. "Bird-Neck maybe's still soberin' up. I'll go up and see how he is atter I quit work this evenin'." I worked on until six o'clock. W'y, old Shep, it 'peared to me, would go into spasms with his long mournful howls. Jist like a cow bawlin' when she's lost her calf.

I walked down off'n the flat into the holler. Then I went up the crick and took th' old yaller jolt-wagon road to my left that went up the big hill to Bird-Neck's shack. I went up to th' old house. The door was open. Shep was standin' in the middle o' the big room floor jist a-howlin' like his heart would break. He warn't hungry. The floor was kivvered with hard corn-pone bread Bird-Neck had baked and left fer 'im.

"Poor old Shep," I thought, "your old master told me the truth last Saturday night. He's sold hisself. He's drunk too much licker. He thought he's goin' to die. He's gone up to Goodland to die in the hospital. I'll jist go to the hospital tomorrow and see about old Bird-Neck."

The looks o' the house was enough to make a man cry.

There was our table and th' empty jug. There was th' ashes of the rich pine torch on the tin pan on the stand table.

I found the doctor at the hospital. "Did a feller by the name o' Bird-Neck Dixon sell hisself to you fer twenty-five dollars?" I says.

"Sure did," says the doctor. "What of it?"

"Well, he's gone," I says. "I was with 'im last Saturday night. We's on a little celebration together on the money you paid 'im. He's tellin' me that he sold hisself and got the money. I didn't believe 'im. Said he paid up his taxes and a few little debts with the money and bought us two gallon o' moonshine whiskey."

"Oh, he did, did he? Now he's gone! I guess we're cheated again. That's the danger about buying a living old cuss."

"You ain't no business nohow," I says, "a-tradin' and traffickin' in human lives."

He stood and looked at me. I got up and went out. Bird-Neck might be hid around there some place. But I'd never find 'im. He'd told me they'd never git 'im, though. I believed Bird-Neck. He wouldn't die off'n his land if he could help it.

Thursday mornin' Bud Travis, Lew Kendall, Flem Sowards, Mort Kenyon, Blade Terry, Ross Perkins, and me all went to Bird-Neck's shack. Old Shep had howled until he was hoarse. He follered us to to the wheat field. We took hands and went around the mountain slope through the tall golden wheat. It was ripe enough to cut, but it hadn't been touched. We went back and forth a-holdin' hands so we couldn't miss Bird-Neck if he's dead on the ground. We went from one end o' the field to th' other, until we reached the top o' the mountain. Old Shep follered us around through the wheat. "He shore to God ain't in the wheat, boys," says Ross Perkins. "He's sommers else."

"What about the cornfield?" says Flem Sowards. "Old Bird-Neck allus loved the cornfields, you know."

177

"Yes, he did. That's right," I says. We went over the top o' the mountain to the cornfield. We began at the bottom o' the high hill. We took a couple o' rows o' corn apiece and went through from one end o' the field to th' other until we got to the top. We couldn't find Bird-Neck.

"He's not here, either, fellers," says Bud Travis.

"Old Shep is diggin' atter somethin' out there under that big shell-barked hickory," says Lew Kendall.

"Jist the shade tree where old Shep ust to sleep when Bird-Neck plowed," I says.

"Guess he's buried a bone 'er somethin' there," says Flem Sowards. We went out and stood under the tree. A swarm o' crows flew over. They saw us under the tree and went on. Old Shep howled. He had a hole dug under the tree big enough to bury a yearlin' calf in.

"You know if Bird-Neck killed hisself," says Lew Kendall, "he couldn't bury hisself. That's a cinch."

"Don't reckon he hung hisself," says Mort Kenyon. So he looked up in the green-leafed tree. "I don't see 'im up there. Tree is a shell-barked hickory and big and hard to climb fer a man eighty years old, nohow."

"We ain't hunted through his house and barn," says Bud Travis. "We ain't hunted over the pastures and the timberlands yet."

Took us all week to search the woods. We went through the pasture fields. We searched the tall-timbered lands. We went over every foot of Bird-Neck's farm. We looked among the tall weeds around the house and barn. We bailed the water out'n the well. Bird-Neck warn't in the bottom o' the well. We couldn't find 'im no place. "He's jist gone," says Bud Travis. "He ain't here no place."

"I 'spect he's went up in Ohio," says Flem Sowards, "to see the children by his first wife. Maybe he went to Oklahoma to see

178

the young'uns by his second wife, er young Bird-Neck by Melvin Sprouse's old mail gal, Martha!"

"He ain't gone that fur," I says, "fer he's told me more'n once he ain't never been a hundred miles from home. You know he wouldn't go off and leave a pot o' corn-pone bread fer old Shep in the middle o' the floor. I know Bird-Neck is a dead man."

The summer passed and we'd never heard no more o' Bird-Neck. No one had seen 'im. My wife Effie wrote to Aaron, Bird-Neck's oldest boy by Widder Jenny, to see if he'd gone to Oklahoma. He hadn't come there. She wrote a letter up in Ohio to his oldest boy, Bill by his first wife Jane, and he wrote a letter back sayin' he hadn't come there.

It was in October; I started shuckin' Bird-Neck's corn. I took Moll off'n the pasture to my barn and was keepin' 'er. No one to take Bird-Neck's corn. His young'uns was too fur away. They'd never come home when they'd heard their pap was missin'. I'd keep Moll and Shep until they died. I'd take Bird-Neck's wheat and corn.

The great sweeps o' fall-time winds would whip like a buggy-whop through the trees. Then the leaves would fall in swarms, jist like birds gettin' ready fer th' South. The treetops got bare.

I was shuckin' corn in the last shock row. I was shuckin' the last shock under the tall shell-barked hickory tree. I heard a rattlin' in th' wind above me. I jist looked up in the tall tree where the wind had whopped away the leaves. Lord, I thought I'd faint. There was Bird-Neck's bones. They were a-jinglin' like a cowbell up there in the top o' the tree. I didn't think a man eighty years old would ever climb a tree like that. Must a been sixty feet up to where Bird-Neck was hangin'. A plowline was holdin' 'im up there. I looked at the body o' the tree and there was a row o' black ants and a row o' red ants a-goin' to Bird-

179

Neck's bones. It was late fer ants, too. But it was a warm sunny day.

It all come back to me. "He'll never get me. The birds o' th' air and th' ants on the ground'll get me." They had got Bird-Neck, too, jist like he'd planned. The wind had swept his bones and bleached 'em. "Maybe it's been his laugh," I thought, "that I've been hearin' all the time I've been cuttin' the corn. It could a been Bird-Neck all right watchin' me work. Jist ramblin' over his old farm.

"Well, it is all over," I says. "I'll call the boys. We'll see if one o' us can climb that tree. We'll haf to cut 'im down."

I brought the boys to the tree that had helped me hunt the place over fer Bird-Neck. Not one o' us could climb it. "I know what we can do," says Bud Travis. "We can get a rifle and shoot the rope in two. That will be a lot easier. I don't see how a man eighty years old climbed that tree nohow."

Bud went to the house and brought back a rifle. He shot twice at the rope and the white bones tumbled from the tree. His bones were clean and white. The weather had made 'em that way atter they'd been picked by the crows and buzzards.

We made a oak box out'n one o' Bird-Neck's oaks. We jist put the bones in it without anything around 'em. We hauled it on a sled from the spot with old Moll. We took 'im back out on th' p'int. We buried him beside his three wives in th' land he loved.

THE CHASE OF THE
SKITTISH HEIFER

From early spring to late autumn, Pa carried salt to the hundred cattle in the big pasture. He'd carry seventy-five pounds at a load up the steep mountain to the long salt trough he'd made of hollow logs. He had cut down hollow trees and split them with wedges, trimmed each split log neatly with a double-bitted ax, and fastened them together. It was a long trough resting on foundation rocks so the cattle could stand side by side and lick salt.

This salting trough was the place where the cattle met in the big pasture field. It was where they got acquainted.

In early spring when Pa put strange cattle in the pasture he'd call to them to come and get salt. At first they didn't know his voice. But a few of our cattle did, and went running for salt when they heard his voice. The other cattle soon learned to follow.

At this meeting place Pa would count everybody's cattle that he was pasturing, to see if they were in the pasture. If one was missing, he wouldn't stop till he found it. Pa soon learned every calf, cow, heifer, and steer in the pasture. All he had to do was look one over carefully and he never forgot it. He knew each of the hundred cattle in the big pasture where thirty belonged to us and seventy belonged to nine different people. He knew and could have called by name, if the cattle had been named, the hundred eighty-seven head of cattle he had in the other six pastures on our seven-hundred-eight-acre hill farm.

But when Pa called for the cattle to come to their salt in the big pasture, all would come but one. That was Jack Remines' heifer with the dots above her eyes. She would follow the other cattle near the salt trough. But she wouldn't come all the way. She'd come to within a couple of hundred yards. Then there she would stand and watch the other cattle lick salt. She'd watch them with her head held high, her neck held stiff as a board, and her black eyes beaming in deep sockets as she looked at Pa. She would never come near him.

"That Remines heifer is a quare animal," Pa once said to me. "Cattle have always liked me. But not that one. She's the wildest thing I've ever seen. I've been a-tryin' to tame her since the day Jake fetched her here. But seems like she gets wilder all the time. Last April she didn't stand more than a hundred yards from the salt trough. Here it is August again and she stands two hundred yards away. Must be the foxhounds a-runnin' through here have made her nature wilder. *But I will tame 'er and have her a-lickin' salt from my hands before Jake comes to get her.*"

That was what Pa thought. But in September the heifer would not come within three hundred yards of the salt trough.

"I can't understand it," Pa said. "That heifer must be a-goin' wild. Out here where she never sees anybody but me and the fox hunters. Out here where she hears fox horns a-blowin' and hound-dogs a-barkin' and wind in the trees! I reckon that's enough to make a brute go wild!"

Among all the cattle Pa was pasturing for other people, cattle that would come and lick salt from his hand, Pa directed all his attention toward the heifer. "I'll tame her yet," he said. "I'll have her so tame that all Jake'll have to do when he comes to take his cattle home is to walk up to her and put his hand on her neck and lead her across the pasture. I've never seen one yet I couldn't tame. Something about me animals like. It hurts my feelings when a brute turns against me. Hurts me more than when a human being turns on me. I can't let Jake's heifer leave this pasture without lickin' salt from my hand."

All through August and September Pa worked with Jake's heifer trying to tame her. When Pa would walk toward her, she'd bristle up like a doubtful dog and sniff the wind. When he'd get within a hundred yards she'd take off, jumping like a deer, with her long tail floating on the wind.

Pa and I agreed we'd never seen a heifer that could run like that one. She'd leap over stumps, rocks, brier patches and go to the tall timber where she'd disappear among the trees. We'd not see her until we went to salt the cattle again.

On the last day of October when Jake came to get his cattle, Pa told him about the heifer. Pa told Jake he'd not been able to get any closer than a hundred yards to her.

"She always had a wild nature," Jake told Pa. Jake pressed the long white beard down on his face. "But my heifer's not got a nature as wild as you say."

Jake paid Pa seventy dollars for pasturing his ten head of cattle for seven months. Jake bragged to Pa about how his cattle had grown. He said they'd put on about three hundred pounds of weight to the animal — all except the heifer. The heifer was standing so far away Jake couldn't see her too well. But the other nine head of Jake's cattle stood close around us at the salt trough.

"Well, let's get her with the rest of my cattle," Jake said.

"I'll fetch her," Pa volunteered.

Pa wanted to show Jake what a man he was for his years. He wanted to show Jake how a lean, bony little man sixty-seven years old could run. Jake wasn't as old as Pa and the hair on his head was white as milkweed fuzz that the wind lifts from the pods and blows away in August. Pa's hair was still black as a charred stump in new ground. When Pa took off running to get on the far side of the heifer and drive her back toward us, he sailed over old stumps, rock piles, and brier patches like a scared fox.

"Look at that, won't you!" Jake said as he watched Pa run. "Your father is a young man for his years. He's younger than you are. I'm an old man beside him."

But when the heifer saw Pa was trying to hem her up, she showed Pa how to run. She wheeled around on her hind feet in one whirl, and it looked to us like her feet were not touching the ground. Looked to us like she was stepping on the wind. Her legs moved like well-oiled pistons and her tail was riding on the October mountain wind like a kite. She was running toward the tall timber. The heifer outran Pa as easily as a fox outruns a slow hound, while we stood at the salt trough looking on. When Pa saw that the chase was useless, he put on brakes and skated like a young skater for a few feet on the damp dying October grass. There Pa stood and watched her disappear under the tall timber. I wanted to laugh, but I didn't. I knew who'd be running after her before we caught her for Jake Remines. Pa turned around and walked slowly and sadly back to us.

"You've done your best," Jake told Pa. "Honest, you can run like a greyhound. You stay in shape climbin' these mountains and carryin' salt to cattle. You can run like a hound-dog yourself, but that heifer runs like a deer."

"Never saw anything like it," Pa said. "I can catch most any of 'em but her. Can't understand what has made her so wild."

"Never worry about it," Jake said. "I'll take these through the gate and drive 'em home. I'll be back tomorrow and get the heifer. I'll fetch my boys with me."

"And I'll come and bring Shan and Finn," Pa told him. "We'll catch 'er, all right."

"Say, come to think of it, Mick," Jake said, pressing the white beard on his face again, "what will you give me for that heifer? I know you deal in cattle, and I do, too. Why not a little trade?"

"What'll you take for 'er?" Pa said in half words, for he was getting his breath hard. Pa's face changed. He smiled.

"She's a nice heifer, Mick," Jake said. "She's young and full of life."

"She's sure full of life, all right," Pa admitted.

"I think she's worth sixty dollars, Mick," Jake said, rubbing his cheek with his big hand.

"Too much, too much, Jake," Pa snapped. "She's not worth that. She's a troublesome brute."

"Well, I'm pricing 'er fifteen dollars cheaper to you than I would anybody else, Mick." Jake looked at the ground and kicked at the brown grass with the toe of his brogan shoe. "She's really worth seventy-five, the way cattle are selling at the market. Little hard to catch — that's the reason I priced 'er to you so cheap."

"That's too high, Jake." Pa turned to walk away.

"Not a cent cheaper," Jake said as he turned his cattle through the gate. "I'll be back to take her away tomorrow."

"We'll be here to help you," Pa said. Pa turned to watch Jake walk away behind his nine head of cattle. One of Jake's big steers turned his head and bawled to Pa as he went through the gate. All of them would lick salt from his hand.

As Pa and I walked along the path home, Pa walked in front. Now and then he let out a little wild laugh. That was the way he had done ever since I could remember, when he was thinking about a trade.

The very next day, Pa, Finn, and I met Jake and his sons, Dave and Bob, at the salt trough. All the cattle had been moved from the big pasture but Jake's heifer. We thought she'd be close to the salting place, but she wasn't.

"Heard her bawlin' out in the tall timber," Jake said. "Out yander on that point."

"She's lonesome for the other cattle," Pa said. "Let's be after her."

Dave Remines was a long-legged young man about my age. Bob Remines was short and heavy. He was a thick young man with big arms and powerful legs. Brother Finn was six feet four and had always been a great runner.

"We'll get 'er now," Pa said. "My son Shan used to be on a high school track team and he used to run long distances in college. Finn's a good runner, too. And I'm not so bad myself for a man my age."

"No, you're not, Mick," Jake bragged on Pa. "And I've got a couple of good runners here, too. Fox-hunt every other night and climb these mountains. They'll be hard men to beat on a chase. I'm not a-sayin' this because they're my boys, either. Guess I'll be the slowest man among you.

Finn and I looked Bob and Dave over. I knew the thought that raced through my brother Finn's mind. He was goin' to try to show Bob and Dave Remines up on the chase after the heifer. We didn't have long to wait for the chase. He had just walked into the tall timber on the Hilton Point when Dave Remines spotted the heifer and we gave chase.

And that is a chase we will long remember. Pa started out leaping over logs and stumps. Dave Remines got the lead. His brother Bob was at his heels. Finn was third and I was fourth. Jake Remines trotted after me. Pa tried to skirt around all of us as the heifer took off like a young deer. She ran so fast we soon lost sight of her. We listened the way she went through the dry autumn leaves as long as we could and then we followed the way of the sound. And when we came to the place where we last heard the sound, all of us getting our breath hard, we picked up her tracks and took off again like a pack of hounds.

When we reached Coon Den Hollow, Pa and Jake were out of the chase. When we followed her tracks up the old log road to Seaton Ridge, Bob Remines fell down, holding his side with his hands.

"Can't go any farther, boys," he managed to grunt.

His brother Dave, who was now following my brother Finn, didn't say a word. He didn't have enough breath to spare. Finn was leading the chase and I was following. We had Dave between us.

"You boys are ridge-runners," he grunted in little half breaths as we topped Seaton Ridge. In the distance we saw the heifer running with all the ease in the world. *She* wasn't tired.

Then across the open field where the land sloped gently, Finn set a terrific pace with his long legs pulling against the wind. Then I got closer on Dave's heels. I finally passed Dave, and he was the third man. Dave didn't have much steam, either – not enough for another three-mile circuit like the heifer had just taken us. Before we reached Hilton Point and the tall timber we met Pa and Jake coming on back.

"She's too much for us," Pa grunted. "We saw 'er, but we didn't give chase. She went over toward Howard Hollow."

Finn went in that direction and I followed. We never saw Dave again – not on that chase. Finn went down into Howard Hollow and I followed him. He found the track again. We followed her tracks up the hill and over into Shingle Mill Hollow toward Coon Den Hollow again. I followed Finn into Coon Den Hollow.

"Why run a heifer like this and kill ourselves?" Finn asked, stopping suddenly. "We could run her all day and not catch her. Run her till we have a heart attack. Run her for what? What's this heifer to us?"

"Not anything," I agreed as the dry spittle flew from my

hot mouth. My tongue was dry. I was hot. I hardly had enough breath to answer Finn. "Let's let 'er go."

Then Finn and I walked up the log road to Seaton Ridge. When we got back to the salt trough Dave and Bob Remines were stretched on the grass resting. Pa and Jake were sitting on big stumps.

"Couldn't you get 'er?" Jake asked us.

"We can't do it," Finn said. "Never saw a heifer that could take off like that one."

"See, I told you, Jake," Pa said. "Yesterday I would have give you fifty for her. Today I won't. I wouldn't give you but forty."

"Oh, that's not enough, Mick," Jake snapped. "I've just been out seven dollars to you for pasturing her this summer. Couldn't do that. We'll come horseback tomorrow and bring my shepherd dog. You come and bring your shepherd."

"We'll be here," Pa said. "We'll ride mules. They'll be better for goin' under the brush."

So the next day we met again. Bob, Dave, and Jake Remines were in good saddles on three nice-looking saddle horses. They had brought their shepherd dog, Jolly. Pa was in the only saddle we had, astride our Rock mule. Finn was riding Dinah and I was riding Dick. We didn't have saddles. We brought with us our shepherd, old Bob. We were off, all of us riding toward Hilton Point. In the open space in a little hollow, and near the tall timber on Hilton Point, Pa saw the heifer.

"Yander she is, boys," he shouted. He pointed in the direction. We were off like a small cavalry, over the rocks, stumps, clusters of briers, and brush. The two dogs knew what we were after and they ran ahead of us. The heifer stood, sniffed the wind, and when Remines' shepherd, Jolly, ran up, she lunged through the air at him. All her feet were in the air when she pinned him against the ground and gored him with her sharp straight horns. Our shepherd, Bob, went the other way, with his tail between his legs.

"She's killed Jolly," Jake Remines shouted. He was weeping when he stopped his horse and climbed from the saddle. He raced toward old Jolly who was lying there kicking and howling. All of us stopped our mules and horses and got down to look at Jolly while the heifer took her time trotting along toward the tall timber.

Jake felt of all the bones first in old Jolly to see if the heifer had crushed any. Then he examined the place where her horns had punctured his tough hide. The spot was bleeding, but not badly.

"He'll be all right," Jake said. "She just took the wind out of 'im and skeered 'im half to death. He's never been after an animal like that one."

"The only way we'll ever take that heifer from this pasture is to take her dead," Bob Remines said. "If I had a gun I'd shoot 'er!"

"Oh, no, never do that," Pa said. "She's not fat enough for beef. You'd lose a good animal."

"Come on, men," Finn said, "let's be after her."

Old Jolly was up on his feet now, barking and howling and ready to follow. Old Bob had taken off toward home, after he had seen what the heifer had done to Jolly. Jake, Bob, and Dave Remines and Pa climbed back into their saddles. Finn and I leaped onto our barebacked mules. We followed the horses that took the lead. A wild grapevine caught Jake under the chin and lifted him from his saddle onto a bed of dry leaves. The branch of a tree that Dave let fly behind him slapped Pa across the face and eyes. We left Pa and Jake, scared but unhurt, and rode after the heifer. I thought somewhere ahead, I didn't know where, if a heifer could laugh, this heifer was laughing at us. We couldn't ride under the trees and through the brush and briers and undergrowth as fast as we could walk. Then a poplar limb with bark almost the color of the wind pulled Bob Remines from his saddle and his elbow hit a rock.

"No more of this for me," Bob said. "Let the heifer go. Shoot her."

We left Bob walking and leading his horse from the thicket. We went on until Dinah fell with Finn when she tried to leap the creek. Finn jumped to the ground and was safe. Dick was sure-footed and I struck to his back. Dave Remines' horse slipped on a steep slope and pressed Dave against a tree. It took the breath from him just a minute. This was enough. We turned back while the heifer ran fleet-footed with the wind, over the dying grass and autumn leaves. She ran somewhere, we didn't know where. We managed to come back to the big grassfield in Shingle Mill Hollow and we mounted and rode toward the salt trough. We overtook Bob Remines on the way; he was still leading his horse.

"Think my elbow must be cracked," he said.

He had only a few more yards to walk to where Pa and Jake were sitting on their favorite stumps near the salt trough. Each of them was holding the bridle rein of his horse and mule.

"No, yesterday I would have given you forty, Jake," Pa said. "But not today. Not after I saw what that heifer did to old Jolly. I believe she's dangerous. I wouldn't give you a cent over thirty."

"Oh, I couldn't take that," Jake said.

"Take it, Pap," Bob Remines said, as he walked up leading his horse. "I've got a cracked elbow over this heifer."

"Take it, Pap," Dave Remines said. "I nearly got a panel of ribs busted when my horse slipped down against the side of a tree. Got the breath knocked out of me. Yesterday I ran after her until my heart nearly stopped. Take thirty bucks and let's get goin'."

"Boys, look what I've got in that red-blooded heifer," Jake

190

said. "I can't take that. I'll take thirty-seven. That's just thirty dollars and the pasture money I paid out on her this summer. How about it, Mick?"

"Too much," Pa smiled as if he were in a position to set his own price. "I'll give you thirty."

"All right," Jake sighed at last.

"It's a bad deal, Pa," Finn said. "You'll be sorry you ever bought that heifer."

Bob and Dave Remines were pleased. Jake seemed pleased to be rid of the heifer. Pa paid him in cash right on the spot when he agreed to thirty.

Pa smiled as I never saw him smile before. I wondered what he was thinking.

Then Jake and Dave mounted their horses. Finn and I helped Bob into the saddle. They rode away with Jolly limping along behind them.

Then Pa climbed into the saddle and Finn and I leaped astride Dick and Dinah and we followed Pa toward home. Pa sat in the saddle laughing.

"What's so funny?" Finn asked. "Tell us and we'll laugh, too."

"I got a heifer that's worth a hundred dollars for thirty," Pa said. "Old Jake has always beat me on trading. Once he sold me a mule with the distemper for seventy-five. Mule wasn't worth ten to me. I've made it back in this trade."

"I wouldn't give you thirty for that heifer," Finn said. "He cheated you again. That heifer just never can be tamed."

"She'll be easy to tame," Pa said. "I wonder that Jake didn't think about it. Cattle often go wild. But there's a way to tame 'em."

"How, Pa?" I asked.

"Just leave 'em alone," Pa said. "Leave that heifer alone in this pasture until the first snow falls. She'll get hungry. And

191

when she gets hungry, she'll be tame. She'll be lickin' salt out of my hand before December." Pa laughed as we rode toward home. "My hundred-dollar heifer won't be no trouble at all."

BEFORE THE GRAND JURY

Steave Sloan, our county sheriff, came up to me last Sunday and says, "I got a summons for you, Jasper Higgins, to be before the grand jury Monday morning at ten o' clock."

I turned and looked at old Steave, the scarred relic of many a bout with lawbreakers, whisky, and women. His face was red from overdrinking, and his belly shook under his blue shirt and brown suspenders like a bag of sand. His blue eyes dodged my gaze and glanced toward the ragweeds by the path when he read my summons.

"What am I summoned before the grand jury for? I can't indict anybody. Who's had me summoned before the grand jury, anyway?" I says to the sheriff. "Didn't my people support you in the election?—and then you take me before the grand jury."

"I don't know who summoned you, Jasper," says Sloan. "I'm doing my duty by handing you this summons. You can't blame me. This is part of the duty of the sheriff. I have to do this. Don't think hard of me."

Old Steave was still glancing down at the dirt. I didn't have the right to rub it in. Maybe if Steave would get shot in a gun fight, then I'd be sorry for a long time afterwards for what I had said to him. I began to draw in my horns and planned to do no more hooking.

"If you don't come to the grand jury, they can fine you," says Steave, "and have you arrested and brought before the grand jury. I'd advise you to come Monday morning and do your little do and get it all over with, Jasper."

"Why can't you tear up the summons and be a sport?"

"I can't do that. You know the trouble I got into once over that Pratt boy, and God in Heaven knows I didn't tear that summons up. I lost it. They put that out on me in the last election and come nigh as a pea sending me up for a couple of years. I ain't taking no more chances."

"It's all right, Steave. You'll run again."

Sheriff of the grand jury Benjamin Harrison William McKinley Rister met me at the door. He too was red-faced from overdrinking and his lips stood blubberly and far apart. His teeth were snaggly and set wide apart. He reached his hand out to clasp mine and says, "You're Jasper Higgins, ain't you?"

"That's what they call me, Sheriff Rister," I said.

"We'll put you right here in the bull pen in just a few minutes. You just wait around here. Don't leave this door. Stay right here where I can call you at any minute."

I saw Fannie Brooker come out of the bull pen and she was crying, "My God, I had to indict my own poor old pap for drawing a butcher knife on Babe Bocook for intent to kill. My God, my God."

Then Percy Ratliff went in when Sheriff Rister called him. He went in with a big grin showing his tobacco-stained teeth. Percy was in the bull pen about five minutes. Sheriff Rister brought him to the door and turned him out.

"Boys," says Percy, "they got our numbers and all our deeds. They know what we know and more, too. They got me. I was in that Cane Creek fracas when Hiram Williams got plugged and I had to indict a whole smear. I hated to do it but I had to. I indicted old Granny Stamper and Tim Rigsby and a whole slew of Cane Creek people. No way around it. I'd like to know who in the hell was nosy enough to turn my name in to the grand jury–damned low-down skunks!"

"Jasper Higgins, next!"

"All right, Sheriff."

Well, there was Fence Porter. He was in a big chair up at the bench. He was foreman of the grand jury. I'd seen Fence before. We'd met on several occasions in different crowds at different places. We just happened to run into each other, not knowing that the other fellow was going to be there.

A right pretty woman was writing down every word I said from the time I entered the room and said "Howdy" to the men–twelve of them, all lined up around the wall, each with a separate spittoon. There was old Sneeze Radform, Tim Mullikin, Henry Divers, John Isom, Foxey Hunter, Jack Cristwell with his snow-white head of busy hair, Felix Middletown, Jason Purcell, Wildcat Robinson, Teddy Newsome, Tiger Hatfield, and Hungry Wakefield.

"Well, what do you know for the good of the country, Jasper?" says Tiger Hatfield, spitting at the amber-colored can and missing it a good foot measured with a rule. "Know anything that ain't right that's goin' on around your farm out there in the Holler?"

"No."

Tiger looked at me. I looked at Tiger. He surely hadn't forgot that I had the deadwood on him. He didn't have any right to ask me anything. Maybe he did it to show the other grand jurymen that his heart was on the right side and that he was earning his two dollars a day. He just couldn't go too far if indictments could date back three years. I thought he'd at least not ask me about a few things.

The boys all looked me over and I looked at them. Jason Purcell said, "Did you hit Lefty Smith's boy Turkey and knock him over that shrubbery back of the schoolhouse last February?"

"A man don't have to indict himself," I says.

Pa had instructed me about this if they ever had me up before the grand jury. I was summoned on Sunday and that wasn't legal either.

"I heard it was you who hit Turkey Smith out back of the schoolhouse that night and that he hadn't been right bright since you hit him. His pap told me he thought his neck was cracked."

I never said a word. There wasn't anything left to say. The woman wrote down what they said. She wrote down all that I had said. She just sat there and wrote and wrote and looked over at the chair where I was sitting. Pa always told me to take my part, and when a man come at me using foul methods, for me to chill him with anything I got my hands on.

"Have you seen anybody with a deadly concealed weapon on their parts," says Felix Middletown, "sich as a pistol, a pair o' knucks, a hawk-bill knife with a blade five inches long, or a blackjack?"

"Yes, sir."

"What did he have concealed on his parts?"

"He had five-and-a-half-inch washers with a wire run through 'em. He had a blackjack."

"Who was he?"

"I didn't know him. He was a stranger to me."

"How come you to see 'em? Was he using 'em?"

"No. It was last horse-trade day and he traded them to boot in a horse swap down on the jockey grounds by the feed mill."

"Has anybody give you pizened licker?" says Foxey Hunter. Yes sir."

"Who was he?"

"I wish I knew."

I wasn't lying. I couldn't lie. The foreman told me to hold up my hand when I first come in the room with the grand jury sheriff, and he swore me to tell the truth and nothing but the truth, so help me God. I had to tell the truth.

They seemed to expect me to say something else, though, so I says, "Boys, I've drunk enough to know good licker. I've tried all kinds and no man had better not try to get any rotten stuff off on me with carbide or coppers in it. I'd go before a grand jury and indict them in spite of hell. I want good stuff when I drink. I've sampled all kinds of licker—I've drunk enough to float a saw log to the mouth of Big Sandy River."

"Have you heard any vile words used in public in the presence of ladies?" says Wildcat Robinson.

"Yes, sir."

"Who done that?" says Wildcat. "And what did they say?"

"When I come down the street a little while ago, a fellow said 'sonofa—' and a woman was passing right along beside of him. She heard what he said."

"Who was the woman?" says Wildcat.

"Who was the man?" says Foxey Hunter.

"Didn't know neither one of them—man nor woman."

"What kind of a looking man was he, Jasper?"

"He was big-bellied with a long sandy beard, had blue eyes with heavy brown eyebrows, white teeth, and a snarl on his lips. He'd weigh about two hundred and fifty pounds."

"That's old Fred Sizemore—I'll bet you a twist of shoe peg it was old Fred," says Tim Mullikin. "He lives up on Slash Branch and he comes to town every Saturday of the world and gets drunk as a badger and gets locked up. He's just got to have his spree every weekend. The other day I saw him all dressed up and started to town and I said to him, 'Where are you going, Fred?' 'Going to town to get drunk, and Lord God, how I do dread it!'"

197

The grand jurymen all laughed. Tiger showed his tobacco-stained teeth that looked like new-ground stumps set in a lobber-sided horseshoe curve.

"Can't do anything about it, boys, if we don't know his name," says Felix Middletown. "Just have to pass it up. Let's proceed to ask young Jasper about Lake Madden's place. I heard he knowed a right smart about the place. Now is the time to find out."

"Do you know Lake Madden?"

"Yes."

"Did you ever go there?"

"Once."

"Did you go to see a woman or buy licker or go for both?"

"Neither."

"What did you go for?"

"To get some phonograph records, 'That's My Baby' and 'St. Louis Blues.'"

"Did you see Babe Madden?"

"Yes."

"Did you buy any licker from her?"

"No."

"Did she try to sell you any licker?"

"No."

"Law's been tryin' to get that woman for the past ten years," says Foxey Hunter, "and they can't get a thing on her. We know she sells that old rot-gut whisky. Didn't Sheriff Barney go over there when he was in the sheriff's office — that's been seven years ago — and look through everything in the house for Babe's rot-gut licker? There was a couple of revenue men with the sheriff. They hunted and hunted and couldn't find a thing. Then they started diggin' in the yard and Babe started screamin' and sayin' not to dig under the peach tree. The boys thought they was right on her licker, but dog my cats! If she didn't run

198

around t'other side of the buildin' and dig up a five-gallon glass jug o' licker and smash it with a double-bitted ax, I'm a liar. It soaked up in the loose dirt. Boys knowed it was licker but they couldn't swear it by smellin' of the glass and the ground. That ain't sufficient evidence in court. She's a bad one. Looks funny, young Jasper goin' over there to get music when he can get a lot more there than music."

"Here's somethin' I want to ask Jasper Higgins," says John Isom. "Did you have a fight one night at a schoolhouse? Didn't you addle a boy with your fist and knock him cold as a beef?"

"I did."

"What did you hit him with—a pair of knucks?"

"No, sir. I hit him with my hand. See this knuckle knocked back here! Knucks won't let you break your knuckles."

"That's right, Jasper, but why did you hit him?"

"He tore up a school program. Come in with a cowboy hat on his head and whooped out that he was the meanest man since Adam. Rest of 'em set around there afraid to move, schoolteachers and all. Wasn't no Law at that schoolhouse. Never is any Law down there. So I thought I'd see if he was the meanest man since Adam."

"Where did you hit him?"

"On the chin."

"How long was he cold as a beef?"

"Till they went and got the sheriff. Had to go a mile and get him."

"Wasn't you afraid of the Law?"

"No. Where there's not any Law to protect a man, there shouldn't be any to prosecute him. We have to protect ourselves in this county. You know that. Shoot a man down, you get one year in the pen. Steal a chicken, you get five years in the pen. No pardon on chicken-stealin', but you do have a chance for a pardon if you belong to the right party when you kill a man.

They need your family vote. The family turns against them unless the killer gets a pardon. Sometimes it's already waitin' in the courtroom soon as the man is sentenced. I've resolved to protect myself first, then my friends second."

"He's right, boys," says Wildcat Robinson. "The boy needs a medal. He ought to be rewarded."

"He ought to be made a Kentucky Colonel," said Felix Middletown.

"He ain't on the right side of the fence. Besides, he's a Kentuckian. That's for outside folks, you know," says Foxey Hunter.

"Man had better never start any of that old Adam stuff with me. That's old as the hills. I'd pick up a rock and cave his damn skull in," says Felix Middletown. "I've seen too much of it around here. I heered that fight kinda settled 'em down at the schoolhouse. Ain't been near so many fights since. People can go there in a little peace now. Twelve men was into that scrap, I heerd."

"What about this Susie Lawthorne that you've been runnin' around here with, the last two months?" says County Attorney Gilmore Hix. "Is she a pretty nice girl?"

"Far as I know she is all right. It all depends on what you call a nice girl."

"I mean the way she conducts herself in public places."

"Have you ever been any place with her away from her home?" says Tiger Hatfield, spitting at the spittoon and missing it.

"Yes, I have."

"Where have you been?" asks Hungry Wakefield.

"I've been to church and to the square dances several times."

"That's all we wanted to know," says Tiger. "We just want to get the straight of these things we've been hearin'. We want to clean up a lot of this corruption from our land and make our county a decent place for a man to bring his girls up in. I got a couple of little girls down there and I'll tell you it's goin' to be hard to bring 'em up in a community where all this blackguardin' and totin' pistols, drinkin' booze, and stealin's goin' on. We ain't here to harm nobody. We are here to get this county cleaned up. We aim to do our best."

"I second the motion, Tiger," says Hungry. "You and me ain't stood together on many things in these last twenty years. But I'm standin' right by you when you are tryin' to do the right thing."

"About all we want with him, ain't it, Foreman?" says Wildcat Robinson. "All them fellows out there a-waitin'. He don't know enough, nohow."

"Dismissed," says Foreman Porter. "Take him out, Sheriff Rister."

I got down off the bench and walked across the room. I didn't go out cussing or crying. I just wondered how many poor devils I had indicted. I hoped I hadn't indicted any.

I remember at one grand jury the county got enough indictments to fill the docket with better than six hundred cases. The district judge couldn't have got through with them all in his whole term of office. They were all for little petty things, too—like carrying a pistol, using profanity in front of ladies, or fighting.

Sometimes the way of the Law don't seem right sensible.

THE CHAMPIONS

"**N**ow, he's a right good man to work," Old Op told me. "Of course he's like myself when it comes to looks. He's not much to look at. But I'm just telling you, if you need a man to help me on the pasture, I'll recommend Young Charlie to you."

There was a twinkle in Old Op's eye the cataract hadn't completely covered. There was mischievousness in his other, almost sightless, eye that stared at me from the deep socket. Long wiry sand-brier-colored beard stood upon his wrinkled face like dwarfed bushes on the wrinkled slope of a rugged hill.

"What are you up to, Op?" I said.

"Well, Young Charlie works around for everybody for almost nothing." He spoke sympathetically, his better eye twinkling with mischief. "I think he's been working for Bill Rouse down on Sandy River for three dollars for twelve hours. He works from sunrise to sunset, by jiminy! Just like the oldtimers used to work. And I said the other day to Young Charlie as we walked up Womack Hollow, 'Charlie, I hear you're Morgan County's champion sprout-cutter. But I hear Bill Rouse ain't paying you much. How'd you like to help me cut sprouts? Six bucks a day instead of three. Work an eight-hour day with me. No one around but you and me. Nobody there to look down your collar. Just you and me in good cuttin' on a clean hill.' Well, you ought to seen Young Charlie's eyes pop out. 'Boy, I'd like it,' he said. Then I told him I'd come and see you!"

"That's not the reason you want Young Charlie," I said. "You've got some other reason."

"Nope," he said. He couldn't hold his lips in place. They bent like rainbows when he exploded with a cackling laughter akin to a hen pheasant's cackling. "Nope, I'm not up to nothin'. I've heard Young Charlie has bragged around that nobody in this county can cut sprouts. Just because he's Morgan County's champion don't mean he's a champion in my county."

"How old a man is Charlie Cotton, Op?" I asked.

"He's only fifty-six."

I'd seen Charlie Cotton, about the size of Op, snake-hipped, beardy-faced, walking along the road with a tall slender woman. They went from place to place, sleeping in summer in barns beside the road or in homes where people would let them stay. He had worked for small wages because he was such a homely man people were afraid of him. He worked in the fields when and wherever he could find anyone who would hire him. She worked in homes, washing clothes and scrubbing floors, if she was lucky enough to get work in the home while Charlie worked on the farm.

When he squirrel-hunted, she took a gun and hunted with him. When he fished in the Sandy River, she fished with him. When he got his small pay on a Saturday and went to a movie, she went too. And they'd take half of their money and buy chewing gum, candy, ice cream, and sodas. Then he might buy illegal wine or whisky from one of the many bootleggers in this dry territory. They'd get imbibed, start home, and not get there. They'd sleep somewhere beside the road.

I'd never planned to hire Charlie Cotton to work for me. I knew people he'd worked for wouldn't have him and his common-law wife staying in their homes unless they were people who were immune to odors. Young Charlie had a beardy face with squinty blue eyes, deep-set above high cheek bones. He had a long straight body minus hips where his legs, swinging like pendulums, hooked onto his torso. His body was longer than his legs. His arms were long, too, for a man his size. His hands were like small shovels.

He worked in tight-fitting overalls, a faded blue work shirt, and a pin-striped cap with a long bill. Two teeth were long and pearly white. Between these two, all his upper front teeth were broken. They looked like short charcoal-black stumps where a row of trees had been cut years ago. Every other lower tooth was dark. One couldn't help but notice Young Charlie's teeth the minute he opened his mouth. Once I met him and his wife walking on the Womack Hollow road. I never forgot this strange couple. I certainly never forgot his teeth.

I knew old Op didn't care for Charlie Cotton. He didn't care for any man he'd ever worked with in the fields. In the last twenty years I had never been able to get a man who could work with gentle old tall-tale-telling Op. He'd tell his tall tales to entertain the man who worked with him. At sunset Op would tell him he hadn't done anything and that he ought to be fired. And if I didn't fire him, Old Op would refuse to work with such a slowpoke another day. This was the way Old Op had treated them all. Once I hired my uncle Jake to help Old Op. Uncle Jake was a two-hundred-ninety-pounder and a neat worker. But Old Op told everybody he had to do all the work while my uncle slept in the shade. Uncle Jake could have worked on for me, but he wouldn't work at the same job with Old Op.

Then I sent Happy Gore out with Old Op once to cut saw timber. Old Op told Happy Gore some new tales until he shook all over. Happy got down on his knees, for he was so tickled he couldn't stand up, to cut the tall saw briers from around a pine tree with his pocketknife. He didn't know while he was down

on his knees shaking all over with laughter, slashing greenbriers
with his knife, that he was entertaining Old Op. When Old Op
got through talking about Happy Gore, everybody was laughing. When people met Happy on the streets they stood back and
laughed. Happy Gore didn't know what the joke was or who had
started it. But Old Op had told the people how he got down on
his knees with a pocketknife to trim the briers from around a
pine before they knelt down with their crosscut saw.

"And we cut only four little saw logs in a half day," Old Op
told his listeners. "That's the slowest man I ever saw in my life.
Gets down and sights over the crosscut like it was a rifle barrel.
I told Shan Powderjay I wouldn't work for no man, look him in
the eyes, and take pay for cutting four little logs size of my thigh
in a half day. No, siree, I wouldn't do it!"

I had to let Happy Gore work with Uncle Jake because Old
Op told so many tales about them that everybody was laughing.
They were laughing at my uncle, who got imbibed over each
weekend and lay somewhere in the woods. One of the stories Old
Op told about him was that he once got drunk and lay in a four-
foot drift of snow. He was so hot he melted the snow for thirty
feet around him and a small river ran from Uncle Jake.

Old Op had told all these tales on men I had hired to work
with him. He had even told tales on me. He's told that the day
we cut eighty-two saw logs in a half day, he had to notch all the
trees because I didn't know how to notch a tree. And when we
put the tiles under the road we built to the Seaton Ridge, he had
had to carry the sections of concrete-steel-reinforced two-foot
tiles by himself while I sprawled under the oak shade. People
started laughing at me. When they did, I said, "Old Op's told you
something. Did he ever tell you about the snake he hit between
the eyes with a fence rail which was so big that it tore down a
two-acre field of wheat after he addled it?"

"Op, you plan to do something to Young Charlie," I said.

"But if he wants to work with you, I'll hire him."

Won't they make a pair, I thought. What a pair! I want the two in my pasture field cutting sprouts together.

I hired Charlie Cotton. Old Op took the new red-handled mattock to the field. He took the bush blades, sprouting hoes, axes, new files, and scythe rocks. Old Op took his own jug of water. Old Op and I always drank from the same jug. Charlie Cotton might have felt the same way about Old Op for he fetched his own jug of water. I went to the field and showed them what I wanted cut.

"Now, you take this side, Young Charlie," Old Op said. "I'll take this one. We work apart so at sundown you can count your many blessings and I can count mine. We'll see which of us is the champion."

I knew what Old Op was up to. He had tried to do the same thing to me. Anybody who worked with him he accepted as his rival. Old Op was a good competitor. I'd never been able to cut as much as Old Op. This was the job he loved to do. He could swing an ax so softly; yet it sank to the eye each lick he struck. When he used a hoe, you wouldn't think he was doing much. But Op always had little schemes he employed to put himself ahead of the others. He used his head as well as his ax.

If he ran into grapevines wrapped around many trees, he started cutting at the outer edge of the grapevine perimeter, going in toward the center from all parts of the circle. Finally, they fell in a big heap. Old Op not only had them down but neatly piled. While we, who used our axes more and heads less, went inside the grapevine thicket, cut from the center, and pulled and chopped until we finally got them cut and piled. Old Op couldn't work with anybody close to him.

The first week, Old Op and Young Charlie cut everything in one little valley. Then they started working on a steep slope. One day when Young Charlie came to our house for more water,

I said, "How are you and Old Op getting along?"

"That old man's the awfulest brush cutter I purt nigh ever seed," Young Charlie said. "He's about got me down. I've had to work to stay with 'im. I like to work close enough to hear 'im talk. But every time I listen he gets ahead of me. So I've quit listening to him. I found out he's a sly old fox."

Young Charlie took his water jug and went back to the field.

The next morning when Old Op walked up to our well in the front yard where he'd filled his water jugs for twenty-five years, he started drawing water. I was feeding the birds. Day was just breaking.

"You're stirring early, Op," I said.

"Yep, I'm a-havin' to do the work of two men to make a showin' in that pasture field," he said. "You know me. I won't work for a man unless I can make a showing. This Young Charlie Cotton is awful slow. Sometime, I'd like to go into the field just with you and show you the work he's done and I've done. I'll show you the difference in the Morgan and the Greenup County champions. If he's the best sprout-cutter in Morgan County, the county judge had better call him home."

I knew what Old Op was trying to do. This was what had happened to all the men who had worked with him. Charlie Cotton was crowding Old Op or he wouldn't be stirring this early. Old Op was getting out early so he could have a through of brush cut up the slope before Young Charlie got there. And when Young Charlie came, Old Op would tell him he'd been there only a few minutes. He had done me this way. It was funny after you caught on to Old Op. But I figured Young Charlie might be a little thick in the head and slow to catch on.

When Young Charlie passed my house an hour later with his water jug, his short legs were swinging like pendulums on his long torso. He waved to me as he went by.

"Seen Old Uncle Op?" he shouted.

"He's already gone to his work," I said.

Young Charlie's legs worked faster.

The next morning Young Charlie went by himself. I didn't see Old Op go up the valley. At noon Old Op came by and filled his jug at the well.

"I'm just like a mule," he said. "When I get used to a good place to drink, I never want to leave it."

"I didn't see you go up this morning, Op," I said.

"Thought I'd better take a half day off and give Young Charlie Cotton a chance," he said. "Give him time to get caught up with me. We've not worked two weeks yet but he's about three days behind me. He won't be able to take it much longer. I'm showing you the difference in the Greenup and the Morgan County sprout-cutting champions. And I'm telling the people, too. Young Charlie can't stand me much longer."

When Old Op left the well, I watched him walk up the valley at an easy gait, swinging the jug he held in his old tough hand that was gnarled like the exposed roots of an ancient beech. His hairy arm dangled in the blue wind like a black stocking. He walked on reluctantly toward the field.

On the second Saturday, I paid Old Op first. Young Charlie came later. I paid him in cash for he wanted money he could see, feel with his coarse fingers, and hold in his hand. He didn't want a piece of paper where he had to make his cross, then have someone sign it for him. After I paid him in cash, he motioned with a sweep of his hands for me to come closer.

"Can I speak in confidence with you?" he whispered.

"Sure you can, Young Charlie," I told him. "Feel free to do so."

"The day Old Uncle Op didn't work, somebody whistled at my wife," he said. "You know where we live, don't you? Down there on the hill in that little house of Fonse Doore's. Well, she

208

said a man stood down in the hollow below the house, motioning with his hand for her to come to him when he whistled."

"That couldn't have been Old Op," I said. "He's seventy-seven and a great-grandfather many times."

"But she said it looked plaim-blank like Old Uncle Op," he said.

"The man couldn't be," I said. "I never heard of his whistling at women."

"But you don't know him," Young Charlie said. "He's been telling me about the things he's done. And that old man can do the work of two men. But I catched on to him a-coming early to beat me. He's found out I can do the work of three men. I'm a-slowing Old Uncle Op down. We're in the third week now. If we get another week together I'll get 'im."

But you'll never get another week with him, I thought. Old Op won't be defeated. He'll still be the champion.

The following morning Old Op didn't go to work. And I saw Young Charlie hurry down the road at about ten. At one in the afternoon I saw Old Op and Young Charlie go up the valley toward the pasture together. They were laughing and talking friendly-like to each other.

That afternoon Young Charlie came down from the clearing first. I stopped him to ask how he was getting along. "All right in the clearing," he said. "But that man has been back whistling at my wife. She said he stood down below the house and whistled again. She said he motioned for her to follow him. She said he looked plaim-blank like Old Uncle Op."

The next morning Old Op went up early. But this time Young Charlie Cotton didn't go up the valley. The next morning he didn't go up either. Old Op passed, filled his jug, while I talked to him at the well. "What's the matter with Young Charlie?" I asked. "Two mornings he's not gone to work."

"He's got more than he can do to work with me," Old Op

209

said. "I don't like to brag on myself but Young Charlie just can't take it. I'm two days ahead of him. He's ashamed of himself because he let me beat him."

The week passed and I paid Old Op, but Young Charlie didn't come for his pay. I asked Old Op if he would walk a quarter of a mile out of his way to their little house and he said he would. He said he would do it on this day and report to me early Saturday morning.

Saturday night Old Op was off to town to see a movie. After the movie he always treated himself to a steak at The Dinner Bell. Then he smoked a half-dozen long black cigars while he walked over town. He was a Saturday-nighter. Old Op never missed a Saturday night western, his steak, and his black cigars. He told me he was always tied to a steak on Saturday night at The Dinner Bell.

"Well, Young Charlie and his spouse have gone," he said. He couldn't hold his lips in place to give himself a serious expression. There was that twinkle in his partly good eye. And the eye in the deep socket with the almost sightless stare expressed happiness too. "See, he just couldn't work with me. He's nearly a week behind up there in the clearing now. Say, you know there's an awful lot of talk about that young booger and that common-law wife! I didn't mean to disgrace myself by working with 'im. I thought I was getting the champion sprout-cutter from old Morgan."

Then Old Op gave that little pheasant-hen's cackle after she's laid an egg. He burst out into an explosive cackling.

"Where did he leave the tools?" I asked Old Op. "I've been up there and I can't find 'em. He's done something with my new bush blade, mattock, sprouting hoe, and ax."

"It's hard to tell," Op said. "You can't tell about these strangers. Not until you test one. He wasn't a champion like he claimed to be!"

210

"I owe 'im for three days' work, too," I said. "He must have had some reason for leaving."

"They're liable never to come back," Old Op said, grinning. "It's hard tellin' where they are."

Another week had passed before Old Op told me Young Charlie and his wife had gone to Dartmouth with some young man, the one who had whistled at her, and they were all arrested and put in jail for drinking. I phoned the two city jails and the county jail and Young Charlie and his wife were not in any jail there.

Then I heard where Young Charlie and his wife had worked a few days for a man in the west part of our county to get enough money to leave. Young Charlie sent me word he would not be back and that he had left my tools by an old stump at the edge of his clearing. I went there and found the tools just where he said he had left them.

Almost to the top of the hill I saw Old Op flaying the sprouts. He was silhouetted against a patch of blue sky. In another hour he would have his half of the clearing finished.

DEATH AND DECISION

"When a man has lived fourscore, ten, and four years he's lived a long time," Pa said to Mom. "I know it hurts. I loved Old Dad like a father. But he has lived a long and useful life."

Finn and I stood lookin' at Grandpa. The wind came through the window and lifted his white corn-silk beard. The big square-shouldered two-hundred-and-forty-pound timber-cutter with the gnarled fire-shovel hands was silent now. His big chest did not expand now like it used to do when he swung a double-bitted ax to cut a giant tough-butted whiteoak.

"You know why Mom is weepin'?" Finn whispered to me.

"No," I said.

"It's Grandpa's funeral," he said. "Bass has notified every-body. They'll soon be a-comin'."

I knew our family would have trouble over whether a minister of the Old Faith or one of the New Faith would preach his funeral. I knew that our people were divided and the two churches didn't agree on anything. And now the time had come for a showdown. Grandpa had leaned toward the Old Faith since one of their ministers had baptized him; yet Grandpa hadn't gone all the way with them since he believed in education. Books were something they had preached against, and when many of their ministers had learned to read, they claimed that they had seen the "light" and just started reading. Mom leaned toward the Old Faith because Grandpa did.

"Don't haf to go to school to larn to read," Uncle Radner once told Finn. "Just have the faith and open the Word and read."

"That's a lot easier than goin' to school, Uncle Radner," Finn said.

Mom wrung her hands and cried until she couldn't cry. She sat in a chair and sobbed, and Pa stood behind her tellin' her not to take it so hard, since Death would slip up on a man most any time after he passed fourscore and ten years. But Mom wouldn't listen. Finn and I knew Mom must be thinkin' about tomorrow.

"I'll have something to say about who preaches the funeral, Finn," I said. "Grandpa told me no longer than last summer he wanted me to carry out his plans."

"Are you goin' to carry them out like he planned?" Finn asked. "Are you goin' to see that he is buried in his shirttail and underwear?"

"He changed his mind about that," I said.

"What about the wild cherry homemade coffin?" Finn asked.

"Don't have the lumber," I said.

"Good," Finn said. "That will surprise the members of the Old Faith. They don't believe in store-bought coffins."

"And I'm goin' to have an undertaker," I said.

"You'll have many of the Old Faith to bury," Finn said.

"And I'm goin' to have Reverend Todd Hunter to preach his funeral," I said. "He's neither a minister of the Old or the New Faith, and this will bring peace among us."

"You'll never do that without a fight," Finn said. "Uncle Radner will never have a minister of another faith to preach Grandpa's funeral."

"What will they say about the flowers?" I asked Finn.

213

"Won't that surprise our kinfolks of the Old Faith?"

"All you plan will go well with our blood kin of the New Faith," Finn said. "But our blood kin of the Old Faith won't have any of it."

"They'll have it too," I said. "We've always done what Grandpa wanted us to do. He wanted me to be in charge of his funeral and I'm goin' to handle it!"

"Look, Uncle Radner and Aunt Mallie," Finn whispered.

"Take it easy, Sall," Uncle Radner said as he patted Mom on the back with his big hand. "Old Dad's better off than we are. He's gone to the Glory Land. He's with Mel Sperry, Tim Cunningham, Alex Spry, and all the old timber cutters who lived accordin' to the Word."

"Yes, take it easy," Aunt Mallie said to Mom. "Pap is better off."

Mom didn't answer Uncle Radner and Aunt Mallie. She couldn't answer them for sobbing.

"Who has charge of the funeral?" Uncle Radnor asked Pa.

"Old Dad told Shan to look about everything," Pa said.

"How did that come about?" Uncle Radnor asked Pa. "What about one of us of the Old Faith?"

Then Uncle Radner turned to me and said, "Who'd ye get to preach Old Dad's funeral, Shan?"

"I'm goin' to get Reverend Todd Hunter," I said.

"He's not a man of our faith," Uncle Radner said. "I won't have 'im. I won't have 'im no more than I'd have one of the New Faith."

"I told you," Finn whispered.

Now the crowd of our blood kin began to walk up the paths to our house. There were long lines of them walking single file up the narrow paths. There were young boys and girls and women carryin' babies and their husbands carryin' one or two who were nearly babies, and there were old men and women walkin' behind with canes. They were all akin to Grandpa by marriage or the blood stream. Most of them had descended from him; fifty-three grandchildren and their families and his great grandchildren.

"We'll talk this thing over, Shan," Uncle Radner said.

"No use to talk it over," I said. "We're goin' to have Reverend Todd Hunter."

Uncle Radner, who was six feet and nine inches tall, stood looking down at me when he talked. Fire danced in his eyes.

We finally compromised on the coffin and flowers, and I was to let him choose the minister. I had to do it anyway, or there would have been a fight in our yard. He agreed to let me have an undertaker instead of haulin' Grandpa to Plum Grove on our jolt wagon with our mules. It would have been a long slow trip. Then Uncle Radner went among our blood kin with a big smile on his face and said that Brother Adam Flint, a preacher of the Old Faith, would preach Grandpa's funeral. I saw many happy faces among our people, and I saw just as many clouded and sullen faces.

Mom must have thought everything was settled, for she stopped weepin'. She talked to many of our kinfolks that she hadn't seen for years, though they lived a few miles from us in another hollow or valley. There was much talkin' and hand-shakin' among us. And as night came on the talkin' died and there were a few songs. Our kinfolks of the Old Faith did their kind of singin'. They read a line and then they sang it with long whines and sobs that sent chills over our bodies. Since we were descended from the same blood stream, our Grandpa, I wondered how we could be so different. And I wondered which side Grandpa would have taken if he could have come to life again.

Just before daylight members of the Old Faith got together in our kitchen and talked to one another. We knew they were up to something. They were Uncle Radner, Reverend

215

Flint, Cousin Erf, Keen, Dudley, Tim, Cy, and Winton Shelton. Uncle Darius, Uncle Pratt, Uncle Sizemore, and Uncle Sneed were tryin' to whisper to Reverend Flint at the same time. Mom wouldn't take either side. Pa wouldn't. But Uncle Jason was on our side. Cousins Ednor, Elva, George, Dave, Edith, Carrie, Nancy, Belle, Lucretia, and more than a hundred others were members of the New Faith. Even Uncle Mace was with us, since he believed in education and had tried to educate his children.

Pa was interested in seeing that everybody got enough to eat and enough coffee to drink after our sleepless night. And as the mornin' came and the darkness cleared away, we knew the day of decision was before us. We knew Mom had always wanted Grandpa to have a good funeral, since he had talked so much about it after he passed the fourscore and ten years. It was then Grandpa was baptized and started thinkin' about the world beyond and how he wanted to be dressed when he entered the next world. And it was then he put his ax, maul, sledge hammers, and crosscut saws away. He said that he had cut timber since he was fourteen and now it was time to retire. He said at the age of ninety a man should stop his daily toil and start preparations for the next world.

I thought of this as I looked at him in his long sleep. I thought of it more after I saw him in the big coffin which was hardly broad enough for his shoulders. I thought it was a terribly small place to put this mountain of a man who was used to the freedom of the ax and crosscut saw and the timbered mountain slopes. I had seen him work stripped to the waist when the winter winds blew and the weather was below zero. I had seen him cut a hundred shocks of corn twelve hills square in a single day when two men workin' with him only cut sixty-nine in the same kind of corn. All this was over. He was confined at last.

"Boys, there is no use to gear the mules to haul Old Dad to that newfangled deadwagon," Uncle Radner said. "He's got

216

enough grandsons to tote 'im."

Just as soon as Uncle Radner spoke these words, six cousins of the Old Faith hurried inside the house to get Grandpa. And six of the New Faith hurried inside too. Mom started weepin' again, and Aunt Mallie wept like her heart would break. There was silence among the funeral crowd. But it happened that three of the Old Faith took one side of the coffin and three of the New Faith took the other side. We walked down the narrow path where the mud was shoe-mouth deep, with the great crowd of our blood kin followin'. We didn't speak across the coffin to our cousins and they didn't speak to us. But they talked to each other and we talked to one another.

When we reached the ambulance at the turnpike and had put Grandpa inside, our cousins of the New Faith, Nancy, Belle, and Lucretia, came with wreaths of flowers and laid them on Grandpa's coffin. There were many clouded faces among our cousins, aunts, uncles, and distant blood kin of the Old Faith. The ambulance took Grandpa toward Plum Grove. When we reached Plum Grove, our kinfolks of the Old Faith took seats on the left side of the church house and we took seats on the right where the winter wind whistled through the broken window-panes.

When Reverend Adam Flint started preaching Grandpa's funeral, he spoke of the visions he had seen when he was a boy in the cornfield. And how he had seen the light when it came to him. And how he had never gone to school but soon after he saw the light he could read the Word. He was a big man, and he looked like a gorilla when he lifted his long arms into the air and shouted his words back at us of the New Faith. Brother Finn nudged me when Reverend Adam Flint said that members of the Old Faith were the only ones with a promise of the Glory Land. Brother Finn's face got red. Uncle Jason, a big two-hundred-and-ninety-pound man, squirmed in his seat. Uncle

Mace nervously fumbled the hat he held in his hand.

Reverend Adam Flint seldom mentioned Grandpa while he preached his funeral. He didn't mention the religious life Grandpa had lived after he had passed his fourscore years and ten. He didn't mention the good life Grandpa had lived in the ninety years before he became a member of the Church of the Old Faith. He didn't tell how Grandpa, who had never gone to school a day in his life, had struggled to learn to read. He didn't tell that Grandpa had read as many as a hundred books a year. He didn't mention how Grandpa had encouraged his grandchildren to go to school and to become schoolteachers.

But Reverend Adam Flint spoke against flowers in the church. He talked against music. He pointed to the organ in the Church of the New Faith and said it shouldn't be there. He looked at the thirty-seven schoolteachers on our side of the church and spoke against the evils of education while we looked at one another and at him. And our blood kin of the Old Faith looked at us across the aisle. Whether they rejoiced watching our faces turn red, I don't know. But Uncle Radner, leader of the Old Faith, rejoiced. While Reverend Adam Flint preached against education there was a new light in Uncle Radner's face. For Uncle Radner couldn't read and write himself. Since he couldn't read and write, he thought education was folly. He thought it was public expense for absolutely nothing. Why we should be hearing all about the evils of education, flowers, and music at Grandpa's funeral was something we couldn't understand. We had to sit in our seats and twist and squirm with our faces hot and then cold for one hour and forty minutes.

"Now I have finished what was in my heart to say," Reverend Adam Flint said. "I have something to read here for the old brethren whose temple of clay we are about to rejoin with the earth." "But," he said, fumbling at his vest pocket with his big gnarled fingers, "I have left my glasses at home and I

218

can't read without 'em."

Then something happened on our side of the church. Everybody relaxed in his seat. And we looked at one another. Many of the schoolteachers looked strangely at each other.

"Reverend Flint, that's Grandpa's obituary you have," Finn said as he got up from his seat. "And, if you don't mind, I'll read it." "You know," Finn spoke softly, "this is where education comes in handy."

Then lights sparkled in the faces on our side of the church. Our aunts, uncles, first, second, and third cousins, and our in-laws on the other side of the middle aisle looked strangely at each other. We could not help looking across the aisle at them. Uncle Radner, for the first time, looked down at the floor. Finn's trained voice spoke the words so fluently that you caught each one and held it firmly in your memory.

"We won't have music," Reverend Flint said as soon as Finn finished reading Grandpa's obituary. "I'll sing you a song from the *Old Sweet Songster.*"

Reverend Adam Flint read a line. Then he tried to sing it. He didn't carry the tune. His voice went high and low. But not one of our side of the church made a noise. We listened intently to his singing. Something happened toward our feeling for him, since he couldn't read Grandpa's obituary. Soon as he was through with his song, Cousin Lucretia arose from her seat and said, "Let us sing 'Rock of Ages.' I'll play the organ."

Cousin Lucretia played the organ softly, sweetly, sadly, and our voices rose in unison from our side of the church. Members of the Old Faith looked at each other. But they held the same respect for us we had held for them. Cousin Lucretia played "Land Beyond the River." We sang it while they had to listen. We had listened to them for a long long time. And we had respected them. Now they were listening to us. And they respected us.

"Now we'll consign the old brethren's dust whence it came," Reverend Adam Flint said as soon as we were through singing.

The same pallbearers that had carried Grandpa from our home to the ambulance carried him from the Plum Grove Church to the cemetery.

Has death brought about a compromise between us, I wondered.

When Cousins Mary, Lucretia, and Glenna put flowers on Grandpa's coffin, our blood kin and in-laws of the Old Faith didn't try to take them off. Uncle Radner had warned us that they would if we brought flowers. When Reverend Adam Flint consigned Grandpa to the dust, crumbling a clod of Plum Grove earth upon him as we stood with heads bowed, we accepted with reverence all he did and said.

"Now we'll take charge of the grave," Dink Wampus, the Plum Grove sexton, said, soon as the services were over. His two helpers, tall beardy-faced men, stepped forward to the graveside with their long-handle shovels.

"And I'll take care o' you," Uncle Radner shouted as he popped Uncle Mace square on the nose with his big fist. "I've been a-wantin' to do this for a long time! Old Dad's under the ground and the time is right!"

At first Uncle Mace was stunned. Then he reached for one of the shovels, but the gravedigger held onto it. Uncle Radner popped Uncle Mace another time on the face.

"You have to fight," Uncle Radner shouted.

Then Uncle Mace came up with a haymaker and Uncle Radner fell across the pile of fresh dirt at Grandpa's grave.

"You've hurt Radner, Mace!" Aunt Mallie screamed.

"No more than he hurt me," Uncle Mace said. "Struck like a copperhead when I was least expectin' it! I ought to bash his damned face in with my heel!"

220

Grandpa's death a compromise, I thought, as I watched members of the Old and the New Faith tangle in the graveyard since Uncle Radner had struck the first lick.

"Boys, be careful with the tombstones," Uncle Jason shouted as Cousins Erf, Keen, Dudley, Tim, Cy, and Winton tangled with Cousins Ednor, Elva, Gleen, Lige, Cief, and Brother Finn. Brother Finn caught Dudley under the chin and upended him. I never saw as many fists flying. I never heard so much screaming.

"Women, go to the church house!" Dink Wampus shouted. "Hurry! Get there!"

Then, instead of trying to fill the grave, Dink Wampus and his men tried to separate the fighting men.

"It's no use," Uncle Sizemore said. "Now is the time for the real showdown between us. Let 'em fight!"

"I'll show you what a real showdown is," Uncle Jason said as he put his two hundred and ninety pounds behind a powerful blow that lifted Uncle Sizemore across two graves. Uncle Sizemore hit between two mounds and lay there. Cousin Cy was getting the better of Brother Finn until he backed Finn upon a grave where Finn had the advantage. Finn caught him with a lick behind the ear and knocked him cuckoo. He fell across the fresh mound beside Uncle Radner.

Uncle Darius, Uncle Sneed, and Uncle Pratt tangled with Uncle John, Uncle Mort, and Uncle Sam. I never saw so many bleeding noses. Everybody was fighting but Reverend Adam Flint and me. All our wives, sisters, mothers, aunts, and great-aunts had reached the churchyard where they stood weeping and watching the fight. Once I thought I'd hit Reverend Adam Flint. Then I saw Cousin Keen Shelton start to hit Finn over the head with a tree root, from behind, since Finn had knocked out his two brothers. I caught Keen on the chin as he was coming over with the root with such a blow that my arm ached to my shoulder. The root fell from Keen's hands and he twisted to the ground like he was out for good.

When Reverend Adam Flint saw me hit Keen he must have thought he was next. He started running down among the tombstones, and Uncle Mace picked up a clod of hard dirt and threw it straight as a bullet at his head. It struck Reverend Adam Flint on top of the head, knocked his hat off, but he never stopped running. He ran to the far end of the graveyard and leaped the low fence and ran down across Barger's sheep pasture toward the main traveled road.

"That's a good riddance, Mace," Uncle Sam said. "Pity you didn't hit 'im with a rock instead of a clod."

The fight started at about four o'clock and lasted until nearly five. Members of the Old Faith had had their way in the church house, but they didn't get it in the churchyard. We had about thirty of their men on the ground at once. Down between the old graves and across graves and every place the ground would hold them. They had twenty or more of our men down. But when Uncle Radner came to his senses and saw all the men on the ground and heard the lamenting cries and wails of the mothers, lovers, sweethearts, wives, sisters, and aunts from the churchyard, he was the first to say, "Let us have peace, brother! Let's stop this fight."

"Have you members of the Old Faith had enough?" Uncle Mace asked.

"Plenty," Uncle Radner said, for he was scared.

Then the fighting stopped. We had to pull several of the men apart and made them stop biting, gouging, hitting, and clawing. There was blood on the ground. Tombstones, pots of flowers, and vases with faded flowers were turned over. Shrubbery and living flowers were flattened on the ground.

"It'll take a long time to straighten this place up," Dink Wampus said, shaking his head sadly. "Never a fight like this one happened here! I've never seen anything like this before. It's a disgrace!"

Then the women rushed back to the churchyard to claim their own. Aunt Mallie ran to Uncle Radner and put her arms around him. And our cousins of the New Faith helped cousins of the New Faith and cousins of the Old Faith helped cousins of the Old Faith. Each took care of his own faith. Not a word was spoken between the factions as we helped our wounded from the Plum Grove graveyard. They gathered their wounded and carried their sleeping from the hill ahead of us. There were consoling words from the women to the men as they left the graveyard before we did. We followed, bringing our wounded and carrying our cousins that had not wakened. We left Dink Wampus and his two helpers shoveling the dirt into Grandpa's grave.

"I'm glad Old Dad is the last one where both faiths have to attend the same funeral," Uncle Mace said as he rubbed his bruised hand gently with his good hand. "From now on, let the Old Faith bury their dead and we'll bury our own."

ALEC'S CABIN

How old Alec ever got on my farm I'll never know. Dad said when he bought the farm for me while I was in Scotland that there wasn't anybody living in either of the shacks, made by the lumberjacks while they were cutting the timber. I know it was a surprise to me that October morning when I went out to round up the cattle and drive them to the barn after the first sharp frost had fallen. For I saw a stream of wood smoke ascending from the rough-stone flue of the one-room shack near the big barn where the lumberjacks had kept twenty yoke of oxen.

Soon as I knocked on the door, the latch turned and I stood facing an old man with black beard and long salt-and-pepper-colored hair. He squinted his black beady eyes as he looked at me.

"I didn't know anybody was living here," I said.

"Well, you know it now." The old man spoke friendly, laughing at his own words. "Ye've got old Alec on your place and he'll never do ye any harm."

I stood looking first at him and then inside at his old pieces of furniture.

"Did you move here after I bought the place?" I asked.

"I don't know," he said. "When did you buy the place?"

"To be exact, four months ago today," I said.

"Oh, yes," he said, laughing. "I moved here a couple of months ago."

"The least thing you could have done was to notify me you'd moved in," I said, my temper rising.

"Thought I might hunt and fish a little," Alec said as I stood thinking about what to do. "And I just wondered what you'd do with that big cattle barn out thar. Thought maybe ye'd want to raise some terbacker and ye'd hang it right thar in that barn."

"That wouldn't be a bad idea," I said. "I'd never thought of that before!"

"Well, ye know that barn oughten to be out here without anybody a-livin' here to pertect it," Alec said. "Thought I could do that much fer whoever owns this land. Remember there's a lot of strangers allus a-prowlin' through these woods."

Once I thought I'd tell Alec to get out. Then I changed my mind. It's not a bad idea to have someone living out here to look over this big barn, I thought. Alec might be all right. And who else could I get to live in a shack like this?

I left Alec standing in the door. I went to round up my cattle, and drive them from the frostbitten brown pasture to the cattle barn. But as I drove the cattle home, I couldn't keep from thinking about Alec. I kept thinking about him and planned to climb the ridge road again to see him. But one morning early when I was taking the ashes from the fireplace before I built a fire, I looked through the window and saw Alec coming down the hollow with a string of fish.

"Thought you might like a mess of fresh bass," he said soon as I opened the door.

"Sure would," I said, looking at the nice catch he'd brought me. "How did you catch them?"

"Hook and line," he said. "That's all I ever use. I can beat the men who set trotlines. They don't know how to fish. They don't know how to bait thar hooks."

"How much do you want for these fish?" I asked.

"Oh, nothing," he said. "Not a red penny. Remember I live in your place."

That was the last time I saw Alec until hunting season had begun. Then he came and brought me rabbits, quails, and he brought my wife a red fox pelt. In late autumn he brought us a bushel of black walnuts, a peck of butternuts, and a gallon of hazelnuts. He brought us pawpaws and persimmons. We offered him pay for these but he refused.

After the snows came I never saw anything of Alec. Although he lived not over two miles from me, I was never near his shack. I heard that he was trapping that winter. Often I'd seen tracks in the snow from one rock cliff den to another and believed these were his tracks. Early next spring after the snows had melted and the water had run from the high hills, Alec came down with some yellow root. He told me if my stomach ever cramped me to chew a little and swallow the juice.

When the trees had begun to bud and leaf, I climbed the high hill to his shack to see what was going on. Without asking me, he had spaded himself a garden and had cut the fence rows from the board fence around the shack, barn, and garden.

"I never liked sprouty fence rows," Alec said. "So I've cleaned this place up!"

"It looks wonderful, Alec," I said. "Look at the work you've done around here. How much do I owe you for all this work?"

"Not a red penny," he said. "When a body's got a home he oughta keep it fixed up, don't ye think?"

Alec talked like the place belonged to him. But I knew the laws of Kentucky well enough to know he couldn't take my land for which I had the deed, until after he had paid the taxes on the land for a number of years.

One day that May when I was in town, I saw Mrs. Harris cleaning some very pretty wild strawberries. I asked her where she was able to get such pretty berries and she told me they came from my farm.

"I've never seen any berries out there this large," I said. "Who brought them to you?"

"An old man by the name of Alec—just Alec," she said.

"Then I'll get him to pick us some," I said. "I'd like to know where they grow."

Alec brought us finer wild strawberries than he had sold Mrs. Harris. He brought us wild raspberries when we couldn't find any on the farm. He knew where they grew same as he knew where to find the butternuts, walnuts, hazelnuts, persimmons, and pawpaws. He knew where all wild berries grew, for he brought us dewberries, huckleberries, and wild gooseberries. When we wanted something that grew wild, whether it was berry, shrub, fruit, or flower, all we had to do was ask Alec to find it for us. When we wanted a mess of wild game or fresh fish, all we had to do was ask Alec to bring them to us.

I never asked Alec to do a day's work on my farm even when I needed help. I left him alone to take care of the barn and shack. For I knew he was past the age when most men retire. But I was surprised when I walked over the big pasture that was near his shack. I was walking along and came to a place where a thicket of bushes and briers had been cut. The thicket had been cut, four acres or more, clean as a meadow. And this was a place in the pasture field where the sprouts and briers were shading the grass. The slopes where the sprouts and briers were not too high had been left alone. When I came to the cross fence, I found the brush and briers had been cut, leaving it clean as a pawpaw whistle. Alec had done it. He worked where he wanted to, when he wanted to, and that was all there was to it. He had cut dead trees near the fence so they wouldn't fall in a windstorm and smash it and let the cattle out. Dead trees near the water holes had been cut. Alec had taken care to see that the cattle wouldn't be in danger of an old tree falling on them when they went for water. I tried to get Alec to take pay but he would not.

"I'm glad I let him stay in that shack," I said to myself.

After he had lived two years on my place, I got better acquainted with Alec. He told me that he was once happily married and that his wife had been dead ten years or more, that his children had grown up and had gone to the industrial cities in northern Ohio. And that he was very happy living alone, without anybody near him. He said he wanted to live where he was living now the rest of his days.

Then came the war, and after I was in it my father and uncle needed help trying to raise and harvest crops. When they called on Alec to help them, he was willing and ready and my father sent me word when I was at Great Lakes Naval Training Station that Alec's help had saved them. Said he could do more with an ax, a spade, or a hoe than any man he had ever seen. Said he was the neatest worker he'd ever seen on a farm. When they hung the tobacco in the high barn, I wondered who would climb up among the stay poles and do the hanging. My mother wrote me that Alec could climb like a squirrel and he had saved the tobacco crop. And then she told me that Alec had two sons in the Army, one in Europe and one in the Pacific. I had never known before about Alec's sons. They had gone into service from Ohio.

When I was in service, my wife couldn't run the place any longer. She moved to town after eight months to live with her parents, and later she lived with me when I was stationed in Washington. She pulled the shades down at our house and closed the doors. But Alec came and cut the grass in the yard so if fire got out, it couldn't come down from the steep hills and burn the house. Alec looked over the entire farm, hunted, fished, trapped, worked, gathered nuts, and picked berries as he had always done. War or no war, he would do these things.

When I was released from the Navy and came home, Alec was not living alone in the shack. His son, who had been in service five years, forty-two months of that time served in the Pacific, was at home with him. I wondered how a young man used to Army life would like a one-room shack without a single modern convenience but Ronald said after his being with many men, he was fond of solitude and loved the one-room shack. Said he would like it for some time to come. In three weeks another son came to live with his father: Dave, who had not passed a physical for military service, but one who had worked for farmers in Ohio while the war was on. Then, I asked Alec if he didn't want to move to the foot of the hill into an empty four-room shack.

"Nope, I won't leave this place," he said. "We are all right. Three can live comfortably here."

Then another son, Tim, came home from the war and this was the only home he had in America, this one-room shack where his father lived, and loved and called his home. Then I went to see Alec to persuade him to move since I knew it was nearly impossible for four to live in one room.

"Nope, we can make it here." Alec spoke for his returning family. "I expect to stay here long as I live."

Why Alec didn't want to move to four rooms down beside the wagon road, where a few automobiles passed, was more than I could understand. This four-room shack did have a road to it. And there was a good well in the yard. He wouldn't have to carry water like he did back on the mountain from a spring nearly a half mile down under the ridge.

But something happened. Alec's daughter, Sue, came home from a city in Ohio where she had worked in a restaurant during the war. She didn't come alone. She came home with a baby and without a husband. He welcomed Sue home and was proud of her baby. He regarded her as a war casualty more than either of his sons. He didn't act like a grandfather to her baby but he acted like a father.

Now I knew his three sons, his daughter and her baby, and Alec couldn't live in one room. I wondered how they would dress and how they would sleep. When I went to see Alec, I found him in the big barn changing his clothes. He had his sons move their clothes to the barn so they could dress.

He had partitioned their one room with sheets and quilts and had a bed in one end for Sue and the baby. Three of the boys were sleeping in the other end and Alec was, I suppose, sleeping in the barn. I knew this wouldn't work. And I told Alec I didn't want anything like this on the place when I had an empty shack waiting for him. But Alec wouldn't listen.

"But your family is back with you," I protested. "How in the world are you going to do it? It's not sanitary! It's awful!"

My patience was tried. I was getting tired of fooling with Alec. I left the hill in disgust.

A week later Alec came down to see me.

"Guess I'll haf to move," he said. "But I ain't moving because of room. My baby needs a room and it can't sleep and so many of us in one room! Just too much noise! Even the foxhounds wake my baby. If I move down at the shack in the gap, we'll hear less of the foxhounds."

"Now you're talking," I said. "You'll need my mules, won't you?"

"Yes," Alec said, shaking his head sadly.

"I'll have Gore to help you move," I said. "When do you want him to bring the team?"

"Oh, in the mornin'll be all right," Alec muttered.

Early next morning Gore and I took the team and wagon

up the old log road to Alec's shack. When we arrived, Alec was out in the yard.

"We finally got here, Alec," Gore said, just as Ronald, Tim, and Dave came out the door.

"The boys will load the wagon." Alec spoke softly. "They got everything ready to load on.

"Ye might think I'm a little contrary about not a-wantin' to leave here," Alec said to me as Gore and his sons carried their scant possessions to the wagon. "I never did tell ye the reason. Reckon I might as well. I built this shack."

"You built that shack?" I asked.

"I shore did," Alec said. "I built it a long time ago when old Sam Dexter owned this land. That was when ye's a little boy living down at the mouth of W-Hollow. Biddie and I lived here twenty-three years. Our young'uns wuz all born in that shack. There's only one tree in that whole house," Alec talked on. "It's a big white-oak. I rive enough boards to kivver it from the two butt-cuts and I had the rest sawed at Dave Snyder's mill. I carried the planks up this mountain on my back. I sold hen eggs fer six cents a dozen and bought the nails."

"I didn't know that," I said.

"I knowed ye didn't the day ye come out here," Alec said. "But I lived here long as Sam Dexter owned this land and timber. And when Jason Radnor bought it, he made me move so the lumberjacks could use my shack. They built that big barn out thar. But I knowed soon as they got the timber cut and got out I was a-comin' back."

"But now your family is too big for one room, Alec," I said.

"Yep, ye're right," Alec agreed. "More a-comin' on and we've got to have more room." But Alec talked as the last pieces of furniture were piled upon the wagon. "Sam Dexter told me that this was my shack and if I ever had to leave it ferever, I could tear it down."

The furniture was loaded, and Gore climbed up on the wagon. He drove the mules away, down the log road toward the gap. Tim, Ronald, and Dave followed the wagon, each carrying a picture, something breakable, or a family heirloom. Sue walked with them with her baby in her arms. When the procession left the mountain, I followed but Alec remained.

We had just time to make the first sharp turn when I heard Alec's hammer and then I heard the boards coming off. Not one of us looked back or said a word. Though this shack was on the land I owned, I knew it really didn't belong to me.

OLD DICK

It wasn't good daylight when somebody rapped loudly on my front door. Wonder who's come this early, I thought as I walked toward the door. When I opened the door, Pa was standing there. He had a worried look on his face. I knew something was wrong.

"Old Dick's awful sick," were Pa's first words. "Wonder if you'd jump in the car and go with me to get Wash. We've got to get somebody since we don't have a mule doctor anywhere in these parts."

"What's wrong with 'im, Pa?" I asked.

"I don't know," Pa said. "For seventeen years, I've gone every morning at four o'clock to feed Dick and Dinah. I've never missed more than ten mornings. And they've been standing wide awake in their stalls to greet me! This mornin' Dinah greeted me. I wondered about Old Dick. I found 'im stretched on his stall beddin'. He got up to greet me. But he had to lie back down. He'd kicked the partition down durin' the night. He'd kicked boards loose from the stall. He'd suffered something awful. It nearly broke my heart to see 'im in so much misery! It was a-hurtin' old Dinah too. I put corn in her box and hay in her manger but she wasn't eatin'. She was a-standin' there lookin' at Old Dick a-moanin' and a-carryin' on something awful at her

233

feet."

"I've not had breakfast," I said. "Would I have time to wait for a cup of coffee?"

"I didn't take time for breakfast either," Pa said. "If we get Wash in time we might save Old Dick. We have to work fast. I can do without the coffee and my breakfast if we can save that mule."

I knew Pa wanted me to go. He wanted me to move in a hurry. I did. I hurried to the garage and started the car.

"Old Dick picked a muddy time to get sick," I said. "This road has never been worse this winter. Lucky I've already got chains on the car."

It was still so dark I had to switch on my headlights. I couldn't see the deep dark ruts well enough to miss them. I didn't miss all of them. I couldn't. The car lunged and plunged from deep ruts to deeper ruts, then came up again with muck dripping from bumper, fenders, and running boards. It was tough driving. I used all the gears and used them fast. Though Pa never liked to ride in an automobile on slick roads he didn't mind now. He didn't grumble and tell me to slow down and watch what I was doing as he had often told me when we were driving over this same road. We were going after Wash Nelson to doctor Old Dick. And Pa told me to step on the gas. Drive as fast and careful as I could and make as fast a time. How I ever got out of W-Hollow was a miracle. When I reached Route 1, a macadamized road, my car deposited a trail of W-Hollow mud for a mile or so. It dripped like heavy gobs of dark rain.

"I got Dick and Dinah when they were five-year-olds," Pa said thoughtfully as I speeded the car down Route 1. "They're twenty-two years old now. That's old for a span of mules. But neither one has ever been sick a day in his life! What a span of mules! Best pair of mules in Greenup County!" "Yes," Pa talked on, "I was a much younger man when I got that pair of mules.

234

I was only fifty then. How I've worked 'em! How they've worked me! I'd get up and go the darkest night for one of them mules!"

"But they're not gentle mules," I said to Pa as we left Route 1 and started up Academy Branch. "Old Dick's kicked you three times!"

"But let me tell you, son," Pa said. "It was all my fault. I never confessed this before. And it's always hurt something inside me that I didn't. But Dick always expected his master to do things right. The first time he kicked me, I went inside his stall and started to put the harness over his back from the wrong side. That's the time he kicked me on the shin and splintered the bone. Laid me up for nearly a month!"

"What about the time you started to put the bridle on him?" I said. "What did you do wrong that time?"

"Had the wrong bridle," Pa said. "Started to put old Dinah's bridle on him. He broke a whole panel of ribs for me that time! Broke five with that left hind hoof. He laid me up for three months that time!"

"I've always been afraid of his heels," I said.

"No need to be, son, if you do things right around that mule," Pa bragged. "I know him. He's a real mule. He does things right and expects you to do things right. The third and last time he kicked me, I made an awful mistake. I put him in the wagon on the off side when he worked on the near side. He really tried to get me that time. He nicked my chin with his steel shoe. He was kicking high for my head."

"And he's kicked several others, too," I said as we speeded over the graveled Academy Branch Road.

"But they made mistakes, son," Pa said. "Don't you ever doubt it."

"Just two months ago, Dick kicked Old Alec," I said. "A month ago Dick and Dinah together got Uncle Jesse's right index finger!"

"Yes, and what was Old Alec a-doin' to Dick?" Pa asked me. "He was down on his knees hittin' Old Dick up under the belly with his big black hat a-tryin' to kill a knit-fly! Old Dick knew that a man was supposed to kill one with his hand and not with a hat. And look what Jesse did," Pa talked on. "When he went after that load of coal, he drove Dick and Dinah under a low coal tipple and their hames caught on the trackin'. That's why they charged when he went to fasten the breast chain and took off his finger. Son, your Uncle Jesse is a mule driver. He knows mules. And he knows he made a mistake. If anything happens to Old Dick, see how hard your Uncle Jesse takes it! He's worked them mules for the last nine years. He won't work the young mules! You know that!"

Just then we reached Wash Nelson's house. I stopped the car. We got out.

"You're stirrin' early, Mick," a voice said.

"Wash," Pa said, "guess we're lucky to catch you. We've got an awful sick mule! Can you go doctor him?"

"You got here just in time," Wash said. "I'd started to the sawmill. Sure I can go, Mick. Wait a minute until I run back to the house and get my medicine bag."

In less than three minutes we had Wash in the car with his little medicine bag. He and Pa sat in the back seat to give me more room to drive. As we speeded down Academy Branch Road Wash asked Pa questions about Old Dick. It didn't take me long to reach Route 1 and speed to the W-Hollow road. The car tossed, skidded, and rocked like a small ship on a stormy sea, but this didn't stop Pa from telling Wash about Old Dick. Finally we reached my home. Uncle Jesse was standing at the gate waiting for us.

"How's Old Dick, Jesse?" Pa asked.

"He's all right, I guess," Uncle Jesse said, his lips trembling as he spoke, and his face was gray as morning mist. "He's dead!"

"Dead," Pa repeated as he looked at Wash.

Then Pa looked at the ground.

"Yes," I went after Gore," Uncle Jesse said. "And I sent Gene after Old Alec. We did all we could for him! In the years that I have worked Old Dick, I've seen him in a lot of tight places pulling saw logs from the timber woods, pulling wagon loads of coal up mountain slopes, but I've never seen 'im in a spot like he was in this mornin'. He wouldn't give up until he had to. We got 'im out'n the barn and he laid down and got up again over a hundred times. He tried to eat and couldn't. Finally he reared up and fell over dead."

"That's awful," Pa said as he kicked at a clod of dirt with his brogan toe. "That's tough. Poor Dick."

"Then there's no need for me to go on," Wash said.

"I'll take you home," I said.

Pa and Uncle Jesse walked silently up the hollow toward the barn. After I'd taken Wash home, I stopped at my home for breakfast. It was still early. And then I went up to the barn where Pa, Uncle Jesse, Gore, and Old Alec were standing looking at Old Dick where he had fallen on the barn lot. There Old Dick lay. It was the first time in seventeen years I'd known him that I had ever seen him lie perfectly still. The old men gathered around him had worked him many a day. They, perhaps, were thinking about the days they had worked him and Dinah. Their memories were going back to other days when they were younger men as they looked at this powerful mule that was at last as silent as the earth on which he lay. Not one of them was saying a word.

But Dinah, still fastened in her stall, was saying plenty. She was speaking in a language I didn't understand. I walked inside the barn and looked into her manger. She hadn't eaten her hay. I looked into her feedbox and the eight ears of yellow corn Pa had fed her at four o'clock hadn't been touched. Dick, for the

first time in all these years, was not by her side. Just yesterday
I had seen Dick and Dinah running over the pasture hill,
enjoying a day of freedom and running like rabbits over the old
trails they had known for a long long time. They were nibbling
each other playfully like two young lambs. They had made
these trails through the woodlands in their pasture that had
belonged to them all of the years we had owned them. Dick and
Dinah knew each rock and tree, each deep hole of water in the
little pasture streams, and the willow shades. These had
belonged to them as much as the two stalls they had kept in the
barn all of these years. We never allowed any other animal to
occupy one of their stalls or know the secrets of their fifty acres
of woodland and grass pasture.

When I walked outside the barn, Dinah was kicking the
plank wall behind her.

"Dinah, stop that!" I shouted, but my scolding didn't stop
her kicking.

Just as I walked back where the men were, standing
silently around Old Dick, Mort Higgins came down the road.

"Lost a mule, Mick?" he said. "Too bad!"

"Yes, I've lost a real mule." Pa spoke softly.

"Say, I'll tell you how to save the trouble, work, and time
burying him," Mort said. "I'm going to town and I can call the
deadwagon and they'll come right out here and get that mule!"

"Mort, I feel like a-sockin' you right on the jaw," Pa said.
"You're a good neighbor, but you don't understand how I feel
toward that mule!"

Uncle Jesse, Old Alec, and Wilfred Gore turned hard eyes
toward Mort Higgins. They didn't speak. They just looked at
Mort with unfriendly eyes.

"Oh, I didn't know, Mick, you felt that way about a mule,"
Mort said. "I'm sorry I suggested the deadwagon."

"There won't be any deadwagon, Mort," Pa said. "This

mule will be buried on this farm. He'll be buried in the dirt he's a part of. Dirt that belongs to him as much as it does to me! Mule that's worked seventeen years for me, I'll see that he's buried when he dies. There won't be any more use made of 'im. I can't stand this idea of workin' an animal till he dies, skinning 'im for his hide, and taking his bones for fertilizer."

Mort knew he'd said the wrong thing. He turned and left us without saying another word.

"Old Dick, you come nigh as a pea a-gettin' me once," Old Alec said. "If you'd a hit me two inches lower you'd a hit me over the ticker and it would've been too bad. But it was my fault!"

"I've made several mistakes, too," Wilfred said. "But I was quick enough to dodge! I learned a lot when I worked Old Dick and Dinah. Best mules I ever worked. Had good mule sense. Knew more about work than a lot of men!"

Uncle Jesse stood there with his hand still bandaged where he had lost his finger. He didn't say anything. He just looked at Old Dick. First time I'd ever seen him shed a tear. For Uncle Jesse was synonymous with this mule team. I'd seen him, a big three-hundred-pound man, wearing a big black umbrella hat, riding on the wagon going over the farm with Old Dick and Dinah. He was working them when I went to college. He had worked them four days ago. I'd seen him ride the mowing machine behind them in the heavy soybeans. I'd seen him drag saw logs from the timber woods with them. And I'd seen him turn the cold March loam over with a big turning-plow in rooty ground on a steep hillside. I'd seen him have them in tight places and they had always come through. When the young mules had stuck with a load uphill Uncle Jesse would never use Dick and Dinah. He would just hitch Old Dick to the tip of the wagon tongue and take the load up the hill. When my car stuck on the muddy W-Hollow road, embedded until mud ran over the running boards, Uncle Jesse would bring Dick to pull me out.

Only once did he fail. That time he was pulling in the direction opposite home. When Dick's head was turned toward home, he was never stuck in his life. He bent iron singletrees and splintered wooden ones and broke hame strings and crushed collar pads and broke collars. Something had to snap. These things went through my mind as I stood watching Uncle Jesse as he looked at his beloved mule, Old Dick.

"Where's a good place to bury 'im, Jesse?" Pa said.

"I've just been studyin'," Uncle Jesse said.

"What about the gap where the cedar tree stands?" I suggested.

"Not there," Gore said. "You once buried a cow there. You know how Old Dick always felt toward cattle!"

"He didn't like 'em," Old Alec said. "I'd be against buryin' 'im there."

"The young mules couldn't pull him up that little hill anyway," Uncle Jesse said. "Old Dick's a big mule. He'll weigh eleven hundred! That's too much for the young mules to pull on the ground!"

"Old Dick could have pulled that much on the ground," Pa said. "He pulled the cow up there by himself that we buried. She'd weigh about that much!"

Drops of cool rain started falling and the soft drops dampened Old Dick's clean hair.

"What about buryin' him at the edge of the pine grove near the gap?" Uncle Jesse suggested. "It's at the foot of the little hill where him and Dinah used to eat fodder and hay. It's the place where they went to play and rest in summer when they didn't work. It's the windbreak where they went in winter when we didn't have 'em in the barn. Seems to me it was Old Dick's favorite spot in the pasture."

"That's the right place," Wilfred Gore said.

"I think it is, too," Pa said.

240

Then Gore, Old Alec, and I got the mattocks and shovels while Pa and Uncle Jesse went into the barn to harness the young mules.

Old Alec picked the spot at the edge of the pine grove for us to dig the grave. Then he started digging with the big mattock while Gore and I shoveled. The big soft raindrops fell from the low clouds that raced over the low mountaintops like long thin-bellied greyhounds. Raindrops hit the green pine needles that swished in the slow-moving wind.

"It's a bad day to bury Old Dick," Gore said.

"But I'd never see a deadwagon haul 'im off," Old Alec said. "Mort Higgins doesn't know how near he come a-gettin' socked in the mouth. I'm a peaceful man, too."

We sank a big hole rapidly into the soft mellow earth. We hit only a few pine roots, but Old Alec cut them with a mattock and pulled them up with his big gnarled hands.

"We want his grave as near the pines as we can get it," Old Alec said.

Before we finished digging the grave, Pa and Uncle Jesse came driving the young mules down the hill, bringing Old Dick. They had fastened a log chain around his hind legs and the young mules pulled him as if he were a saw log. That was the only way we could haul him. We couldn't load him on the wagon. But the young mules, Rock and Rye, knew instinctively they were not pulling a saw log. They whiffed the wind. They pranced in the harness. Pa had trouble holding them with the lines.

"You can't fool a mule," Pa said. "These young mules know that Old Dick is dead. He never had any respect for these young mules after he pulled the first wagonload of coal they stuck with on the hill. He pulled it from the tongue tip. After that he'd never let these young mules come around him. But they respected him after he pulled their load."

"Every animal and person on this place respected Old Dick," Uncle Jesse said. "Old Dick was like a good apple with a few rotten specks in it. He had his faults. He wouldn't hold on a hill. Had to chock the wagon when he rested. But the catch was"—Uncle Jesse talked on as he wiped rain from his brow—"Old Dick just wouldn't rest on a hill. Dick and Dinah always took their load to the top before they stopped."

"The grave is ready," Gore said.

"Listen to Old Dinah, won't you," I said to Uncle Jesse.

"She broke out of the stall twice," Uncle Jesse said. "Mick and I got 'er back in the barn. She run out to where Old Dick was a-layin' and sniffled and sniffled and took on something awful! We've got 'er in a new stall. I don't think she can break out now!"

Dinah was braying mournfully. She sounded like a mule crying. If mules could cry I'd say she was crying.

Pa drove the young mules across the little valley to the edge of the pine grove. Then he angled them left and drove them up among the tall pines so Old Dick would be on the upper side of his grave. Then Gore unhitched the log chain from Dick's legs and Pa drove the mules to one side to let them stand while we rolled Old Dick over into the big hole. We heard Dinah kicking the wall of the barn. Then she stopped braying.

"She's learned that she can't get out," Pa said. "I feel sorry for her. She's lost Old Dick. I don't know what I'll ever be able to do with her now!"

We were getting hold of Old Dick's legs to turn him over into the grave. Old Alec and Gore had his hind legs, and Pa and I had his forelegs. Uncle Jesse couldn't do much since Old Dick and Dinah had charged with the wagon and he'd lost his finger. And then something happened. Old Alec saw her first.

Dinah had kicked the heavy planks, nailed with spikes, from the side of the barn, since she didn't have room to leap over the top of the stall because the barn loft was too low for her to leap. But she had kicked her way out and had followed the trail, smelling like a dog, with her nose on the ground. She had come to see Old Dick buried. She didn't bray or cry as long as she could see Old Dick. The young mules, Rock and Rye, turned around and watched too. The three mules stood there silently watching us as we lifted Old Dick's legs and he rolled over into his last stall. Then Dinah moved up closer and looked in.

Uncle Jesse shed more tears. And Pa wiped the rain from his beard with a big red bandanna and he wiped his eyes too.

I watched him when he lifted the check lines to drive Rock and Rye to the barn. Old Alec and I shoveled dirt over Old Dick until he was hidden from Dinah's sight. Then she turned and followed the young mules back to the barn as if she understood.

GRANDPA

Grandpa was sitting on the back porch. His dim eyes surveyed the knob of tobacco just set out on the hill across from the house. He looked toward the pasture field where the cows were around the black-oak stumps – stumps where Grandpa had cut the trees in a timber job fifteen years ago.

"Son, I could tell you a lot," Grandpa said. "There is not much use, for you will find out. You are young and eager."

Grandpa kept looking toward the tobacco field where the heat glimmered above the soft black-locust and shoe-make loam. Wilted burley plants grew on this hill, deep-rooted in the loam as Grandpa has been deep-rooted in the Kentucky earth.

"There's where I'd like to be," Grandpa said. "I'd like to be there behind that mule. I allus did like to raise terbacker. I love the smell of young terbacker. I love to see it standin' under the sun in twisted rows around the mountain and a lazy mule easin' the cutter plow against the stumps. Now I haf to sit here waitin' fer the Master to call me. I don't like it." And the vision from the blue-dimmed eyes, from beneath the long frostbitten eyebrows, beheld the faint rays of a setting sun.

"I can't do much with Pap," Mom said, for Grandpa was too deaf to hear what she said when she spoke softly. "Pap's got so he cries because we won't let him get out and walk to the wheat fields. He sits out here on the back porch and counts the furrows the Brown boys plow in their terbacker patch over there on the hill. Then he will say, 'Can't turn out no work. Just forty-six furrows around that hill in a half day. That's not any work.' "

Almost a score of years over his threescore and ten, Grandpa sat on the back porch and looked at the sunlight on the tobacco field.

"I've weighed over two hundred pounds all my life," he said. "I'd never been sick enough to have a doctor until I was eighty-four. When I was a young man, I didn't know how strong I was. I could lift a barrel of sorghum molasses and drink from the bunghole. But now my people are gone. Pap left the family tree at eighty-seven, Brother Douglas at eighty-nine, Sister Nance at ninety-two, Sister Salina at eighty-eight, Sister Victoria at eighty-five, and Brother Willison at ninety-three. Brother Douglas would a made the fourscore year and ten all right if it hadn't been fer a log rollin' over him when he burnt the new ground.

"I married Violet Pennington," Grandpa continued, gesturing with his big hands. "She was a child of April. They named her atter the violets on the hill. I went to housekeepin' in a one-room shack. We didn't have a bed. We slept on the floor. We just had two quilts. One to go under us, one to go over us. Good thing we got married in May; we didn't need much kivver then. We didn't even have a table in our house. We et off'n a big goods-box. Didn't have a tablecloth until Violet wove one. She was a pretty woman. She was only thirty-nine when she died. She got her feet wet and took the quick consumption."

Grandpa wiped the tears from his blue-dimming eyes with his big fire-shovel hand.

"You've seen her picture, son, in there on that easel that her cousin Riley Pennington painted," Grandpa said, as he looked toward the heat-glimmer over the wilted tobacco stalks. "She looked a little like your ma. Your ma is about as tall and has the high cheekbones and the coal-black hair your grandma had. That's the reason I stay with your ma instead of the other children. She looks so much like Violet. Violet was a wife her a livin'. I worked; she saved all I made. We raised seven children."

"I can remember when Pap wouldn't take an easy job," Mom said. "He took the hardest jobs at the sawmills. He offbore the slabs. When he cut timber on cold winter days, he'd go out with his shirt unbuttoned and without a coat, and he never wore socks. He'd go out on the coldest days when the timber would be frozen and work from daylight until dark."

The hills that stand against these skies are more durable than the oak trees that hide these backbone ridges. Grandpa has battled among them from sun till sun with the ax, cutter plow, maul, crosscut saw, sledge, and wedge. These rugged hills have been salted by the sweat that trickled down his beardy face to the ground. But these hills have kept young while his eagle eyes have grown dim. Grandpa has seen the earth take back his sweat and give him bread in return.

"And when Ma died," Mom said, "I remember what a time we had. For seven years, Pap toiled for us like a brute. I remember how we'd have fried apples for breakfast, hot biscuits and butter and coffee. I remember a little apple tree where we'd go to get the apples. Mary got married and left the house to me. I had to take care of Brother Jiles, for he was a baby then. A duck laid every morning that spring in the chimney corner and I'd fry the duck egg for his breakfast."

Grandpa was now looking into space, looking at the tobacco on the hill, the green rows with the leaves flapping in the wind. Grandpa was chewing tobacco from those hills on his natural teeth, while his youngest daughter, my mother, was trying to keep him from walking to the wheat fields and to Uncle Mel's house a mile down the hollow.

Grandpa

"Now, son, that man over there plowin' that second mule is a lazy man," Grandpa said, gesturing with his hand. "I've watched him day in and day out and I know he won't work. Wish I had that hill and could recall ten years. You know, I was runnin' Pap's farm at sixteen while he's out preachin' the Baptist doctrine. I hated to do it, but he made me do as he said until I was of age, which was twenty-one. It was my legs that got me at eighty-two. If I could just have new legs I'd be a good man yet. I'm gettin' soft and my wind ain't good, just huff and blow every time I go up a little hill. It's your ma keepin' me in. That's why I'm soft. I could do more than that fellow over there right now."

There was a time, Grandpa, I thought, when you nearly killed me. You were seventy-five then I was sixteen. That was when you built this house, and I helped you. You'd back me up against the hill and I'd have to saw down a saw log with you without resting. And by the time I had my side of the log scored, you had your side of the log scored and hewed, and you were right at my heels with the broadax, hewing on the side of the log I had scored. You would get mad and throw the sledge hammer over the hill when the tree pinched the saw. You'd cool down and make me go and hunt the sledge hammer. When I found it and carried it up the hill to you, you seemed pleased. I remember how I tried to keep a row of corn up with you and you nearly killed me. Finally, I had to let you lead me, for the sweat got in my eyes so I couldn't see. Even the sweat bees didn't sting me that day. They lit on me, drank all the sweat they wanted, and flew away. What a man you were—a mighty mountain of a man.

"Pap, it's time for supper." Mom spoke loudly so he could hear. "Supper is on the table."

"I'm not ready fer supper," Grandpa answered. "You go ahead and eat now if you're hungry, but I want to watch that mule stumble along in the terbacker row. I want to watch that lazy man. Wish I could get between them plow handles and could recall ten years. That would put me back until I'd just be eighty again."

Mom persuaded Grandpa to leave the porch and go to his supper.

"I just want buttermilk and corn bread fer my supper," Grandpa said. "It's the grub I was raised on and I still love it. Don't pour my glass quite full, Mitch."

Grandpa put a thin slice of yellow butter on his hot corn bread. He was ready to eat.

"Life is just like a day," Grandpa continued at the supper table as he ate. "In the mornin' we are young and we want to get out and turn over hills to see what is under them. Before the long day is over we get tired, just like the sun that rises in the east and comes over to the west – comes over the big sky. That is just like life. I've loved my journey across the sky. I am the last leaf. I'm waitin' fer the Master's call. He will call me, too, when he wants me. I'll hear His call. I'll heed that call, fer I am ready. I've cheated no man. I've given away in my lifetime. I have come to the end without land or money. I've wronged no woman, killed no man, stole no chickens. I've cut as many saw logs and cleaned as much of briers and sprouts and trees as any man in Kentucky. I've done as much as two ordinary men from the age of sixteen to eighty-four and I'm not braggin'. Wish I had new legs; I'd show you yet."

The sun had gone down beyond the Seaton hill, dragging a patch of sky with it. From the kitchen window I could see the green tobacco plants between the plowed furrows. I could see them flap their leaves in the wind as they breezed against the radiance of a sundown sky. I could see the great hills, the trees on their backbones, flanks, and fingers – trees with green growing leaves in this new season. I could see the snags of old trees desolate and forlorn; but around the fertility of their bodies the new stalwart trees had sprung with new leaves in the new spring season.

THE DEVIL AND TELEVISION

Everyone wondered what would happen as Mom, Pa, Brother Tim, and I walked into church. Because Pa was on trial. All eyes turned toward us. We couldn't sit too far away from the other members of the congregation because our church building was a house. Our Church of the Old Faith was in the largest house in Blakesburg. When the house had been put on skids and moved out of the way for a new street, the elders in our church saw a bargain and bought it for a church because there was plenty of room upstairs for our moderator, Egbert Chanute, and his nine children. There was enough space downstairs, by removing the partition, to have one big room for worship.

The house had fourteen spires. Two old people had once lived in its twenty-seven rooms with twenty-seven cats. Some said the house was haunted and the spirit of a witch was in each cat. They were afraid to go near this house. But when Moderator Chanute, who was holding services in the homes of the members of our church, heard the house was for sale, he said if there were evil spirits in the house, he had what it would take to make them leave.

Now, because our church had a lot of strict rules, my father was on trial. That was the reason all eyes were turned toward us. Even Moderator Chanute, a big man with busy eyebrows and deep-socketed black eyes that shone like ball of fire, watched us as Pa found seats as far away from the pulpit as he could. Pa hadn't done as bad things as some members had done. Pa hadn't attended a circus. He hadn't gone to a movie. He hadn't seen a horse race. He hadn't smoked or chewed the fragrant weed and drank the violent water. Pa hadn't even read the funny papers. He had tried to go straight according to the doctrine of our church, the policies our moderator had laid down to his members. Pa would have gone straight if it hadn't been for one thing.

Percy Cadden, a short fat redheaded man who smoked big cigars, had brought television to Blakesburg. He had built a store and he installed the sets. He put them in people's homes just for trial. If the family liked television, then the set remained. And I have my first time ever to know of a television set being taken out of any home where Percy installed it. That's where Pa had made the mistake. Nobody in our house liked television more than Pa. He would laugh, slap his knees with his big hands, and twist in his chair, holler and laugh more than Mom, Brother Tim, or I as he watched a baseball game, wrestling match, girls dancing or singing, or any program that came on. I never saw anybody enjoy anything more than Pa enjoyed his television. He couldn't wait to finish his work at the store and check his cash register to get home to his television.

"This is a serious moment in our lives," Moderator Chanute announced after we were all seated. "When we pray, I want every praying member to pray aloud for a lost and backsliding soul in our congregation."

Then he lifted his big hands and I never heard such prayer as our moderator prayed. I couldn't follow the words for there were too many others praying too. This was one of the times when Pa didn't pray. Everybody was standing and Pa stood there and listened and he looked down at the church floor. Pa

251

had joined in prayer once when a member had backslidden when we went to Cincinnati to see the Cincinnati Reds play the Brooklyn Dodgers. Old Bill Hinson was an old-time baseball player and he loved baseball. That was before television. And on that day Old Bill Hinson was "churched." But he repented of his sin and came back to us after many evenings of special prayer. Caleb Atkinson was "churched" for going to a circus in Dartmouth, Ohio. After his backsliding, and Pa had helped pray for him, he didn't get back into our church for he went to another circus in Auckland, Kentucky. Caleb had always loved the circus. When he was a boy he poured two gallons of moonshine in a tub of water the trainer gave the elephant and the elephant got drunk, grabbed Clinton Wiggington, our druggist, and threw him over a small tent but didn't break a bone in his body. The elephant went down the street breaking windows in the stores of Blakesburg and Caleb left town while the street-carnival people pulled up the stakes, folded their tents, and left Blakesburg. Caleb Atkinson was the only back-slider that had never come back.

Gladys Griffee, Anna Burton, and Murtie Garthee, three young women in our church, were "churched" for seeing a movie and Pa had helped pray for them. I'll never forget how Pa had prayed that time for I stood right beside him. I thought of all this because I couldn't hear the words of the prayer they were praying for Pa, who had backslidden for his first time. I could hear "worldly things" shouted above the other words now and then for everybody was praying his own prayer and my father just stood there and trembled as he looked down at the floor. His time had come and he knew it. We knew the sermon to follow would be about television. For when one had backslidden, after the prayer, Moderator Egbert Chanute preached a sermon on the cause.

There had been more than thirty out of a membership of

sixty who had been "churched" for partaking of worldly things. Half the members had been "churched" at one time or another and all had gone back, had been reinstated by prayers of our moderator and the faithful members of our congregation, who prayed with the sinner, in the church or at his home until he did repent. While the great prayer of many mixed voices went on, Pa stood there and trembled. But Mom didn't tremble. She didn't belong to this church that was Pa's choice. She belonged to another church in Blakesburg that let the members of its congregation go to baseball games, football games, wrestling matches, movies, circuses, street carnivals. Mom's church let its members enjoy television, checkers, rummy, dominoes, authors, and other things that members of Pa's church considered "worldly things." It seemed odd to me, after going to Pa's church, to see members of Mom's church go on the street smoking big cigars, pipes, cigarettes; even some of the women smoked and went without stockings to cover their legs and sleeves of their dresses to cover their elbows. No woman did this in Pa's church. So when Mom went to Pa's church with us, she always wore a dress almost to her ankles and sleeves that came to her wrists. Mom did this to please Pa.

When I looked up at my father's face, I noticed the sweat drops didn't come together and trickle down in little streams but they just stuck there as if they were glued. Pa was going through something terrible as the prayer got louder and more furious. When Mom looked at him, her face was very sad. She hated to see Pa go through all this among the members of his church.

The deafening shouts of prayer went up to the low ceiling and out the raised windows to the people passing on the street or riding down the highway. Only a week ago Pa had been addressed as Brother Thomas Bowling, now he was only Thomas Bowling.

Then I started thinking about when television first came
to Blakesburg. Pa had first seen it in Wiggington's Drug Store
when he stopped there one night to buy ice cream for us. Pa just
stood there, and marveled at this newfangled creation. When a
beautiful young woman sang—she was in short sleeves too—Pa
stood there with his mouth open and never batted his eyes as he
looked and listened. And after her singing, two men, wearing
black suits with big-legged pants, danced. The way they could
keep time to the music caused Pa to tap his feet. After this, a
magician came on and did a lot of tricks and Pa tried to guess
what was going to happen with Brother Tim and me and he
never guessed the magic at all. He'd laugh as I never heard him
laugh before. We ate more ice cream as we watched this
program. Three times we ordered ice cream. And the last thing
on the program was a beautiful girl playing the piano, and four
young beautiful women singing. It was a song we'd never heard
but it was called a hit by the tall skinny man that announced the
program and the song nearly melted Pa. When the program was
over, we left the drugstore. And Pa was in a big way. All the way
down the street home, he talked about the singing, the magic,
the dancing on the television program and Pa wondered about
this newfangled thing he had heard about but had never seen
before.

When Percy Cadden came to our house one evening, he was
very slow about telling Pa what he wanted because he knew Pa
was a deacon in his church and his church didn't go for worldly
things. But Brother Tim and I knew why Percy had come and
Mom knew why and we just stood there all excited looking at
each other and wondering what would happen. We didn't have
long to wait.

"Percy, I know what you want," Pa said with a big smile.
"You want me to try television, don't you?"

"That's it," Percy said softly, looking down when he spoke

to Pa.

Now Percy never traded at Pa's store because Pa refused to sell the fragrant weed in any form, to smoke, or to chew. And we had the biggest store in Blakesburg and Pa was Blakesburg's most successful merchant.

"Well, Percy," Pa said, "install a set here and let us try it out."

This was the mistake. For the next day Percy installed the television set. That evening we didn't have to go to Wiggington's Drug Store like a lot of Blakesburg people. We sat in our home and watched and listened. Pa carried on more than ever. There were not a lot of curious eyes looking on at Deacon Bowling as he clapped his hands and shouted at a wrestling match between two gorillalike men. When one hit the mat Pa shouted as if he were wrestling. When the young beautiful women in long dresses with short sleeves came on and danced and sang the new songs, Pa enjoyed himself most and he got up close so he would not miss a thing. We saw baseball games, horse races, wrestling matches, dancing, heard music and songs, and, honest, our home was a new place. We couldn't wait to get home from school and Pa and Mom couldn't wait to get back from the store.

"Your father is hungry for these things," Mom said to me in the kitchen one evening when she washed the dishes and I dried them. "We used to go to movies"—Mom smiled and her face brightened—"a long time ago. Your father loved movies. He loved baseball, football, and wrestling, and he liked to watch the horses run at Coney Island." "Oh."—Mom laughed—"we used to have such good times. It's all coming back right in our house. Television brings back memories to us." And then she added, "I don't know what Moderator Egbert Chanute will say. I can pretty well guess. Television is a worldly thing."

Before Percy Cadden came back to see if Pa was going to keep the television set, people in our church had started talking. Not the people of the other churches but the members of our church. The women whispered about Pa's television over the back-yard fences. The men talked about it where they worked together or whence they met on the streets. They said Pa had gone "worldly" and Moderator Chanute would "church" him. But before Moderator Chanute got word what Pa had done, Percy Cadden had come back to see what Pa thought of television. It didn't take my father long to tell him. He'd never asked what the price of the set, the best Percy had, would be when Percy had installed it. He asked Percy and when Percy told him the price Pa didn't say a word but got up and left the room. In a few minutes he was back with the money and he paid Percy right there. That was Pa's way of telling Percy what he thought of television. Soon as Moderator Chanute heard Pa had a television set in our home, he came in person and told Pa he was "churched."

Now the long prayer had ended, and there were many "amens" coming from the congregation. Men and women pulled handkerchiefs and bandannas from their pockets and purses and wiped perspiration from their flushed faces. Pa pulled a handkerchief from his pocket and wiped the beads of sticky sweat too. Then everybody sat down and there was silence. Everybody, especially Pa, must have felt what was coming and anxiously waited for our moderator to announce the text of his sermon. Then Moderator Chanute, who towered high above his pulpit, laid his hands on his Bible and said: "I will preach this morning on 'The Devil Has Many Faces.'"

"Amens" went up as men and women still wiped their sweaty faces after the long loud and exciting prayer. "The devil is in so many places these days. He walks among the men that wear the checkered suits, the loud neckties with diamond stickpins, men with the big cigars in their mouths at the race tracks. He is at Coney Island. He is at Churchill Downs. He is at the Hilldale Theater in Blakesburg every afternoon and night in the week and especially on Sunday afternoon and Sunday night. He is at weekly baseball games but he is there with a selected group of his angels from hell. He gives them a break to let them see their future brothers and sisters who will soon join them. The devil is at the Sunday bathing parties along Big River. And never did a woman walk down a Blakesburg street in a pair of shorts that the devil, though unseen in form, is walking beside her and urging her on. Because the devil is of the flesh and he loves to look on the bare legs of women, and low-neck dresses are his special delight. And he loves the short sleeves too..."

And it quickly flashed through my mind about the meeting we once held at our church, when men and women came from the hills and hollows and the little towns along Big River and drove in all sorts of good cars and old cars and by horseback, muleback, buggies, and on foot, how Sherd Hylton looked them over when he was standing beside a filling station just across from our church and said, "They look like people from another world. I can remember when women dressed like that. That was more than fifty years ago. It's like turning back the clock."

Sherd Hylton didn't know that I went to church there and was on my way to the meeting then. But what he said had made me think. I'd never noticed it much, but then I compared the way my mother dressed to these women and I thought he was right. The women were dressed in long black dresses that swept the street behind them. The sleeves came down to their wrists, too. And the men were dressed in dark suits and there was not a rose in a coat lapel. My father and mother dressed differently. The dresses Mom wore were no match in length for the dresses of the women who had come to this meeting. My mother had not turned back the clock to another day and another time. And she never would. And my father hadn't exactly turned back the

257

clock for he wore a nice dark suit and a collar and tie.

"The devil loves company and he is always with the crowd at these places of amusement. If he was there walking among these people they would run and scream. And God's Houses would be full and running over with people. But that's not the way the devil does things. He is a devil with many faces, visiting many places. And now the devil has the slickest way he has ever had before of getting into the homes, homes of good people, religious people. He comes in this newfangled thing called television. I believe that's what it's called. I've never seen it. But these places of amusement, these singers and dancers and baseball players and wrestlers and women in shorts and low-necked dresses and sleeves above the elbows are brought right inside the homes for the family to see. Brothers and Sisters, the devil has pulled a fast one."

Moderator Egbert Chanute had to stop for the "amens" going up from all over the church while Pa just sat there like a man on trial for his life. He looked at his feet and Mom looked at him. Mom hugged closer to him and I leaned over against him because I loved my father. I knew Pa had once been a man of the world. Now that I had grown up and was in my first year of Blakesburg High School I'd heard the things my father had done. Nothing really bad but he had drunk the violent water and smoked big cigars and things like that. He had danced many a night all night with Mom before and after they were married. And I knew the one thing that had caused him to join this church. I never told my father that I knew.

Pa had bought a new automobile and he had tasted of the violent water and let the car get out of control. And it hit a woman who was walking beside the highway. She was coming from church. Nor our church but the same denomination Pa belonged to now. It was beside this woman, whom Pa had knocked unconscious with his new car, that her brother and five

258

sisters, also coming from church, gathered. They looked Pa over and saw that he had had too much of the devil's temptation. They didn't have Pa arrested. They took him from the car, formed a circle around him, and prayed for him until morning. And it was on this night Pa joined their church and became a saved man.

He prayed for Bertha Jenkins, the woman he had hit, mother of five children, while she hovered between life and death at the hospital. When she got better, Pa said his prayers had been answered. Then Pa became the biggest contributor in the church of the same denomination in Blakesburg. Pa's reckless driving while intoxicated was dismissed because it was the work of the devil and he was never indicted and brought before court. He was never sued either though Pa had his car insured. Pa said this was the real thing and from this time on, until television, he was a devout member of his church and loyal in every respect.

"Yes, the devil has many faces," Moderator Chanute shouted as Pa sat there on trial. "When he can get into the home of a deacon in the Church of the Old Faith, he has to be plenty slick."

Pa moved his feet on the floor. Once he coughed and swallowed. Mom looked at him quickly, then turned her eyes away. Mom had her hand in his hand and I leaned over closer to Pa. I was on his side and I was on the side of television, this wonderful magical thing that had brought the entertainment of the world into our room at night. And I thought about the way we had enjoyed it and how Pa had laughed more than any of us, as we sat here in a huddle while Pa was on trial. How will it all come out, I wondered.

I knew one thing was in Pa's favor. He gave as much money to our church as all the other members of our congregation put together. But our moderator wasn't thinking about what Pa had done for the church, how he helped pay for the building, had it remodeled himself, and bought the seats and song books, and had paid most of Moderator Egbert's salary. Pa was the biggest of the ten merchants in Blakesburg before he joined the church and now he was doing nearly as much business as the other nine merchants combined.

"I tell you the devil has many faces," shouted Moderator Chanute. "Yes, when he can fool a member of this church and move in and sit with God's people and laugh to himself and chuckle them under the chin while they laugh at the things the devil is feeding them over the air waves at night, it's time something has to be done..."

The drops of sweat stood on Pa's face again. They were bigger drops of sweat and they were closer together. They looked like little bright haystacks on a dark gray autumn piece of land. That's what I thought as I looked at Pa's face. And as Moderator Chanute preached, more and louder "amens" went up from all over the house and everything seemed to get warmer suddenly as the members of Pa's church were fighting the work of the devil. While Moderator Chanute preached louder and white dry cotton spittle began to fly from his mouth and after each sentence he went "ah-ah," I wondered if Pa would fall to his knees and begin to shake and ask forgiveness as the other backsliders had done. I wondered what the verdict of this trial would be. For the time would soon come when our moderator would call Pa's name and ask him what he had to say for himself. Then he would announce Pa was "churched"—that is, if Pa didn't fall to his knees pretty soon and start praying as many of the others had done, all but old Caleb Atkinson. And I thought of old Caleb, as Moderator Chanute shouted and raged on.

"When the Lord is in this house and the guilty is not touched to fall to his knees, to pray for his evenings of pleasure in the presence of old Beelzebub," Moderator Chanute shouted,

The Devil and Television

"I think old Beelzebub is in your presence and he has his hand upon the shoulder of our deacon and he is whispering something very soft and sweet in his ear, something such as he has sent over the air waves of night and it's time..."

Before he finished that sentence, Pa made a start for the aisle. I wondered if he was going to the altar. All eyes were turned on Pa. Our moderator must have thought Pa was coming to the altar and members of the congregation started shouting "amen" and "glory" as Pa entered the big aisle in the middle of the church and Mom's eyes, my eyes, and Brother Tim's were following Pa. When he reached the aisle he turned toward the door, and everybody got real quiet and Moderator Chanute stopped preaching and watched Pa as he went out the door with his hat in his hand. Then Mom, Brother Tim, and I followed and the people looked at us with tear-stained eyes and solemn faces as we walked out into the bright summer air where Pa was waiting for us.

"Come, let's go to your church for a change," Pa said to Mom. "I'm not movin' my television set out of our home. And I'm still goin' on to church. We won't be late for the sermon."

"Or we can go home, Thomas," Mom said. "We've been gettin' some good church services over television."

"Who would ever have thought a member of my family would rather look at a newfangled invention than go to Sunday church?" my father said. He was shocked. He stood there looking at Mom.

Then Mom smiled, and said, "Let's go to church."

My father and mother, arm in arm, walked down the street. My brother and I followed. We hadn't gone but a little way until Pa turned around and said to us, "Remember, you're never goin' to let the devil pull a fast one on you."

PLOWSHARE IN HEAVEN

"I'm not goin'," says Pa. "I just hate it. That's all. You go with your Ma, Shan. You know I can't stand to go around when a body has passed to the Great Beyond."

"I just couldn't believe Dave," says Mom, "when he rode the mule up here and said that Phoeby was dead. Last week we talked about plantin' our pole beans fer next year. I give her some of my bean seeds fer some of hers. We sat before the fire last Sunday and smoked our pipes and talked about plantin' next spring."

"She won't plant any more beans," says Pa. "Her plantin' here on earth is done. Phoeby was a good woman and a good neighbor. I'll pay my last respects. I'll attend to diggin' the last piece of ground Phoeby'll own. I'll do it tomorrow."

I put on my overcoat. I put gloves on my hands and a scarf around my neck. It is cold. The December winds whip mournfully among the barren branches of the oaks above our house. We can hear the moan of the wind from where we sit inside our house by the good wood fire. Sometimes the wind tries to come down the chimney and it blows out wisps of blue smoke that makes tears come to our eyes.

"You'll need the lantern," says Pa. "The stars ain't enough light fer your Ma's eyes. It's in the dark of the moon, you know."

I get the lantern, lift the globe, and light it with a stick of pine kindling from the hearth. I let the globe down.

"I'm ready," I says to Mom.

"Just a minute," she says.

Mom fills her pipe. She takes a stick of the rich pine kindling from the hearth, sticks it in the fire, and lights her pipe. Her scarf is wound over her head and wrapped around her neck. We walk out into the cold December wind. We leave Pa at the house. We walk past the hog pen and go across the pasture to Dave Lester's log shack on the creek.

The wind whips through the bare oak limbs above our head. It is a cold December wind and it nearly brings tears to our eyes. It stings our faces so. We leave the woods now. We walk the hard frozen path across Dave's wheat field. We can see the little green stems of winter wheat by the lantern light. The trees around the wheat field look like high dark palings around a garden. They are high and dark and move back and forth by the strong puffs of wind against the starry December sky.

"Phoeby allus wanted a good funeral," says Mom. "She ust to tell me about it. We'd smoke our pipes and sit under the peach tree in her front yard and talk. She'd say, 'I've worked hard all my life. I've got my children raised up big enough to take keer of themselves. Now I'm savin' fer my own funeral. I've saved a little bit every fall when I sold my turkeys. I've saved back a little of the money I got fer eggs. I want a pretty coffin with silk linin' and bright handles!' "

We walk under the pine grove now. The wind *oooooooo's* through their tops and lifts the shaggy arms of the pines toward the sky. It is so lonely and Mom talking about Phoeby's coffin. I just think, "What if we would meet Phoeby on this path? What if she would come up to Mom and say, 'I allus knowed you would come if I died first. You said you would. I am so glad to see you goin' down to the old shack. You will see me in the coffin I allus wanted. You will see the pennies over my eyes that I saved and sewed the black cloth around. You'll see me in the dress I saved the money to buy—the dress I want to wear in Heaven. It is a pretty dress and I know you'll like it. You'll like my coffin. It is so pretty. It's not a homemade coffin. I never wanted one.' "

It is silly to think this. I just wondered if her and Mom would smoke their pipes again together and blow the smoke into the December wind. I would see a lot of ghosts in the wind then. I think about last summer when I went to Sandy to fish and I saw Phoeby in the cornfield. She was hoeing corn and she says, "Shan, your Ma and me are going down the hill. We ain't as strong as we ust to be. I've had eleven children and your Ma has had seven."

I can see her now. Her face is red. There are little drops of sweat on her red face. They look like white soup-beans sticking there. She has the handle of the hoe in her hand. It is a one-eyed sprouting hoe. She is barefooted. The sun is hot. A lizard lies on the top of a stump above her. The lizard is sleeping in the sun and waiting for a fly. The corn rows beneath Phoeby are clean. The weeds lie wilted in the sun. Dave is up on the hill plowing. Dave is saying, "Ghee, Barnie! Ghee! Ghee!"

Then Phoeby says, "We'll have the corn fer this winter if we get a good season. The ground is good. We've got enough planted. All we need is a season. It's a lot of work but I don't mind. I nearly got overhet a time or two, Shan. You know it's a long way to the top of one of these cornfields just takin' three-foot wide back and forth around the hill. My heart ain't as good as it ust to be. It bothers me some."

"Shan, we'll soon be there," Mom says. "I can see the light from the winder."

When Mom says this I don't see the ghost of Phoeby any more nor I don't see her in the cornfield. I can see the narrow path ahead of us leading to Phoeby's shack.

"I guess Phoeby was right," says Mom as we walk into Dave Lester's yard, "when she said that when this little cedar she planted here got big enough to shade her grave she would die. When Phoeby moved from her old home place on the other side of Little Sandy she brought this tree with her. She said, 'It's just somethin' I wanted to carry away from the place where I's born and raised. It's just somethin' to remember it by.' She brought a little bunch of broad-bladed grass, too, and set it out by the door."

"Come in, Martha, you and Shan," says Dave. "The place won't be the same now but come in."

We walk into the house. The Turners, Sheltons, Tates, Crums, and Hustons are here. The house is filled. The people are silent. They sit before the big log fire. All of Phoeby's children are here, Mel, Wid, Sid, Levi, Grace, Ester, Essie, Ron, Donnie, Ted, and Kate.

There are two chairs in the back of the big front room. On these two chairs is the coffin. A chair holds up each end. It is a pretty coffin with bright handles. It is a bluish-gray-colored coffin and it has a glass lid. Mom walks back and looks in it. She stands silently and does not speak. Phoeby is in the coffin. I know she is in the dress she told Mom about and she has the pennies that she covered with dark cloth over her eyes. I do not go back to see. Mom comes back up before the fire and Ted Lester get up and gives her his chair.

"Thy will," says Dave, "will be done."

After this I beheld, and, lo, a great multitude, which no man could number, of all nations, and kindreds, and people, and tongues, stood before the throne, and before the Lamb, clothed with white robes, and palms in their hands.

Phoeby will be lost there. It will not be home unless she can walk barefooted over the fields of growing corn and feel the soft earth beneath her feet; unless she can feel the handle of a hoe

265

in her hand and smell the good clean wind of a Kentucky spring; unless she can smell the silking corn and hear the cries of the wild birds. How can she take a cedar tree, or just a little wisp of grass, from the land she loved and plant it there? How will she feel among strangers from all lands and in a great multitude of people? How will she feel among many tongues when she has only heard one?

Surely the dark Monarch Hills will call her back! They have owned her; they have possessed her! The log shack with the clapboard roof, the wrens that come back each year to build in a coffee sack of rags and a rusted coffeepot hanging on a nail in the smokehouse, and the trees that Phoeby could call by name and the laughing April streams filled with clean blue water. Surely these are Heaven to her. They are Heaven to all of us! How can we ever leave them and the wild flowers that bloom in the spring when the hill world awakens from sleep!

Therefore are they before the throne of God, and serve him day and night in his temple: and he that sitteth on the throne shall dwell among them.

They shall hunger no more, neither thirst any more; neither shall the sun light on them, nor any heat.

For the Lamb, which is in the midst of the throne, shall feed them, and shall lead them unto living fountains of waters: and God shall wipe away all tears from their eyes.

No more days of Kentucky sunlight, those golden sprays of warm spring sunshine on the white wild crab-apple blossoms, and the pink crab-apple blossoms, and the wild plum blossoms, the red bud, and the white lilting sails of the dogwood blossoms that spread in the wind like wide snowy sheets! Surely, for a hill Kentuckian God would let us have our Heaven here in Kentucky! We have lived in it so long, shut away from the outer rims of the hills, that we do not know it is Heaven until we get away!

Our Monarch Hills feed us. We are their vassals. Have they

not fed Phoeby and Dave and their eleven? Have we not lived slowly with the years and the old have ripened sweetly with the years at the end of their season? They have been cruel to us but they have absorbed our tears! We have hungered and we have thirsted but have not our hungers and our thirsts been quenched? Have we not walked by the living waters and heard their cries? Have we not felt the warm sunlight and loved it? And the heat has been both kind and cruel!

Cannot we return again to the Monarch Hills that have enslaved us, that have fed us, that have held us for generations? A land that we cannot escape no matter where we go! Can't we return as a vapor, a thin ghost of smoke? In any form so we can return and see the land we had to leave, the Heaven we left and never knew it was Heaven until we got away? It is our land after all and you never hear one of us speak against it when we are away. We tell you that it is our land, that we are a part of it, and we show you that we cannot escape it no matter how cruel or how kind it has been to us. How can we be contended among a multitude of strangers and many tongues?

"His will," says Dave, "will be done."

The night is passing. We sing songs before the firelight. Mom does not sing. She looks at the firelight. The flames leap brightly up the throat of the chimney. The men that the hills have made are here. They are hard men from the fields and the plow. Their hearts are tender as a spring flower in the time of sickness an distress! Men who can be as kind or as cruel as the hills that have made them!

It is four o'clock. Mom and I start home. I light the lantern. We walk out of the shack. The sky is filled with stars. The Dipper is in the sky on the west side of Dave's shack. It hangs above the brown broom-sage field where Uncle Mel used to grow his corn.

We walk up the road. Mom smokes her pipe. We come to

the little hollow and we turn to our right and walk up a little path across the cove where the Indian turnips are first in bloom in spring. Now it is bleak and dark under the winter starlight and the tall white beeches look grim and bare. We walk until we reach the pine grove. The wind is still now. We cross the rail fence by the white oaks and cross the wheat fields. I walk in front with the lantern. I can see the little stems of wheat are white with frost. On a far hill we hear the *who-who* of an owl. It seems to sliver the silence of the morning. Our roosters are crowing. We walk under the oaks around through our pasture and come to our hog pen and then we cross the barn lot. We can see a light in the house. Pa is up, has fed the cattle and the hogs, for we can hear them eating their corn.

"Poor Phoeby," says Mom as we walk from the barn to the house. "She's better off than we are. She is beyond the starry skies."

I do not answer Mom. I carry the lantern and light her way into the house in the cold stillness of the morning hours.